Match Frame

Match Frame

PAUL OSBORNE

Library of Congress Control Number:		2008907326
ISBN:	Hardcover	978-1-4363-6362-4
	Softcover	978-1-4363-6361-7

To order additional copies of this book, contact:
Xlibris Corporation
1-888-795-4274
www.Xlibris.com
Orders@Xlibris.com
52617

for Jeanine

MATCH

"14. *Patternmaking.* A form so shaped as to support a pattern made of plaster of Paris, sand, or a mixture of sand, litharge, and boiled linseed oil. It is attached to a ***match frame***, which serves as the bottom of the mold."

Webster's New International Dictionary of the English Language
Second Edition Unabridged

"One step forward, two steps back . . . It happens in the lives of individuals, and it happens in the history of nations and in the development of parties."

Vladimir Ilich (Ulyanov) Lenin 1870-1924

I encounter millions of bodies in my life; of these millions, I may desire some hundreds; but of these hundreds, I love only one."

Roland Barthes 1915-1980

1

The thought of being watched was disquieting. With the window unscreened, she lowered the lights before they removed their clothes. Blurring of contours reduced chance of recognition, but vulnerability increased when making love. They acted brazenly, as when going past the guards before and on the morning after. It added a sense of bravado in their tempestuous mood. He wondered how they might look to them. Compared to the view of a spectator, close-up for an actor on stage can be confined, obstructed by another performer. That is how it was for them, on their arena in front of the bookcase. For a rooftop observer watching from a building behind, armed with a night telescope, the interior panorama would be intact between the un-drawn curtains. The rug, in position away from the wall, would appear square, its rectangular shape foreshortened by the shallow angle of the line of sight. Against this backcloth, she would be less noticeable, unless silhouetted above his chest, or caught resting on his stomach. From afar, images of moving figures locked together might suggest conflict, but in the tenebrous lighting, outlines would be unclear. Shadows, cast from the lamp beside them on the floor, could map the lines of backs and fronts pressed to one another, or torsos tied by limbs. Among this tangle of human parts visible from the distance, an observer might pick out the distinctive triangle of her pubic hair, passing briefly across the field of vision—geodetic reference point, marking a peak in the landscape. Everything may appear an indistinguishable disarray, constantly varying forms unidentifiable in the dimness. What would the anonymous viewer think, standing in the night air, barrel of the telescope gripped between numbed fingers?

When I saw her first, it should have been clear that my times in Moscow would not change. It was in a restaurant—underground, with arched ceilings, picked for visitors, not far from where I stayed. I went by foot through fresh snow. The largest table was taken by locals and beside their boisterous vitality, another looked abandoned. I noticed the bare, unmarred tablecloth on passing, but facing away, immersed in conversation, was not aware that people arrived and sat there. When a colleague pointed, I perceived some men, probably foreigners. Dishes were not visible and they seemed unconcerned by the lacking service. Then turning, I saw her sitting in the chair behind mine. Her appearance was a surprise in an environment of controlled moderation. Tall and slender, she had a complexion to be envied—a subtle shade of ochre. "It's disconcerting," was my guarded response. As she talked with the man on her left, I noted the delicate features of her face, framed by the straight dark hair. It fell over the nape of her neck, which I could see when I twisted further in my chair. She wore a simple red dress, and her elegant shoulders emerged from two wide parallel straps. While I watched, she turned and saw me. Our eyes met, but for an instant. My companions were on a first visit to the Soviet Union. I had to untangle discontents, after a day of meetings to discuss a venture, fraught with obstacles. As she continued talking with those at her table, I observed the way the line of her hair played with the angle of her head. The movements drew my attention and once I caught the smooth contour of her cheek in silhouette. I do not know how many times I looked during the evening, but when I did, she was in conversation and gave no sign of noticing. Turning once more, I saw the table empty, dishes and glasses gone, tablecloth removed. She was nowhere in sight. She disappeared with the people with whom she emerged.

Next day the image persisted. Although we sat in neighbouring chairs, we exchanged no word. I did not know who she was, or where she was from. I realized we would not meet and I would not know her name. She was likely a visitor herself, and already packing to leave. In a city of millions, it was absurd to think our paths might cross again, but what I learnt earlier suggested the reverse. When I saw a woman who stimulated me, I would see her a short while afterwards. Though contrary to the laws of chance, this came from a game to ward-off boredom during the years as schoolboy. I used to go to town with my mother while she was shopping and sit alone in the car, watching women walking by. I could pick any and make love with her, but just her. It was then too late for something better—the rules allowed only a single choice until the car moved. If caught at the finish without having made-up my mind, I must take the last to pass 'regardless' and make love with a person, who might be repulsive. To avoid the risk, I had to be less demanding and pick someone sexually attractive, not necessarily good-looking. To win an inspiring woman called for patience and persistence. It was necessary to disregard the 'merely satisfying' and hold out in the hope that an 'outstanding beauty' would ultimately appear. It was possible to park freely in the streets and I could repeat the game, whenever left somewhere new. Occasionally, I won a jackpot and a woman who aroused me intensely, came into view. Then it was not a single 'lovemaking'—her image remained in my mind. Unplanned encounters were unlikely in a town that was neither large nor small, yet after seeing a woman who excited me, I would run into her a second time, under different circumstances the next day, or within two days. I could not explain the illogicality. It happened so often, I began to wonder whether our thoughts could in an obscure way, interfere with actions of others.

Moscow unsettled me. Contrasts and opportunity to be close to the centre of a power ruling half the globe were animating, but Westerners were 'enemies of the State'. Outside official meetings, fraternization was resented and could put others at risk. I felt alienated. The Russian spirit seemed masked and interest to explore was subdued, besides, a false step could jeopardize the future. The city seemed a place without time and wherever I went, I faced stretches of waiting to fill its absence. Whenever there, days laboured. It was hard to say when anything might start and whatever happened, the outcome would be unpredictable. The visits followed a pattern. They started under pressure, summoned for a meeting, always on Monday. When I arrived and phoned whomever I had rushed to meet, an assistant would inform me: "He had to go outside the city. We will call you when he returns, Gospodin. Give me your room number. Please wait in hotel!" I longed for the exception, where postponement would be a day or two, but the pattern was played-out. When told: "We expect him by the weekend, you will be contacted in room," I knew a further spell of confinement was starting. I was prisoner in a hotel room, waiting for calls that might not come, or at best would confirm appointments on Saturday. First day was for telephone calls and though only a handful, they filled the void. When the operator rang to confirm lines were busy, it was time to ask again. Later, another secretary would admit someone else I wanted to contact, was not reachable. There was no telephone book for the city and when a person moved, a succession of enquiries was needed to obtain the new number. With options limited, foreigners had to go to restaurants when they opened, to get in. The menu was the same, apart from prices left blank, for what was unavailable. Then following a long delay at the start and more waiting between courses, the evening was lost. After years of toiling on the minutiae of immense centrally planned undertakings, there were instances in which the thousands of packing cases involved were discarded at isolated sites. They sat forsaken, while the weather took revenge, destroying contents and until everyone forgot, why they were there.

Involvement in the city was unexpected. The firm, with its base in central London, controlled from another continent, had earlier sought an orthodox candidate for the unorthodox domain, but jealous protection of his expertise made him more secretive than his counterparts and raised suspicion. After two years without results, they fired him and he left the same day. Potential was anything but realistic and my participation was rated temporary. The Canadian chief called me to his office: "Howell has gone. I need a fill-in. Make an assessment, but treat it short term."

Then, as was his wont when discussing matters of confidence, Calvin stepped to my side of the desk, to lean forward, his head a foot from mine. Looking directly in my eyes, he conceded: "Howell was used to a different culture. He set the wrong bait and couldn't see the whales. The fairway's clear! You have to float it around current engagements and it may call for personal sacrifice. You have my word, it won't be for nothing."

The second day at the ministry with my companions, showed neither advance nor redress. Discussion dragged, wrangling over obscure regulations that blocked the way ahead. In spite of disagreement, they offered tickets to the Bolshoi at the Kremlin Palace. The long performance times overlapped restaurant hours, but in the interval, visitors could ride escalators to lavish buffets on the top floor of the grand building. Struggling to regain our seats through crowded aisles, I saw her—swept in a counter-direction. Our eyes met again, but there was no possibility to stop, or speak. I did not see whom she was with, or where she sat. I simply knew she was somewhere in the mass of rows behind. After the performance, I looked back, but did not see her—she had left once more without trace. I thought of my game. The opportunity was lost.

The city proved expensive for visitors, who had to pay with cash. Black-market trading of foreign currency or goods, merited summary arrest and the exchange rate was less than a rouble for one dollar. Having to cover the bills of my colleagues, I was running short. Sole source in the Metropole gave an excuse next day, to escape afternoon discussions. Collecting documents from the National, I went to the other hotel and took the lift to the second floor. To reach the exchange office, I had to traverse an imposing corridor, lined each side by doorways. On arrival, it looked empty but as I walked along the half-lit expanse, I noticed a figure and the silhouette appeared familiar. The person, seen in the restaurant and glimpsed in the crowd at the opera, was approaching from the other end.

2

The randomness of collision between our movements in space and time should not be different, from those of particles of matter in a gas. Without containment, paths would be un-deflected in straight lines. Einstein told us these curve and eventually come back from infinity, to go through their starting point. Probability for encounter would be higher when enclosed and paths deflected at the boundary. With no such limit to confine our courses of motion, the random paths of others should be like comets, which having passed the point of intersection for their orbits, disappear in space until trajectories bring them back again. In a city as large, the likelihood of successive meetings between persons unknown to each other could not be coincidence. Were earlier fantasies of remote influence materializing, or might direction be contrived?

"Hello! Left to fate, another meeting would exceed the scope of possibility!"

"Is it fact, or an invitation?" She asked with a smile.

"I am disconcerted. You are too conspicuous to monitor me."

"Wait a minute! I work for the other side—attached to the embassy, the American one, I mean."

"I am curious! Can I invite you to the restaurant here—or somewhere more suited to a soft interrogation?"

"It could be challenging, but today is not possible. Tomorrow might be different."

"Tomorrow, then! How about seven o'clock and where can we meet? I am at the National."

"It's safe here, downstairs in reception. Seven thirty might be better."

"Seven thirty then! I look forward to an evening that will in no way disconcert. Oh! I almost forgot. What's your name?"

"Max De Sousa," she added. "Max is a nickname. I prefer it to the real one. What's yours?"

She was not an agent, but American and living in the city. I would let her choose the restaurant.

This was not a cellar and smaller than the hangar-like places familiar to me. In the lobby, a white-gowned woman took our coats at the check-in desk. I wanted to meet earlier, to avoid risk of not getting-in wherever she suggested. Surprisingly, there were vacancies. As she walked ahead of me into the room, I noted she wore a two-piece black suit. Below the trim-cut skirt, I saw the long slim legs that earlier, I had observed folded and pointing in obscure directions, as they hung suspended from the chair behind my own. Striking, as the first time, she did not disconcert, or disappoint. I do not recall the name of the restaurant, but picture it—austere and rectangular, with observation limited by thin, grey steel columns, evenly spaced through an otherwise undivided space. I led her to a table in a corner, the most remote and private I could see and with two chairs, to ensure nobody joined us. Apart from the usual bare tablecloth was a single flower in a glass vase. A menu lay on another empty table nearby and I got up, to bring it over. It was in Russian, the place was not intended for foreigners. When the waiter finally appeared, I let her order. He brought vodka and we asked for wine. Now, there were opportunities to talk. We had plenty of time until the first dishes arrived, not to mention the long pauses, inevitable between courses. As I looked across at her, it was hard to acknowledge that the person in my thoughts over the last three days, glimpsed fleetingly, was sitting on the other side of the small table. It was vital nothing damage the fledgling relationship. Probing must be avoided, I rehearsed—better explore coherences.

She told me she came to Moscow as teacher at the school of her embassy. She lived in one of their flats, not the principal staff residential building, but a small block of apartments, previously a terrace house and since converted. It was in my preferred section of the city. "Although the first time intentionally, tonight is the fourth time I have seen you. It must be a lucky number." I volunteered.

"I hope you are not trying to puzzle, but four is interesting—with four points in a square, symmetry is matched."

"Yet, balance is not perfect. Points along the sides are equidistant, those across diagonals more remote."

"Positions can be varied, without disturbance of the sum."

"I was thinking about time, not place—the repetition, I mean. Doesn't it entitle us to feel less estranged?"

"I wouldn't disagree, though place is also relevant."

"What is your relation to the square?"

"On the diagonal in a phase of exploration, naturally, an exposed position and somewhat out of joint. You might say: I am 'a free soul in an environment of totalitarianism'. It was calculated. I took the job to rattle dogmas."

"You must be part of a preserve, you are too attractive to be otherwise."

"How about you? You need not say however. You can leave me to surmise. I can speculate on issues that may be purely theoretical. For me, what you refer to as the preserve has another significance."

"I see! But I hope the suppositions don't make you, want to move out of the square."

"That pattern, seems to be looking somewhat triangular, but on the subject of place, I have to say my friends back home, consider this an outlandish spot to be."

"You mean—far from home, or too isolated?"

"You must experience alienation on your visits, for my needs though, it has advantages. My posting was set to continue four years, maybe five and I am not yet half way through. How long have your visits lasted?"

"Six months so far. The future depends on success. My predecessor stayed two years. He produced nothing and was turned onto the street."

"Will it go better for you?"

"Better doesn't seem to apply, the task is daunting and I need luck. Sometimes the difficulties seem impenetrable, but you know how, when something goes to the limits, it can become the antithesis—like extreme bitterness tasting sweet. I cannot help feeling, if at the boundaries of impossibility and with good fortune, it might in the end, prove straightforward. With a breakthrough, it could be significant."

As we talked of hopes and interests, I discovered her love of books. She read and collected contemporary literature. We shared authors. We had read some of the same works. In spite of the duration of any dinner in that city, the long span of this one stole by. As we finished the last course, she said: "You must excuse me. I have to get home—I need to start early tomorrow."

"I'll call for the bill." I gave a sign to the waiter. After paying, I asked her, "Is it something special?"

"Quite mundane. I take the children on a trip. We go outside the city. There will be a bus. It's a tortuous journey and we leave at dawn."

"Can we meet tomorrow evening, when you get back?"

"It's unreliable. We may be late. I'll give it a rain check."

"And the day after?"

"Why not? Same place? Same time?"

"Sure! Let me see you out." I accompanied her to where she parked. As she bent down to open the door, she looked up expectantly and for the first time I kissed her. The lips touched briefly. The street was quiet and appeared deserted, but I felt uneasy. We could be observed from many angles. She got into the seat and started the engine. I watched her, as she drove slowly down the road and around the corner out of sight, realizing I was sad, she had left me. I comforted myself—I was going to see her again. It was only two days. In that city of timelessness, such a period was nothing. I was accustomed to waiting.

Entry for Westerners in the Soviet Union was limited to officials, or those with justification for a visa. Getting there was seldom straightforward and once inside, it was forbidden to leave the capital without a permit, almost unobtainable. On most days, the skyline merged seamlessly into leaden skies, but at night, tops of buildings were marked by red stars, glowing resolutely above. With little green visible, the grey panorama of government offices and sprawling blocks of flats appeared broken only by the characteristic red of the Kremlin's walls. With its castellated ramparts and medley of spires and rooftops, peeping over the curtain of stone masonry, it looked seductive, belying the power behind. I could see it across the open space of the 50-letija Okt'abr'a ploshad, next to where the Moscva hotel was since built and taken down, or catch glimpses on taxi rides sometimes of its southern face, as it rose above the curving river. The city landscape was embellished by skyscrapers—bizarre reflections of 1930s New York. There was the Foreign Trade building at Smolenskaja-Sennaja place, in which many of my contacts had offices, or the Hotel Ukraine, to which they routinely directed Western businessmen. If you took the trouble to count from outside, there seemed one more storey than the number of buttons in the lifts. According to rumour, the extra floor was where they housed the listening and recording equipment. I preferred the National, but it was normally a struggle to get a room. Sometimes, they put me in the Minsk. Though new, its lift was an anachronism after Gargarin's launch in space. When trying to stop, the iron cage would drift upwards, floating perilously between floors to imprison passengers inside. The air was different in this city and its habitual, slightly acrid reek, lingered through the atmosphere, affecting visitors and residents alike. With time, the senses deadened and it became less noticeable. Moscow was a city of unseen eyes and hidden microphones, but also a city of patterns. The street plan, with its arteries radiating from the centre, intersected by ring roads, was a web. For me the patterns were circles, defining the annular bands to which I did, or did not go. Among the latter, was the innermost, containing the Kremlin and landmarks like Red Square. If anything could be termed home, it was the band, about a mile to a mile and a half deep, directly encircling this inner core. It was the zone 'between the boulevards', which included the downtown area. I needed to go nowhere else, my government contacts and hotels were located in its west, or north quadrants. A wider band beyond the boulevards and extending to the outer ring road, ten miles out, was for me: 'back-of-beyond'—I rarely went there. On the other side of the outer ring road was more, but this could have been 'outer space'—I could not go there. This indistinct and seemingly remote region was 'out of bounds'. I merely passed through it, as an object bonded and sealed by customs on arrival, or when leaving at the end of my visits, from Scheremetjevo airport on the road to Leningrad.

Two days later, when I asked her: "Where would you like to go?" She smiled then said: "Hey, would it upset you to go to the place we saw each other first? I mean the one downstairs."

"Why? I would enjoy that."

"Jump in!" she said. "I'll drive you there." So, we went to the Aragwi, the Georgian restaurant in Gorky Street, but not to the same room. We sat at a smaller table, from which the earlier ones were out of sight. After getting through ordering, I looked around and realized that had I sat there the time before, I would not have seen her. "Was it intuition that led us to the other room, or might there have been some leprechaun involved?" I asked.

"For sure it was no Fairy Queen! She would have done a better job than having us end back-to-back, only able to converse with others. We can be thankful though. Now, we are face-to-face and there is no one to interrupt, except the waiter." She reached across and touched my hand. While talking about the place, she commented that the separation gave it intimacy. For me, the stone structure conferred a feeling of protection. I said: "It makes me conscious of being underground."

"Really! But on that subject, have you been to the important place?"

"You mean Red Square? I could not face the queues. I have enough waiting."

"You can go to the front. It's our privilege as foreigners. We are given precedence."

"It doesn't make sense to give us 'slaves of capitalism' preference over 'citizens of a free democracy'," I teased.

"They are realists—they know foreigners wouldn't go, if they had to stand in line." When I admitted I found tombs depressing, she told me it was more than a burial place. She did not know how the embalming was performed, but reminded me that apart from the Pharaohs, the concept was original. At the lying in state, nearly a million people waited five hours at thirty below zero, to view the body. Continuation of memories had powerful symbolism for the people and she thought it reasonable for them to nurture legends and immortalize Lenin, as founder of the communist state. She suggested I see it personally and volunteered to be my guide. "To go with you, makes it less forbidding. Next time I am here for the weekend, I will remind you!"

Afterwards, she took me to her flat. She drove without hesitation from the street, through the pillared entrance into the walled courtyard in front of the building. I could see the fur-hatted uniformed guard, standing by the sentry box beside the gate. I noticed him as we entered. He noticed me that night and for the first time, I saw him look at his watch, then record my description and time of arrival, in his official report notebook.

I was many times in that flat and picture it with clarity. It was small—two rooms, but large by local standards. The authorities would have allocated at least four people to live there. Bizarrely unique at the time, were the custom-built white kitchen and state-of-the-art bathroom. Appliances, every tap and each of the fittings, must have been brought across the world, for installation in this and other apartments of the building. A small hallway separated the bathroom and kitchen from the living room and along the division wall was her bookcase. I recall some of the books it contained. She had works by Balzac and Kafka. There were Russian books, like the works of Gorky and others I had not seen before, in particular Sholokhov's bulky novel *And Quiet Flows the Don,* as well as two volumes of *Tales from Life* by Konstantin Paustovskij. The bedroom was small with a single bed, so when we went to the flat, she used to lower the lights and spread a rug on the carpet, just below the bookcase. She would place the gramophone on the floor and set a record playing. That first night, it was a recent Russian recording of Bach's cello suites. Later, I bought one at the Melodiya shop in Kalinina prospect, to keep as memento. After she arranged the rug, we would stretch out on it together, talking and listening to the music. We might pick a book from the shelves and while turning the pages, talk about its contents, or the author. Sometimes we would take-off our clothes, lying together directly on the surface of the rug in front of the bookcase, making love. Through the night, we would remain on the floor. We did not need the bed. The heating was powerful in the city and it was rarely necessary to use a blanket. As we lay, I could gaze at her skin, wondering at the contours and graceful proportions of the body it covered faultlessly. There was no deception, the perfection unmarred by silhouette. I would study her belly, her hips, her breasts, the nipples gently protruding. We grew to make love compulsively, submitting to a desire that seemed not to abate.

When in the middle of the night, she woke and we might start once again to make love, she would leave the light extinguished and we would feel each other silently, in the darkness.

3

Intimacy was antidote to the sense of isolation on earlier visits to the city. Then, the alienation confounded me, now it was cancelled by fascination. My attention was held by a desire, where all seemed reinvented. Among millions each different, the odds to match affinities of individuals can exceed the realms of chance. Even with those close, who can hazard why from 'hundreds', one should draw more than others, or which from a number someone else might choose? Incidence is willful and when missed, there is no assurance of repeat. When happening after commitment to another, what rule applies?

Her presence in the city was an enigma, hard to understand. How could someone as gifted and qualified forgo opportunities in America and face the restrictions of the Soviet Union? Her action must have been motivated by personal issues and I was keen to know what she meant, when we talked about 'preserves'. She admitted, the two years of marriage until she walked out, left scars and that it was not the first time she recoiled from a man, important in her life. The sense of failure from the separation was reflection of an earlier loss. Her father abandoned home, when she was a child. She didn't say why he went, but it happened abruptly. After her divorce, a friend told her about the diplomatic teaching posts and when she called Washington, Moscow was sole vacancy to fit. It scared her and she dropped the idea, but the possibility remained in her thoughts. She tried to distinguish between popular concepts of the socialist society and possible realities. Surrender of what fellow countrymen declaimed 'a free country' was not entirely valid for her, as she explained: "You have to have the means to use liberty, and back home availability may not be as egalitarian, as seen from outside. I had a sneaking hope that once in Russia, the restrictions of the communist state might be the fake side, and after the leveling impact of the revolution, people prove more liberal and tolerant, than in my country." From there she came to regard an assignment, a benefit: "An unusual way to promote a rebirth," as she put it. "The extreme isolation could make it a recuperation station and I could view the posting like a stay in a sanatorium." She arranged an interview. Practical issues, the apartment and the vehicle, made it less threatening. When told she could bring her books, it tipped the balance. "I thought of Russian literature and took the gamble, but did not know what I was letting myself into," she confessed. I told her that on my first visit, I felt like a conscript sent to a war zone. "Come on, you can't say that! You didn't have to wear a uniform, or carry a rifle," she laughed. In practice, it was no different—I arrived in the city with a suit, carrying a briefcase. With my repetitive trips, there was no acclimatization. She had a base from the start and did not have to battle with the solitude of a hotel room. Life on the inside was familiar—job, apartment, language and textbooks, even food cooked in an American kitchen. For her, it was similar to a sailor, going to the front accompanied by the trappings on the ship. "With your books, pictures and gramophone, it's a home, a position of privilege. But you're not alone, I feel fortunate now!" I touched her hair. She bent over and I felt the light pressure of her lips on my cheek, before she added: "It may be beginner's luck. Take care!"

"Now, I can afford danger! I found a refuge in the midst of a disconnected landscape. Maybe one day, we'll be allowed to discover the country outside, surrounding us."

"It could be a revelation! We must keep it as a promise for the future."

"And in the meantime, there's something else I value about this refuge—the freedom from the microphones. It's the only place in the city, where I am relieved from the bugging."

"Why should this be different?" She asked to my surprise.

"The building was fitted-out by your embassy. It must be safe."

"Don't be so sure! For them it's ancillary. When revamped for diplomatic use, the Russians did the rebuilding and wiring can find a way in. Our security guys checked it out, but they work at different levels. This was low priority. The staff housed here is not politically sensitive. The apartment may be no more secure, than your hotel room."

"You mean there could be devices under the floor?"

"I am no expert, but I understand it is not the preferred location. Probably, it has to do with resonance. They place them high up, in ceilings, or tops of walls, where they can be concealed in the plaster without being muffled."

"Did you examine the surfaces, before your things arrived?"

"I looked in likely spots. When I measured-up, a neighbour loaned me a stepladder. But, you must be used to having them follow and observe you.

"I value the thought we are alone."

"Maybe we are—but you cannot rely on it. Does it matter, if they listen? Records of your visits by the guys at the gate must be uncompromisingly exact."

How many times did they record me, entering and leaving that building? It stirred innate anxiety each and every time. I could not recognize individual guards. The disguise of their uniform, ankle length greatcoat, and oversized fur-covered hat, made each indistinguishable. They sought comfort from the sentry box and liked to stay within, or close-by, stepping outside to peer obstinately in our direction. It was unusual for them to venture far from this cover. The notebook would be visible, usually in the left hand, so that an entry in pencil could be made with the right. They must have patterns those notebooks. They could not be filled with plain paper, for random annotations, scrawled haphazardly across the pages. No, they must be arranged symmetrically, to assure an ordered execution of a strictly regulated system of entries. They must be lined, and have headed columns.

How did they start? Did they insert date, before time? Because they checked the watch, time was probably first—whilst fresh in the memory. Date was possibly inserted earlier, as a line item made at the beginning of each shift and needing no repetition in individual report notations. How did they describe me? In the appropriate column, this might need more than one line. Perhaps numbers were used that referred to fuller descriptions at the end, or by coded reference to an indexed dossier at headquarters. Could it be that my real names are written under separate columns, designated: 'Family Name' and 'First Name'? Their file on me must be large. The appropriate department could inform guards of my name, simply in respect of the circumstances. What special identification did they add, when I came out in the morning? Was there another column to be completed with a penciled tick, when a visit lasted overnight? Would any visit, lasting a few minutes after midnight, qualify? Maybe they labelled it without ambiguity: 'Intercourse'. How could this be properly determined, hours before midnight could also call for circumspection? Perhaps there was a designated band of time, say from start of the 4 p.m. watch, until the new shift at 8 a.m. next morning? Did they subtract departure time from arrival, to give duration in hours?

4

As I lay, I noticed the light streaming-in through the three tall sash windows that symmetrically divided the wall opposite the bed. Without raising my head, I could see the trees screening the river, as it silently and relentlessly flowed towards the city. Everything in the room was bright. The soft shapes of the old pine panelling that enclosed the room playfully reflected the light around me. Its white painted surfaces contrasted with the fresh green, of newly opened leaves on trees outside. There was little grey visible. For a moment, everything was quiet as I continued to lie, gazing at the view. I thought I was alone in the house, but silence was short-lived. I heard a door slam and a clatter of feet, running up the old wooden staircase. I could feel the wide boards under the bed shake, echoing the sudden movement on the stairs. The door opened with a rush, to shrieks and shrills of laughter and both collapsed into the room, falling over each other. "Hello Daddy! When did you get back?" asked Natalie perkily.

"Come and give me a kiss both of you. I got back late and you were fast asleep. We didn't want to wake you."

"Where have you been for so long? You missed the sports day at school! The other parents were there," questioned Katie with an air of complaint. "Mummy says you must come down at once. She's taking us shopping."

"You can't come, because you won't be ready in time!" echoed Natalie.

They disappeared behind the door, to scuttle back to their mother below. Lottie, the Swiss au pair, must be with them in the kitchen. I got out of bed and staggered down the half flight of stairs to the bathroom. I needed to splash cold water on my face, shave and have a shower, before I could properly place myself, get awake and confront the new day. It was a different reality—this one foremost, existent, tangible, the other removed and fading fast. As if there were two people—me and 'him' over in Moscow with 'her'. I called it splitting. The present is here now and it happens to be first. At this moment, he, she, and the 'other world' seem compressed to a nucleus, as if non-existent. A day before, the reverse was true. Strange, the match time and distance play—one with another.

After the shower, I felt revived. I got dressed and went down to the kitchen. Katie was guarding the breakfast left on the table. There was no sign of the others and I asked why she wasn't at school. "Mummy has gone to drop something in to Laura. Natalie went too. Lottie has gone to a lesson. Daddy, it was end of term on Friday. Didn't you know the date?"

"I didn't remember the date, but it is good the term is over and you are at home. So that's why you told me you are going shopping," I said, sitting down at the table and pouring a cup of coffee from the pot kept warm with the old tea cosy.

"Why were you so late Daddy? I was coming to the airport, but Mummy said I must go to bed."

"A plane broke down. I had to wait hours in Warsaw."

"Where's Warsaw? What were you doing there?"

"It is in Poland Katie. I couldn't get a direct flight home and had to switch planes. That was the one that broke-down and they needed a replacement. It took four hours and we had to sit at the airport, without anything to eat or drink."

"That's a long time to wait. But you haven't said where you were."

"Don't you remember? I told you before I left—I was going to Russia, that big country behind the Iron Curtain. It's very strict there. Do you remember the man on telly who took his shoe off, to hit the table?"

"Yeah! That was funny. What was his name?"

"He was Mr. Khrushchev. Russia is his country. He was big boss there."

"Oh! I remember. Aren't they the enemy?"

"Sort of—but it isn't a real war. They are not so friendly. It's different there."

I heard the rear entrance slam and when I looked up, saw them walking past the magnolia tree, towards the kitchen. "They call it a cold war Katie," I added.

As Anna stepped in through the door, she said: "What's this about a cold war? There will be a war here, if one of you doesn't get this cleared away. It is almost midday. You had a long sleep, so how do you feel now?" She continued, as she bent over to kiss me.

"What happened Daddy? Why were you late?" added Natalie, interrupting.

"I was just telling Katie about it Natalie. A plane broke-down and they had to call another. It took hours, but I've recovered. It was good to sleep late."

"Hey Daddy! We're shopping with Mummy and taking Lisa. Are you coming too?"

"Yes, can't you join us? You should not go to the office after that!" said Anna.

"I'd love to, but I have to go in."

"For goodness sake, why?"

"Because Calvin is leaving for America tomorrow. I have to brief him and the others about what happened in Moscow. He is planning to be away two weeks."

"You complain that everything takes so long in Russia. You said that time does not matter there, so why can't you make them wait a couple of weeks more?"

"It doesn't work like that! To win there, it is their rules that count."

"Can't you delay once? I promised to pick up Lisa. Why don't you take the children there? It would be fun for them—you can walk along the river."

I remembered, Calvin had a lunch date and was unlikely to be back before three. "It's a good idea. Come on girls, let's go!" They were pulling me out of the kitchen, through the hall towards the front door. "Bye! We'll be back in half an hour," I called back to Anna, just before we went down the stone steps into the lane.

5

Familiarity with the area 'between the boulevards' grew. It was the zone of the city, with which he was conversant. Apart from time trapped in hotel rooms, earlier visits allowed taxi rides along the boulevards or streets and wandering by foot through back alleys or *pereuloks*. With her apartment in the same zone, the intimidating landscapes encircling them, seemed further removed. From their meeting, all appeared reinvented. It was his turn for revolution—as if there was one. He became interested to explore what initially was unnoticed, obscured or intimidating.

He had avoided the innermost zone of the city. Of course, he saw Red Square with the Lenin mausoleum, crouching rat, with its tail of party loyalists waiting to pay homage, watched by unblinking guards. It was hard to pass-by without images of May Day parades, heavy tanks and rocket launchers assaulting the mind, but he would be skirting around, or looking across. He did not have to go there. It was the same with the Kremlin. Most was closed to foreigners and sections used by the leaders, including their luxury shops were strictly off-limits. Apart from occasional visits to the opera in the Kremlin Palace, he was not tempted to go beyond the gates. Now, the sullen complexion mellowed and he went to the inner core with her, the following Sunday. They entered through the Spasski Gate next to St Basil's, closed and boarded-up, as if quarantined. Inside, they passed three more churches, likewise sealed. They walked through confined, twisting streets between old stone buildings. On one corner, a small tower projected from the wall and fixed to the weathered brickwork he saw a notice, unexpectedly familiar—a theatre poster for *A Midsummer Night's Dream* with the Royal Shakespeare Company. The text was in Russian, but layout and names were the same, transposed from the other world. Could it be a warning? He thought. "It must be their first time in the city, a sign of good luck," she said. "We should see it together!" While thinking how to extricate himself, she pointed to the notice, adding to his relief: "Look, the date has passed. A near miss!" They went somewhere else theatrical, a museum, with halls arranged in ascending chronology. The first contained implements of torture used in earlier periods, but having read Solzhenitzyn, he wondered how the room could portray reality in the Gulags. They wore cloth slippers to save the old parquet and the hushed shuffling shadowed them through the building. It was apt accompaniment for a fanciful long robe worn by Peter the Great—a costume better suited to the world of fairy-tales. She pointed to the shoulders "If so narrow, how could he be great?" It was unusual to see something not concerning the revolution, yet a reminder of its origins. Final room showed Tsarist extravagance, each exhibit competing in lavishness and walls as black as the coffin shaped bed-sit of a solicitor, next door to a friend in London. He went to work in a bowler hat and when asked why he painted them that colour, asserted that it fitted a disposition to coat molten chocolate on his member, for consumption by young clients as fee. She drew his attention to the Fabergé eggs. "Most here would rate them symbols of greed, by a degenerate society," she said. He told her of an artist, who referred to egg-shaped paintings as 'his Easter eggs'. His words were in jest, but the intemperate critic used them to humiliate. "It's not only here, we have to worry about those with power," she commented.

Outside was the red granite of the Lenin Mausoleum, its inevitable line of queuing visitors, leading across the square, out of sight. The moment had arrived and he felt a sense of apprehension. She took his arm saying: "As promised, I'll go with you." When they got level with the guard near the head of the line, she showed her pass and they exchanged words. He held back the rest, beckoning them in, near the front. In ten minutes, they were proceeding under the low doorway, passing between motionless guards with bayonets and fixed gaze that he earlier observed with a mix of curiosity and unease, crossing the other side of the square. As they started down the steps, he felt a chill. It was completely quiet, save the muffled sounds of feet, this time shoe soles slipping over stone surfaces. There was a slight dampness, but no trace of formalin, or whatever chemicals the preservation needed. The dim lighting was reflected off shiny granite walls. Standing alongside the plate glass catafalque, lit from a diffused source above, he could view the familiar profile. Was it real, or imagined reflection from statues, banners and plaques seen in the city? The shoulders were broad, or was it illusion after the robe? No deterioration seemed apparent in the elegant hands. Where was Stalin? He saw no trace.

Back in the noise and glaring daylight, she anticipated his question. "Did you realize that earlier there were two inside? Stalin used to be there alongside Lenin. Both lay together beside one another."

"That's what I thought. Wasn't it Khrushchev who had him taken out?"

"It was one of his last acts, before being removed himself."

Whilst in the area, they went to a museum dedicated to Lenin. After the clean line of the mausoleum, stripped bare except for the body, this seemed cluttered with belongings, yet forsaken by the person. The exhibits included the Rolls Royce used by this man of the people.

Vladimir Ilich Lenin, inspiration of the Bolshevik revolution, died on 20th January 1924. Seven years earlier in the spring of 1917, he was put aboard the sealed train, which transported him back from Switzerland through Germany to Sweden, from where he could enter Petrograd unnoticed. The October revolution appointed him first head of the new Soviet state, but time at the top was limited. Already in late 1921, health problems forced him to rest, and on May 22nd 1922, a stroke left him partially paralysed, with speech impaired. His last visit to the Kremlin was to retrieve papers from his office, incriminating to Stalin. To soften the ride his aides filled the tyres with sand, but the trip was in vain—Stalin got there first.

By December, Lenin's deteriorating health forced him to give up political activity. Desperate that Trotsky or Stalin might succeed him, he dictated his 'Testament' to the Congress. Stalin sought too much power, he warned. An addendum, completed days later was more direct. It urged his colleagues in the Council to find a way to have Stalin, now described 'uncouth', removed from his post. Stalin proposed the mausoleum and embalming at a closed doors meeting in 1923, when he realized Lenin might die.

Josef Stalin, whose regime lasted a quarter of a century and saw the Soviet block a world power, died on March 5th 1953. Within four years of Lenin's death, he had centralized power and taken control. From the 1930s onwards, his purges exterminated more than seven million people, put twenty million in labour camps, imprisonment, forced collectivization and exile. Stalin's body was sent for embalming within days of his death. The preserved corpse was placed in the mausoleum after State funeral and remained there for eight years, an unintended juxtaposition of the poles—creative intellect of Lenin and ruthless autocracy of Stalin combined for the faithful and the fearful.

It was five years after Khrushchev's denouncement of Stalin's cult, before they secretly removed his body and buried the remains under the Kremlin walls. Lenin's body was again, alone.

6

The new life in the city offered contrasts. Fresh patterns replaced those of before. Earlier patterns, depicting comfortless days in hotel rooms, were concerned with distribution of time—arrangements of data in rows and in columns. Filled spaces represented repetitious events, blanks the emptiness. The new patterns depicted lovemaking in front of the bookcase. They would be juxtaposed within the three-dimensioned space, immediately above the surface of the rug, spread in its usual position on the carpeted floor. Because the two figures barely remained stationary, the fourth dimension was necessary, to define them in respect of time. Images of uninterrupted motion were multifarious, continuously fluttering forms of a cinema screen. Individual descriptions are not possible, as before one could be fixed, it had moved and been replaced, perhaps not to be repeated in quite the same combination. Generically, these patterns, which occurred in her flat, usually at night after dimming the lights, were tempestuous.

The term should not imply conflict, for there was none. The word is used figuratively, to portray the nature of the patterns. These were unconstrained by rules, or definitions and without bounds to the uniqueness of the configurations. Viewed from above, alongside or in front, they might seem unconventional, impulsive, or unpremeditated—sometimes across the warp of the rug, diagonal over its rectangular outline, or outside its boundaries altogether. As uncontained extrapolations of spontaneity, they could be turbulent and just as the energy of vapour increases, when liquid approaches boiling point, so did the concentration intensify, when stimulation approached its peak.

Without warning, his latent fear of clandestine strife with the other side, took a step towards reality. She wanted him to see a large development, built by the authorities in the north of the city. When both had time-off, they made a sortie into the region, which he considered 'back-of-beyond'. On the way, she pointed out the recently built *Ostankino* television tower, the country's highest structure—tinted orange by the setting sun. Continuing their northerly direction, they arrived at the blocks she mentioned. There was no denying they were large, for anywhere outside America. From the distance, the symmetry of the clean rectangular outlines, unbroken except by the uniform patterns of windows, looked imposing. She told him "It's a favourite for politicians from abroad." He asked if they were residential and she got out of the car saying: "Come see!" They stepped carefully around large cavities in the concrete slabs of a wide walkway that led up to the nearest of the blocks. She went alone to the entrance, as if looking for a doorbell, or one of the mailboxes. In the waning daylight and with the porch area in shadow, he couldn't decipher what she was doing. While waiting, he looked more closely at the nearest building. From there, defects were visible, windowpanes smashed, missing, or blocked-up with cardboard and ahead, a broken door hanging at an obscure angle with a hinge snapped-off. When she returned, she led him behind the front building to an area that divided it from the next. Here there was a general air of desolation, with an unimaginable assembly of faded washing, on a jumble of lines. "Do you notice the lights?" she asked. It was now getting dark and he could see them shining inside the buildings. When he asked if she meant the number, she pointed out that a light was visible in every window. There was no separate space. People lived and slept in the same room—generally two, or more in each. Not one room was in darkness. Thousands had their home there. She told him that the party guides drove foreign visitors past to demonstrate the progress of communism. Then, she turned to lead him back between the blocks. As they reached the corner of the first, on their way towards the street, she pulled her hand abruptly from his. Surprised, he asked what was wrong. "Look ahead! We have visitors," she whispered. "Don't you see the police car parked behind mine?"

As he looked, the lights came on inside a jeep-like vehicle and two uniformed policemen stepped out on either side. They went over to her car and circled it with the interest of sniffing dogs, peering through each of the windows. On seeing them approach, one shouted sharply. She went to her car to get the documents. She took her passport, asking him to give them his, but the hotel had kept it. They were ordered into the back of the jeep and detained for almost an hour, repetitively questioned and filling-in one form after another. When eventually released and the police out-of-sight, he asked: "Did they tell you what offence we committed?"

"They said we behaved suspiciously."

"Did you make a drop in a mailbox?"

"Just pretending—I thought someone from inside might wonder what we were up to."

"The militia wasn't around when we stopped. We were behind the building and out of sight."

"True! Somebody inside must have reported us."

"Did they say what will happen?"

"The guys made it clear, they can prosecute, but did not say whether they would."

"Let's hope it's only a threat. They should be straight and let us know."

"People in their position probably don't have the authority— everything gets referred upwards!"

"Maybe we won't hear again."

"If we don't get a charge, we will be left in suspense. It's the way things go here."

"It's callous—a lesson to keep our heads down and stay invisible."

"I didn't expect this. You are right, we must take care in future— anywhere outside the apartment."

It was his first brush with the Soviet police. With or without a charge, names would be linked in a report that sooner or later will end up on his file, as well as hers. Somewhat jaded, they returned to where they felt safe. As she drove back, he scolded himself: I must avoid anything that can draw attention.

The shock of her arrival in Moscow was self-imposed, but earlier traumas were the result of other people's actions and besides the desertion by her father, she experienced abuse from another trusted person. She became close with a school friend, an only child living nearby and was welcomed in their house almost as daughter. Her proper parents had difficulty supporting two children and there was no money to take them on holiday. The school friend's family rented a house by the sea and invited her to spend the summer with them. An old building on three floors, it was directly opposite the boardwalk that ran along the shore. This was the first time she had a room to herself and wasn't afraid to sleep alone—it was 'like home'. The sun blazed from morning until nightfall and the two could run across to the beach, to spend the days with other children. In the evenings, there was a routine, going back at six, to join the parents on the veranda for long drawn-out family meals. Afterwards, the girls went to bed in their attic rooms. For the first month, the regular programme continued unbroken. One night, she was awoken by a tapping and assumed it was her friend. She got out of bed to let her in, supposing she could not sleep and wanted to chat. It wasn't she. It was the father. He stood wearing a dressing gown and without a word, pushed his way around the door. He leaned back against the doorframe and pulled her against him, his hands on her back, clasping her. She felt his hardness through the thin material and terrified, burst into tears. For a time he continued gripping her in the same position. Then, after she started to scream, he backed away, looking angry and muttering apologies. She felt damaged.

When all was quiet, she ran into the water. Only after the waves covered her head, did she swim back. It went no further, but the experience confronted her with a new vulnerability. She was ten and for her, childhood ended that night. She didn't tell her friend—she thought it unfair. Away from home, there was no one she could confide in. The man became hostile and the remaining weeks were torture. Soon afterwards, her father left home taking his belongings, including the books. He went back to South America. Although she was not told the reason, his loss and the incident with her friend's father, were then connected in her mind. The vacant space in the bookcase was a reminder. She had to learn to live with empty shelves.

He was familiar with her bathroom and relished the flows from the adjustable showerhead. Its bottom surface was flat and homogenous and the water ran through small holes, arranged in six symmetrical circles, set flush in the shiny chrome. The small lever mounted on its side, was similar to a safety-catch on a gun. When turned, six bullet-like plungers, each with its eight channels, emerged from behind the rings, breaking the sleekness. They moved in perfect unison, like conscripts on a drill ground, as the handle advanced towards the stop at the other end. In the normal position, the pattern was orderly. Soothing, fine bead-like droplets would spread outwards in a cone, whose base was wide enough to surround and enclose his frame. Looking upwards, he would see a circle above his head, dropping vertically downwards, over and around him. The fine particles soothed the skin, wet its surface and trickled down the limbs, to collect beneath the feet, before running away. In the other position, the pattern of the flow was unruly. The water would rush in full flood, from the channels around the distended protrusions. Convoluting briefly, before falling like strands of an untwisted rope, it would lash his body as if a punishment. He avoided this and left the setting in its normal position. If tired after sleeping badly, or being awake with her much of the night, he might edge it to some mid-way position, so the jets would concentrate on his head and the stream across the eyes be faster and more intense.

Her shower was different from those in the hotels. Frequently they would not function and it was necessary to put water in the bottom of the bath to splash oneself. When a shower did work, there was no uniform distribution. Operation would be hesitant, often intermittent. Occasionally, it would stop completely, without warning.

7

Sometimes lying with her at night, he would raise his head and look towards the bookcase directly in front. Although concealed by the darkness, he would stare into the shadows trying to decipher the familiar pattern, finding reassurance in the solidity of its frame and the constancy of its form. He would try to identify the parallel lines of the straight white shelves, by watching for reflections from minute traces of light, penetrating the room, as they struck and collided against books with glossy jackets, or bright, glimmering spines.

There were nights when the moon was strong. It would shine through the window into the flat and light their reclining bodies. He would lie gazing at the singular shade of her skin, contemplating the soft malleable contours, randomly highlighted by the intrusion. Sometimes, he would study the contours of her breasts, or observe the triangle of her pubic hair, faintly visible in the suffused reflected light.

"I didn't realize you had the book of *Marienbad*. We can play the matches game," he said, when discovering her copy of Robbe-Grillet's text for Renais' film *Last Year at Marienbad*.

"Have you read it? The atmosphere is haunting."

"I have not seen the book before, but the film was impressive and I remember the game of matches. I played it with friends. Such games can be a power test, but this one is an illusion. As well as rules, it has a trick and anyone working this out, will win."

"Then you probably deciphered it." He remained silent, recalling: I had to see the film three times, to do so. When they took the book and lay together on the rug looking at the illustrations that showed stills from the film, he momentarily thought about another life that seemed unconnected. For no apparent reason she got up and went into the kitchen. Did she apprehend? He continued holding the book, its text triggering the memory for rules painstakingly worked-out a few years before. "I think I have it—the layout and basic rules of play, I mean. You got matches?" He called to her.

She seemed to recover from whatever upset her and brought the matches. He took sixteen from the box and laid them evenly spaced in four parallel lines, with seven then five, three and a single one as the last—in the form of an arrowhead. "Doesn't it matter, at whom it points? That must be important. I mean the position in respect of us both."

"No, it is irrelevant, it can point at either player. The starting arrangement is always the same—with no exception," he explained.

"Who goes first?"

"It depends on chance. We can draw for this. Afterwards, it alternates."

"What happens then?"

"Each time, you can take one, or as many matches as you like, but from only one of the four rows. The restriction is the line in which they are placed."

"I suppose the person with the most at the end wins," she suggested.

"Numbers are of no concern. It's like here—the rules are contradictory. You don't win by beating. You have to get the other trapped. One player has to corner the other into taking the last match. Whoever does that is loser, not winner." He concealed a match in one hand and held both out to her. "Left or right?" He asked.

"I'll back left!" she said. It was correct and she started. She took the single match in the last row. "What do you do with the ones you select?" she enquired.

"Once picked-up, they have no significance. They can be kept undercover until the game is finished."

He took one of the seven, from the first row. She followed with two from the same row. He took two matches, from the five in the second row. She thought for a moment and picked-up one, from the third row of three. He took three from the second row. She took one from the third row. He took four from the first row, leaving her with the single last match. "I see," she said surprised. "You've won. Is it beginner's luck? Perhaps you worked-out the trick!"

"No comment!" He responded.

"I want to try again. This time it's your start. I will be more attentive and observe each move," she said, anxious to recoup her disadvantaged position. He took six matches from the first row. "Well if you are going to act like a despot, so will I," she said, taking all five matches from the second row. He took two matches from the third row. She realized she had lost. Whichever of the three remaining matches she took, he could then pick up either of the two left and she had to take the last. "There's no justice here!" she exclaimed. "There is something underhand. You seem to take advantage. It's insider knowledge. You have to make a disclosure!"

"Tomorrow!" He said, inwardly ashamed at enjoying the power play. Why didn't I admit and explain? He asked himself in silence, while she carefully replaced the matches in their box and returned them to the kitchen.

He thought of another occasion, where pieces were set in strict formation. Sheard laid out his, to satisfy a particular eccentricity. They were not matches, but canes and not in an arrowhead but parallel. He devised a way to transform a simple school beating—to a flogging with a thirty-foot run. By marking the canes with chalk, he could ensure that successive strokes were aimed at the wounds from before, to multiply the pain. Corporal punishment was an arena for deviation. Sheard had a reputation to be feared and I was ill fated to fall victim under his 'reign of terror'. Like in Moscow, it was necessary to keep out-of-sight and adhere to the rules. If picked, you were doomed. I could watch between my straightened legs, as thrashing like a machine, he beat the air to practice each stroke. The speed increased, until ten yards later, the lash tore into the tightly stretched skin. Like in a ritual, he paced back to meticulously pick another. It took three weeks for wheals and cuts to heal. Repetition on the open wounds had to be avoided. It was fortunate they were only canes. At the Lubyanka, specially designed implements replacing those in the museum, must achieve levels of suffering far exceeding 'flogging'. With the matches—it was a game.

One evening, she suggested a new restaurant, further out in 'back-of-beyond'. It was the Baku on ulica Svernika, in a south-easterly direction from the centre. She wanted him to sample their Azerbaijan cooking. She promised to book the table, but the evening had a bad start. She was almost forty minutes late, where they were to meet and he felt vulnerable, waiting exposed in the street. By the time they arrived, delay had grown to an hour and the waiter responsible for bookings, had given the table to someone else. It was impractical to go elsewhere. Encouraged by dollar notes, the waiter went to a small table, where a young man sat alone, with a glass, guarding a carafe. Following an angry exchange, he picked up the vodka and dragging his feet, shuffled to join a group of older men. The waiter put-on a new cover, straightened the seats and beckoned them over. She sat next to the rear wall and he opposite, with the sidewall to his right and his back to the room. The delay annoyed him more than it should have. After a trying day, he was looking forward to be with her and in no mood for unexpected irritants. He couldn't blame her, as it was she, who ferried him around, wherever they went. She was rarely late. What upset him, were her implausible explanation and refusal to discuss it. She became evasive and talked about the antics of a child, who played-up at school.

"Hi honey! How's it going? Haven't seen you around for months." The loud, grating voice made him shrink. It came from immediately behind, the accent obviously American. He turned around to see someone short and stocky, with hair sprouting back from a ravaged temple that crowned a worn face. Looking at least twice her age, certainly over fifty, the man wore an ankle length, dark leather coat and clutched a fur hat in one hand, only inches from the food on the table. He felt angered, unsure whether this was from further disruption to an evening, which started badly, or from the familiarity with which he addressed her. The thought of him being other than a casual acquaintance was disturbing. "Hi honey! It's great to see you! I need help," the voice continued.

"Curtis! What a surprise! I thought you left town. Come say hello to a friend from the outside. This is Curtis Weltler. He's been around a real long time."

"Good to know you fellow. But honey I wasn't kidding. I do need help. I haven't eaten and they want to throw me out. The place is full to the eaves. Mind if I join you, the waiter can bring a chair." It was clear that the longed for seclusion with her was being trespassed.

"Sure Curtis! Make yourself at home!" He listened to the words, powerless to intervene, silently murmuring assent, as they slid their chairs across towards the sidewall and the waiter set another at the end. It was not only their peace that was being shattered. At this small table, I felt trapped—there was no escape from this loud, expansive man. It was as if he were climbing into bed with us.

"So tell me honey what have you been up to?"

"I have been here throughout. Everything's been normal. But where were you, since I last saw you?"

"I was home seven months. After a break as long, I've lost the sense of place. It's spooky!" They talked about people he had not met and of happenings, or events with which he was unfamiliar. He felt increasingly alienated. Perhaps to satisfy curiosity, or show faked cordiality, he interrupted: "Where is home?"

"Baltimore, you been there?"

"I passed through on the way to Washington. I didn't stay."

"Curtis is bluffing," she commented. "Home is here. He's an old timer. This city was home to him for years. How long was it Curtis?"

"Almost five. Maybe I'll be staying some more now. I have to see how things work out." Sensing he was ill at ease, she added: "Curtis is knowledgeable about the city."

"Oh! Is that so!" He said dismissively, then recanting to try for a friendlier course: "How did you pick-up the knowledge? It's not easy to draw people out beneath the camouflage."

"Quite the reverse! It's real hard to be long term, without learning a hell of a lot along the way. Besides, if you need to survive here as I do, you have to want to understand things. You can't fight the system—you have to go with it."

"Stories circulate by word of mouth. People living here don't talk about much else. The political scene impinges everywhere," she intervened.

"Have you seen differences, over the period you have been here?" He asked, feigning interest.

"Maybe some names are new. There's been some musical chairs at the top, but nothing else."

After a pause, then turning to look at him directly in the eyes, he added in a lower, but compelling tone: "Change is a mirage."

He looked around the room, before continuing in a half-whisper: "It doesn't exist. In the scene here, the power of the system is immutable."

"That's a surprise to me! The fellows I meet for my business repeat the line of how egalitarian it is. They even claim that decisions can be influenced by the rank and file."

"It's crap! Have no illusions! Anybody can make suggestions." He lowered his voice further, as he continued: "Woe betide anything abnormal—it can be labelled 'deviationist'. It's not healthy to draw attention to yourself. It can put a person in real deep water."

"You mean everything goes on, the same as before."

"Absolutely! The built-in systems resist novelty."

"It happens everywhere. Nature reacts to change. A law says: 'changes towards order' are reversed to the previous state of 'disorder', but to label natural order—disorder, is absurd."

"Maybe, but who says nature is more important than the party?"

"It's a matter of broad and narrow. Nature is universal, the vision of most politicians limited, or they would not make change towards a so-called 'order' that in fact is 'disorder' and vulnerable."

That was a conversation stopper and he let them continue their chatting. From the self-assured manner, he assumed their tablemate was a diplomat, but deciding to check, asked: "Are you with the embassy?"

"No Curtis is in business," she intervened. "Curtis has to battle with the trading corporations like you. He has been fighting them for years and could probably teach you a thing or two."

"I have a current problem. Could it be something you would know about?"

"It depends on which business and what problem, but don't let's talk here!"

"I have my car, Curtis. Why don't you ride back? I can drop you where you're heading and you can talk on the way," she suggested.

"That's fine by me!" Curtis responded. "This place must be about to close for the night. If you're ready to go, I'll skip the coffee." Concerned they would be stuck there for another hour or so, he turned to attract the attention of the waiter, and saw the tables were empty. The waiter's attentiveness and the speed he brought the bills, were unusual—he was waiting for them to leave. As they went to the car, she asked: "Where do you want to be dropped Curtis?"

"I am at the Metropole," he replied.

"I can drop you out front."

When safely in the car, he told Curtis the problem—a common one. The trading people wanted to talk about commercial matters and there was nobody, ready to discuss fundamental issues of the business.

"Behaviour of those guys seems oftentimes illogical, but they have support from up top. Undermining negotiations that go well is official policy. They know the longer the delay, the better the terms they can extract. Other stuff gets kept behind the scenes. I don't know anything about your field—it's a long ways from mine. There will be a specialist institute involved and if you want to influence progress, you have to find out where it is located, most are outside of Moscow. You'll need a permit to get there."

"The trading fellows would block a visit by me."

"It's the way the rules are set. If you want to make things happen, you have to go see the experts."

"They would not allow me to make contact," I said.

"You have to beat the system."

"But it's not possible!"

"Nothing's impossible! It's just harder," he responded. "There's a way with these things."

"It sounds convincing, can you expand?"

"As I said—first, you have to know who the right people are and second, you have to find a way to get there, so you can meet them."

"But can these people make decisions that contradict the others?"

He hesitated a moment. "You need to understand the way the political guys and those behind-the-scenes, inter-relate here. According to the system, power in economic affairs is concentrated with the party officials. In practice, they pass responsibilities downward to the specialists, who we foreigners are supposed not to meet. It's they, who have gotten their heads on the line."

"You mean the party people don't have authority to make the decisions?"

"I didn't say that! I didn't say they don't have it. I said they use others, so they can lay-off the risk—pass the buck!"

"Then, to whom do they refer it?"

"The guys we're talking about, the professionals. They carry the blame for whatever goes wrong, so they have the motive to get it right and if not—are in deep trouble."

"If the specialists take the responsibility, it must be impossible to achieve anything without meeting them."

"You got it!" He snapped. "Hey! You can drop me on the corner here. I hope it gives you a lead to work on."

"Thanks! You planted new thoughts."

He clambered out of the car saying: "I'll see you honey!" She drove away at once and he watched Curtis walking along the pavement, but said nothing when he noticed him going in the wrong direction, away from the hotel.

As she drove, he stayed silent. Curtis seemed versed in the political scene, but I didn't trust him, he appeared to be playing a part. It was helpful to give tips for the business, but were these genuine? If so, they could be useful and it was thanks to her—it was she, who encouraged Curtis to talk.

"Guess what play we are reading at the school next term?"

"I have no idea! Could it be something by Shakespeare?"

"Getting warm!"

"*A Midsummer Nights Dream?*" He offered.

"Right! From the many possibilities, it's peculiar! I get the feeling I am re-crossing lines. I know there's this theory that one half of the brain senses something, a split second before the other and gives a false sense of recognition."

"I know what you mean—it's as if loops keep intersecting."

"In this case, not people—only a play!"

When they got to the flat, he questioned her about Curtis being in the CIA. She denied it and seemed to resent the insinuation, insisting he was a casual acquaintance and as a businessman, part of the scene there. She often ran into him at parties among the American community and they had mutual friends from that circle. When he pressed further about what he did for a living, she told him he was a trader and gave the bizarre story that he imported ladies underwear from American manufacturers. A mutual acquaintance had told her that for his particular line, he was the principal importer in the Soviet Union. She seemed to believe this, adding that when it came to underwear, people close to the centre of power, preferred the American products. They liked the artificial silky materials, durable and easy to wash—forbidden fruit, with strictly limited access. It was absurd, but he didn't openly challenge her. He raised the matter on several occasions, to see if she gave a different answer and each time it was the same. Was she involved with him in something he didn't understand? The thought of her embroiled in spying, was not merely unbelievable—it was surreal.

If not watched through a telescope, lovemaking might be monitored with a planted microphone. When it came to recording the human voice, with its many scales and shades, the Russians were practiced and resourceful, but at such times, words were superfluous. In the dimmed lighting in front of the bookcase, they communicated with eyes and touch, watching or feeling each other's bodies in their nakedness. Dispensing with a bed was not planned, but expedient—eliminating giveaways. They felt protected on the rug, it deadened sound and muffled movement. Listeners would need patience for monotonous sessions of near soundless playback. But he overlooked, they probably did not have Dolby systems for removal of noise from the raw tape. Then, it would be a struggle to endure the impenetrable hiss and maintain their concentration, as the unprocessed tape laboured its way through equipment that was lacking.

8

When thinking of times in her flat, the image of the bookcase often comes to mind. The symmetry displayed by its structure, characterized by the definitive arrangement of its parts, resembled the ordered and reproducible distribution of events, during earlier visits to the city, or the uniform page layouts in the notebooks of the guards outside her building. It was a matrix, the columns, represented by the four vertical sections and the rows, by the six lines of parallel shelving that together divided the whole, to its twenty-four components. From arrangement of the individual elements, allocation of smaller books in the higher narrow ones and larger volumes, in those wider spaced lower in the structure, may have suggested a design or orderly array, but the distributions appeared accidental, the shading, jacket designs and angles of repose, random in their disposition. In some compartments, books might be placed at odd angles, horizontally across the tops of others or as supports, propping items where the space was incompletely filled. In others, patterns were variegated as those of the lovemaking, directly in front. They might be constrained by the area of the rug. So were these, but by the frame of white painted wood that surrounded each. Within the confines, designs were unlimited as regards their creativity, colours and haphazardness.

"It intrigues me how you got into books," she said one evening, while they sat together by her bookcase. He explained it was connected with time. For her, books were reminder of a void, for him they filled one. At the age, she was forcibly confronted with sexuality—he was exploring second-hand bookshops, some cavernous, unending. His final trophy was a book about the French revolution—a two-volume edition with portraits of leading revolutionaries. He only made it halfway and for years did not buy another. After the gap, there was theatre—Brecht, T.S. Elliot and Jean Anouilh, whose plays led him to the French contemporary writers, but elsewhere. "What do you mean—elsewhere?" She asked. Elsewhere was afloat, strung beside a jetty in a neglected port. Monday to Friday, minesweeping exercises were conducted at sea. By five o'clock every evening and through weekends they were abandoned, tied doglike to an iron ring. Curiously, the ship's name was 'Pluto'. It wasn't the monotony, but encouragement from a companion, a rebel forced to serve by an obstinate father. They spent hours discussing books, most new to him. He learned the differences, between the idealists and materialists, about existentialism—Hegel, Kiergergaard. He discovered Sartre and Camus. There was no space for the books, but he kept a list for years. It filled his void. "It sounds more like a monastery than a warship, but we can keep the subject for another time. I should get ready for bed. We need to leave at seven tomorrow."

She went to the bathroom and he heard the familiar sound of water running from her shower. The pitch altered, she must have switched to the second position. Normally she used that in the morning. While he lay waiting for her to return, he thought of what she said. She would not have used the strange term to describe life on the ship, had she known the facts. Alongside, most of the ship's company ended up in bars, which were everywhere in that town, many dilapidated. When drunk, the sailors liked to brawl. Once away from the watchful eye of the CPO and with libido loosened by alcohol, it could be savage. There might be thirty or so in one bar, in a mighty free-for-all. I thought of the time they went for Marsden. They threw him through a plate glass window, clean out into the street. A favourite was the bottle game. They broke the end off, and rammed the jagged edges into the opponent, aiming for the face, particularly the eyes.

His gaze returned to the bookshelves high up, wherever books lay casually pushed between others, or in spaces above. She came back from the bathroom and squatted next to him. "Have you thought they could have planted a camera in the bookcase? You wouldn't see it there, with the shadows. They could be watching us when we make love. Maybe they can see us now."

"Come on!" she replied. "What's got into you?"

"I felt uneasy. It's dark there—an obvious place to hide one. When did you last remove books at the top? Someone could have got into the building, when you are out."

"Impossible! Most reliable feature of this building is the locks, highly special and top security. They can't be tampered with."

"What if a key gets lost?"

"There are safety procedures. We have a 24-hour emergency back-up service from the marines. No one can get in. It's possible they can listen, but they can't see us."

"They could photograph through the window with a telephoto lens."

"That's different! But so what! They know I'm here and that you are with me. What do pictures add? From the archive of your visits, they can prove you sleep here. You'd have a hard time denying it, besides, there's no law against making love in this country."

"I hope they can't film us," he said, concerned.

The following evening, she mentioned the ship and wanted to know who else had interest in books. He told her, many must have known of Herman Wouk's *Cain Mutiny*, because the First Lieutenant was nicknamed *Queeg*, but he had to disappoint her, probably few read it. He mentioned two, who might have featured in novels—the first, from the pages of Henry Miller, was forever in search of women. He broke the rules bringing them to his cabin, sometimes two at a time. They made so much noise—the bo'sun threatened mutiny from jealousy. Most nights, it was someone new and flaunting his success, he proclaimed: 'it was the first time that excited'. "Each was likely the bigger disappointment," she commented. The second, an older fellow, became lodged through disillusionment in his own *Catch-22*. Dragged from a childhood sweetheart in the war to go to sea, he returned three years later, finding her settled with his younger brother. After drink drained the savings, a new life-style consumed the pay. He was trapped—same as the people in Joseph Heller's novel. Then, unexpectedly, he quit to captain one of the floating palaces, tied up in Monte Carlo. 'It would be Paradise after that'—to use his words. "A bedtime story for adolescents!" she smiled. "I have to think of my kids and need to check texts for the class. I must do it now, before I get tired, or forget. Give me five minutes, then I'll put a record on."

She took some papers and went over to sit on her bed. He settled on the rug. She was right about the one with the girls. I knew about his ghosts. He was brash about the time he joined-up as a seaman, recounting how when his carrier went to New York to show the flag, the young sailors were enticed into limousines by cashmere-coated cruisers, offering to show them something more. He argued it wasn't for the money, but the curiosity. 'You couldn't imagine the luxury of those pads, and the size of their automobiles,' he quipped. I was glad to answer her question, without disclosing the script. She didn't need to know, why the other was caught in the *Catch-22*, 'programmed' on a four-day cycle. It was every fourth day he took the train to London, shuffling down the gangway, muttering disdainfully: 'I always say—four days is the absolute maximum!' Spitting the words from the corner of his mouth, as he headed for the big city, where the four-day's accumulation of semen would be spent inside one of the spectral women, who waited for him there. Reinforced by a few drinks, he returned relaxed and breezy, but the poorer. Such incidents seemed remote, but made him conscious of how happy she made him.

A day or so afterwards, they discussed the *Outsider* by Albert Camus. He noticed a copy on her shelves, and was interested in her opinion. "I haven't looked at it since I came here, but I remember the unsentimental account of the mother's funeral at the start, and the colourful description of life in Algiers," she remarked.

"It doesn't seem a particular favourite."

"We worked on it at college. The author was considered important as an existentialist, then Sartre distanced himself, suggesting Camus be classified elsewhere and I don't know how the dispute ended. As regards the book, I warmed to the narrator for his intense outlook on life. A particular sentence encapsulated this. I believe it ran: 'One day of experience in the outside world, is enough to provide thoughts, for years in a prison cell.' The main character said this shortly after he was put in jail."

"I didn't notice that particular statement. I saw the book as an account of injustice. The description of pious lawyers distorting truth was poignant and how an act of chance was twisted, to become premeditation. At the mother's funeral, behaviour of the man in the dock was exaggerated almost to the point of matricide. They tried to portray him as a monster to the jury and later scenes are reflections of what can take place in any so-called 'court of justice'."

"I am no judge. I have little familiarity with that scene. I find courts scary and like to keep away."

"For me the book is an unsettling study of victimization."

"That was the part that disappointed me. Once the main character was arrested, he seemed to give up. He did little to help himself out of his plight and his passivity and naivety seemed to go too far, to my mind a touch implausible."

"It's odd you should mention implausibility, because something referred to as 'the story of the Czech', relates to this, remember? A man, returning home with a fortune after years abroad, is not recognized by his family and killed by them for the money he carries. The narrator admits it could be believable, or unbelievable."

"Maybe he questioned the nature of reality. Personally, I felt the second part was incompatible, a story of pessimism and hopelessness."

"I don't believe the author saw it as pessimistic, or hopeless. In an introduction, Sartre explained how Camus wanted to present death by execution as heroic, opposed to death by suicide, which Camus referred to as: 'cowardly . . . with farewell notes and resentments'—whereas the man condemned to death: 'acts with dignity and achieves true freedom, to rise above those, who condemned him'. But he had to admit not understanding, how a condemned person can achieve freedom after execution. She suggested this remain a literary dilemma.

Another time, she said unexpectedly: "The stories of your companions on the ship disturb me. I can't imagine women acting this way. There has to be something other than physical need." Defensively, he suggested, indulgence was not a male prerogative. When she would not agree, he recounted an incident that happened when a student: "Two girls shared the flat above. We were on friendly terms and chatted on the stairs when we met, or borrowed things from each other. They had regular partners and were frequently at parties. Late one evening, the older of the two asked to come in. She was leaving the next day, about to get married at the weekend and wanted to say good-bye. I offered her a drink and asked about her future husband. He was a politician and she seemed proud of him. After saying this, she made no move to go and we carried on talking well into the night. At one point, she said I must be tired and should get into bed. She sat on the floor alongside and we continued the conversation. Then she put her hand under the bedclothes and felt me. Without a word, she undressed and joined me in bed. It was before the time of the pill. I had not anticipated this and she let me make love to her without protection. It was less than a week to her wedding and she could have had my child!"

"Her fiancé could have been a good match, but maybe she was not sure. A friend at college told me she went to bed with someone three days before her wedding. I quizzed her about it. The commitment scared her and she thought the experience with the other man would help the decision." When he asked about the outcome, she added: "The friend got married as planned, but there was a problem. A mutual acquaintance saw her going into the man's house and told her fiancé. He got suspicious and there was an unholy row. He wouldn't believe they hadn't gone to bed, and almost broke it off."

"In both cases the girl's behaviour appears compulsive. Perhaps you are right—motivated by fear. But you have to admit, sex like death is a levelling influence that applies to all!"

"Yeah! To everyone, everywhere, regardless of creed—capitalists, even communists!" She laughed, then continued: "And you could say that sex is as pervasive and covert as the party here!"

"Indisputable!"

"There's something more you can add. From all of them, there can be no one, who doesn't have something to hide."

9

We went down towards the river holding hands, turning right at the bottom to take the road that curves between the high walls, dividing the gardens. We passed under the stone bridge, with its gracefully twisting carved balustrades that linked the park with the gardens alongside the river. All was bright—the lush leaves on the bushes, blossom hanging over the walls and mellow pink of the old bricks. As we reached the churchyard, Natalie bolted up the steps. "Let's go through the graveyard, it's quicker!" said Katie. When I got to the top, Natalie was nowhere to be seen. "She's hiding. You have to find her before I count ten, it's a game Daddy!" Said Katie, a note of challenge in her voice. I thought of the matches game—this time, I must not be winner. I saw a small coloured shoe, projecting from behind a large tombstone and pretended not to notice. I went in the opposite direction, around the building and the heavy old gravestones, to the other end of the churchyard. "Fourteen, fifteen, sixteen, seventeen . . ."

Walking towards where I saw the foot, I grabbed it, shouting: "Gottcha!"

"That's not less than ten. It's eighteen! Daddy is the loser," proclaimed Katie, proud to be arbiter.

"What is the penalty?" I questioned.

"A new uniform to play 'Nurses & Patients'," cried Natalie.

"Well I suppose it's my fault for being slow. The gravestone you hid behind was very large and old, I couldn't see around it. We had better go to the toyshop, as they may close for lunch," I said, looking at my watch.

"Yes come-on," screamed Natalie racing ahead. "I want to see if they have other bits for my outfit."

The girls found what they wanted, to pay off the penalty and something else, to compensate for returning empty-handed. I liked to bring presents, though Moscow was difficult. There were those egg-shaped painted dolls, concealing six, or as many as ten inside. You had to split the outer at the waist, to find the next inside. I brought these after the first trip and put them with their Easter eggs. They were fascinated, opening one after the other, each time discovering a smaller doll inside, but it could not be repeated. I took the girls home, fetching what I needed for the office. There was a meeting that afternoon.

When I returned that evening, Anna was in the kitchen preparing dinner, but Lottie was absent. "I forgot to ask this morning, where's Lottie?"

"She's at Michelle's. It's the third time—she went for the afternoon. It's more than two days now. I am not going to permit it. She is here as au pair and is supposed to look after the children. I'll call the agency in the morning. I will ask for a replacement."

"But Lottie has been good with the children. They love her," I said.

"She was reliable, but seems another person since Michelle got after her. The first time, she went for a couple of hours to do the ironing and came back the next day."

"I don't understand. Michelle is such a beauty. You think Lottie sleeps with her?"

"I know she does. You've seen their flat. There's only one bed. The chairs in the sitting room are too uncomfortable."

"Maybe she sleeps on the floor. Their flat is large and there must be space."

"That's absurd! Nobody could sleep on a wooden floor, even with carpet. Imagine how hard it would feel. It's impossible."

"I suppose you are right, but perhaps they are in love. It's odd, because Michelle could have any man she wanted and she has Lars. Where is he?"

"Away making a film, as usual. He travels continuously. Michelle said she feels for him, but it need not be exclusive. She admitted she's bi-sexual. I got cool, when I thought she was after me, but she can afford to forget me now Lottie is star attraction. She has no right to seduce our au pair and leave me to do the work."

"If it goes on, her parents might find out. Thank God, she won't get pregnant!"

"The next one will be so plain, Michelle won't be interested."

It happened fast. Two days later, we said good-bye to Lottie. The children were sad and Natalie cried when she left. The agency happened to have a new Swiss girl available. Anna saw a photo and said, she had a plain face and wore heavy spectacles. It sounded rather forbidding. Her name was Heidi and she would start the following Monday.

I couldn't help wondering what 'she' might think, if he told her about Michelle and her affair with the au pair. Anna's remark about being unable to sleep on the floor would amuse her—but I must not tell her. I cannot protect only the one sheltered by vows and the law. Neither pole of a triangle can be overburdened. Rules of splitting apply both sides. Despite her understanding about my family, she does not know them, nor has she seen them. If he spoke about them, she might form pictures in her mind. Better, keep images bland . . . devoid of contour, or substance. At this moment however, I should not be thinking of her.

10

The monotony on the first visits to Moscow, made his life there moduled as those of the Russian guards, keeping watch outside her building. He did not make entries in notebooks, but they shared an awareness of boredom. Like them, he experienced the protraction of each day and was conscious of how long he had to wait, for what happened, or might not happen, next.

After meeting her, the correlation differed. The earlier void was replaced by a perception that all was fleeting. Things happened instantaneously and a feeling of transience prevailed throughout. He was aware of the lightness of time. Time became fugitive.

Staff at the ministry responsible for the convention, were steadfast in maintaining their incognito second role, a closely guarded secret. Unexpectedly, it was leaked by the foreign press. A Westerner was arrested for espionage in Budapest, and his Russian accomplice in Moscow was shot. The man worked in the same department of the ministry, as those he dealt with. The newspapers reported names and positions, also the surreptitious roles of others, some participants at the meetings. The adverse publicity soured relations and evasiveness increased. Two months before the sanctioned date, Thornton and Brandon accompanied him for a meeting, to settle the final differences. The ministry stubbornly withheld the facts, significant or otherwise. Although venue was agreed for the capital, they refused to name the building, or announce its whereabouts. They stayed silent and when prodded, response was the same: "*Nichevo*! It does not matter. It will be selected to suit the number attending." Thornton was upset. When they boasted of more than one hundred specialist institutes, spread through the sixteen autonomous republics, he pleaded: "You must say how many will attend!" He seemed unable to rest without an answer. Brandon and he led Thornton up the back stairway from the hotel, down the rambling corridors and not having been in that part before, he had no conception where he was. When they opened the door and put-on the lights, his jaw dropped. "Good Lord!" He exclaimed. "Has someone died? Those black chairs, it's a setting for a funeral oration!" The chairs suggested the order of play. He counted fourteen in his suite and Brandon across the corridor, had twelve. With four more from the corridor, they arranged them as an array—four columns with seven rows, each identical and set symmetric from the back wall. With a small table and two more chairs in front, the place looked distinctive. As Thornton stood, with downcast eyes roaming the neat display, he muttered: "They said there would be several hundred." It was surprising that he seemed to believe it. Did he not realize it was a game? "They argue that numbers have no meaning!" They bluffed to continue the pretence. "Narrowing attendance focuses audience attention."

"How can we justify the cost?" Thornton sighed, adding with resignation: "You fellows go without me tonight, I'm meeting someone." From two short visits, he had little opportunity for private contacts and was unlikely to know anyone. Hopefully, he will not out of pique, allow himself to be chaperoned by one of the Russian courtesans, in the foreigner's bar at their hotel. It would be dangerous and not for him alone—it could jeopardize the venture. A year or so earlier, a Western politician was victim. They handled this professionally, returning him drugged and photographed to his room. The evidence was sent by diplomatic bag to the newspapers, with copies to his minister and his wife. Thornton must be more astute, but for the present, there was a bonus. At dinner, Brandon and he would be alone. They could cut corners and he could be in time to go to her place for the night. Setting-out, he contemplated the wantonness—the empty suite, chairs in their neat rows and abandoned microphones.

How could mutual attraction, between comparative strangers, be as strong? Formative years and transition to maturity were hardly more diverse, but when it came to residual confusion, comparisons existed, albeit in opposite directions. I didn't suffer premature confrontation, but was sent to a male boarding school, in denial of the female world. At the age that she was forced to adulthood, development was put 'on hold'. It was a source of chagrin and disappointment, but when fifteen I received a tutorial. During school holidays, a friend of my mother's, in her thirties and recently divorced, invited me to lunch with my elder sister. Midway through, she got a telephone call and had to leave. I stayed on as Grace, that was her name, was fun to be with and outspoken. While finishing lunch, she asked what I knew about the facts of life. I told her of the ten-minute explanation from my father and stories that circulated among boys at the school. When she teased: "I bet you got up to things with girls," I confessed in all honesty that it was not possible. She disapproved of boarding schools and considered it unfair, to expose young people to the isolation. I decided to hang around with Grace, until she asked me to go. After clearing the table, she noticed me standing in thought. As if on impulse, she led me down a corridor, to what seemed a spare bedroom with single divan and fitted counterpane. She sat down and leaned back against the wall. Then, raising her legs and folding her arms around her knees, she said, looking at me: "Do you want to try something with me?" Although she probably missed my barely audible response, she sensed my eagerness and leaned over, opening my belt to let my trousers down. She could see I was stiff and calmly pulling her dress over her head, slipped her underwear off. I tried to touch her breasts, take the brassiere off, but it was forbidden. Instead, she pointed at my white underpants, saying: "You don't want these!" As I awkwardly lowered them, she slid along the undisturbed cover, to lie flat and spread her legs. Moving past, I stood staring in bewilderment, seeking an expected straight wide opening. Beneath dark hair, I discerned an area of pink, convoluted folds of crumpled skin, with a line that meandered back and forth, as it extended down and receded out of sight—roadmap of alien terrain. "What are you doing? I don't like you staring at me like that," she said. Her voice startled me and I stepped back to the side to lean over her, taking care not to touch the forbidden breasts. In what seemed an ungainly manner, I climbed on top of her. Apart from seeming short, I don't remember much else. I admit a degree of excitement, or perhaps fear? If pleasure, it was obscured by feelings of embarrassment and shame. As I gauchely helped her from the bed, she comforted me matter-of-factly: "It feels a bit strange the first time, but after a while you'll get to enjoy it." Two days later, I tried to phone her from a call box, but didn't reach her. I returned to school and when home again learned she moved and went back North. I felt timidly grateful for this first encounter into a world that might have remained secret for sometime yet. When thinking of her prostrate form, almost stationary on the neatly covered divan, I was confused. I couldn't help imagining a body laid-out for the final view. The fact it proved my last sight of her, was significant. Could perplexities from earlier years affect barriers that, as with magnets, force-apart or draw-together, according to a juxtaposition of polarities?

Books were important. Her father had many and she learned to love them from an early age. When he left, their absence seemed to evoke the guilt she felt for his desertion. Her own first volumes were childhood presents, or bought for school. Those in her bookcase were from her college years and the times that followed. With literature her subject, they were expected: 'part of her professional package', as she put it. In his case, books were considered an oddity, 'non-conformist' and often treated with suspicion by those he worked with. Yet, had they known about his relationship with her, few would consider it questionable.

Preoccupied with the restrictions of the power encircling them, he said to her one-day, probing: "What if we were told—it had to stop? Imagine if they refused access to books, and prohibited us from making love. What could we do?"

"I suppose we could go to lectures and hold hands." She reached forward to take his. "That would be safe even here, but unless we could outwit the authorities, sharing of thought would be the monosyllabic exchanges of the visitor's room at a prison. Meetings, or contact would be taboo."

"We would be separate beings, with no means to bridge the gap," he added.

11

"Why are these books in the hall?" Anna asked in irritation. Everyone was out when I returned from the office. I bought some books and left them on the hall table, to use time while the house was quiet, to read an urgent report and hear a recent record from Moscow. Anna burst into the sitting room as she asked the question. I told her, I went to Pools at lunchtime and took the opportunity to buy books, I was looking for. "Why do you need that number?"

"They are interesting, I'll deal with them later."

"You have loads of books and nobody touches them."

"I read each one eventually."

"Well I don't see you reading."

"Either television is on, or something is happening. I read books when I travel. I take at least two, every time."

"I thought people read magazines on planes. Have you worked out how much they cost? Why not spend the money on things we can all enjoy."

"When the girls are older, the books will be a source of knowledge."

"That's what you think! I bet they won't touch them. And you have to take the record off. I promised the girls, they could watch television for half an hour. Heidi's getting them ready. I said they can come down in their dressing gowns."

"OK I'll take the books upstairs and sort them in the shelves at the weekend." I put the report away. I would read it later. I took the record-off, carefully putting it into the plastic bag inside the sleeve that Supraphon provided with their LPs. The protection was important, they scratched easily. Afterwards, when I went to the hall to take my purchases upstairs, I ran into Natalie coming down from her bedroom.

"Hello Daddy what are you doing? We're going to look at the telly. Are you coming to watch?" she said gleefully.

"After dumping these, I will be right back," I replied, trying to open the spare room door, without dropping the volumes stacked in my arms. I lowered them on the carpet, wedging them in a corner inside, so they would not topple. Then I went back to the sitting room, where the girls were tucked-up next to each other on the newly upholstered sofa.

"Hi girls! So, you're ready for bed. That was quick! What are we going to see?" I said from the armchair, where I sat before they got home.

It was later, while Anna and I were watching a television play, that I remembered the report. "If you don't mind, I'll go up now. I need to read some papers, before I go to sleep. If I wait till this is over, I'll be too tired."

"What a shame. It's very good—it's a pity to miss the rest."

"I know, but it may go on for an hour. I'll see you later, you can tell me how it ends and in case I drop-off, I'll say goodnight now." I bent over to kiss her. The children went to sleep hours earlier and Heidi, who said she was tired, had gone to her room before the play started. She slept at the top of the house on the same floor as the children. When I got to the bedroom, I threw the report on the bed and started to undress. A moment later, I heard the floorboards creak on the landing. Thinking it must be one of the children, I threw my dressing gown over my shoulders and looked around the door. Heidi was standing there with a slightly impertinent expression on her face. It seemed as if she had been looking through the crack, between the doorframe and the half open door. She was wearing a long nightdress and I could see the nipples of her small breasts, pushing out from behind the flimsy material. "Are you alone?" she asked in a low voice.

"Yes, Anna's downstairs watching television. Are you looking for something?" I asked.

"No!" she responded thoughtfully.

"Well! What is it you want then?" For a moment or so, she said nothing. "I am thirsty. I wanted a drink."

"Why don't you get something from the kitchen?" She stood for a moment without replying, and then said: "I will!"

"Goodnight then," I added, as she turned and went downstairs. I closed the door and lay on the bed reading the report. I would go to the bathroom later.

When Anna came up, I told her. "I believe she was spying on me. I am sure she was watching through the crack in the door."

"Spying? My God! You're getting a complex from too much time in Russia. She is extremely well brought-up and in no way as familiar as Lottie. You misjudge her!"

12

Life had been uneventful during his absence, she told him. She sat in silence with her eyes on the rug and he realized it was so. He told her that on the 'other side', it was different—a close colleague in the firm had been assaulted and seriously injured. Visiting one of the States in the south, he took a rental car at the airport and planned to leave it in the hotel parking lot. As he got out, someone slugged him from behind with the butt of a revolver. He lost consciousness and woke in hospital. There were head injuries and doctors had not determined, when or whether he could continue his job. A month earlier, another person in the firm on a working visit in the Midwest, took his wife along. They booked into a motel, went downtown for the evening and on getting back, disturbed a break-in. Shot on entry, he stumbled and the wife rushing to support him, was killed as well. There was no arrest. The police report coldly noted that an unidentified intruder killed both, to eliminate a witness.

"Maybe, we have to be less critical about life here", she remarked. "It appears that hard pursuit of materialism can turn anyone to a casualty. Perhaps their term 'slaves of capitalism' contains some truth."

"Violence seemed remote on the other side, but these incidents demonstrate—I could be next!"

"Here, we may worry about being bugged or followed, but can walk in the streets without fear of being shot. With that many regulations, we seem better protected."

"Under Communism, there could be danger from ideological faux pas, but with no political agenda, it would not be life threatening."

"Yet, we are supposed to be the free ones. We may have means to travel and less restriction, but if risk is disability or loss of life, benefit is questionable."

"Perhaps, it's the misconception over change. I don't mean Curtis' remark, but the opposition by nature" he said, continuing: "Alleged advances get diluted."

"Swings and counter-swings in my country are less marked though,"

"With political transformations—like the Soviet revolution, change can be eroded by a combination of regressions, unnoticed individually."

"It seems that the differences between the two 'sides' are less distinct than politicians would have us believe."

As time for the convention drew closer, Thornton repeatedly complained. He appeared to take comfort from threats to withdraw. It was not possible—commitments were in writing. No one disclosed location, until a couple of days before. It was central, in the ministry's own building and as final concession, they allowed entry two hours before the start. The hall was large and reasonably full. There were a few hundred people, maybe a thousand, hard to judge—counting was not allowed. When someone made lists, they snatched notes away. "Release of information is contrary to regulations", they curtly announced. There could have been extras, brought around the corner to fill the empty seats. Only recognizable faces were those known before—the party members from the trading corporations. Experts exhibited proficiency and not just academic. They had to keep machinery running under extreme conditions in farthest corners of the territory. At evening receptions, security agents were noticeable, moving among the visitors, jotting notes on scraps of paper and slipping them guiltily into side-pockets.

Where was the information directed? Was it for records of the so-called technical institutes, or somewhere else? Most likely, it would land in files at headquarters of the Committee for State Security—to give the KGB its official name.

Her complexion was component of her uncommon beauty. She mentioned inequalities in the democratic country from which she came and her hopes that the classless communist world might prove more tolerant. It was in her country that prejudice coined the term 'wasp'. She might have suffered affronts for that gift, that colour, which nature gave her. Should I have questioned this? Initially we talked of the past, but interest was displaced as the time that mattered unfolded. Mutual interrogation was taboo—like his children. They did not belong to the new life. They were a separate chapter with different actors, beyond the scope of this particular world, and accepted *fait accompli*—or it's what he understood.

He watched her, as diligently as her gate guards, but with another kind of intensity. His observations, scrutinizing her gestures and behaviour, were not for shift-reports in a notebook, but for storage as patterns in the mind. Those created with her on the rug, during their spell of tempestuousness, were a source of euphoria, but that was the stage of his visits, when time charged unbridled. He had every ground to be content—yet flirting with dissatisfaction, yearned to return to the periods, when movements of the clock seemed almost to stop. Timelessness was a part of his earlier stays there and seemed to belong in that city. Why could he not have it now? How inspiring to have it in the patterns with her. It should not be just emptiness and periods of waiting that are drawn-out. It ought to be possible to stretch time in moments of fulfilment or satisfaction and let it extend, like metals when heated. Nature should be sporting and provide balance, then the fleeting instants in this wilderness of sensation would be prolonged, to continue-on without break, without stop, on to infinity, for ever and forever.

One night, he acted carelessly and they caught him on film. The opera was among few entertainments they could visit together. This time, at the Kremlin Palace they saw a production of a Russian work, unheard of by him. Exhausted from a day, unexpectedly filled with meetings, he almost fell asleep during the first act. "Sorry! I need the restroom. Why don't you go up for the food? I'll see you by the buffet on the left side," she said. It was the interval and although the work was little known and rarely performed, the place was full. He manoeuvred his way back towards the escalators, but when he reached the top, access was blocked, choked with stationary people unable to move. As he looked for a way through, he saw Curtis, about ten rows ahead. When calling him, he turned his head, but didn't respond. After trying a second time, Curtis swung around, stared directly at him, gave no sign of recognition and then pushed forcefully between people in front, to disappear in the crowd. He was perplexed, but gradually, the mass thinned enough for him to move. Minutes later, he was obstructed again, this time behind a line of people, shoulder-to-shoulder with their backs to him. He got closer to check and being tall could peep on tiptoe over their shoulders. They were standing behind others, who sat on a row of chairs—as in a group photograph. There were both men and women and among them some Africans in colourful costumes. It must be a group of visiting dignitaries with their Russian hosts, and he leaned forward with interest, curious to see who they might be, watching them talking through interpreters and switching positions at the front. Only then, did he raise his eyes and note to his alarm that he looked directly into the giant lens of a film camera. From its position ahead, he realized the viewer must include him, as well as the posing group in front and he ducked, immediately. As far as he could judge, he was near the centre of the row, no more than a few feet from the influential persons, whoever they were. The camera must have filmed continuously, while he stood there. It vexed him that he hadn't noticed from the start. Keeping his head low and out of view, he worked his way as quickly as possible, around and away from the group. With a wide detour, he was then able to reach the spot where they agreed to meet. He saw her arranging smoked salmon and caviar canapés, on a plate. She looked-up and called across the crowd of waiting people: "It's late! Could you get the champagne? I'm taking care of the food."

Finding a quiet corner, he was anxious to tell her of his escapade. "I couldn't get through. You won't believe this. I may be on the news."

"What happened? Did you get stage fright?" She joked. He described the crush of bodies and then the people lined-up for the filming. "With so many trying to get to the buffets, it was crazy to block-off access. How could they allow this?"

"I didn't notice. All was normal the other side. It must be someone important. They would only do this for VIPs."

"I assume it was the television, or could it be something else?"

"No idea, but you don't often see film cameras, unless it is the TV. We can look when we get to our seats. If important, they will be in the VIP box," she said.

"It's the last thing I need in my position, to be seen snooping behind a group of VIPs. It could spark unpleasant enquiries."

"Trouble is—you don't look very Russian. Your face will stand out like a foreign flag, waving from the Kremlin's walls. Those guys must be pretty wary and if you are in the scan, may spot it."

"They won't be able to recognize me!"

"You can't be sure. They must have photographs on your file. After the number of visits you've made here, they probably have a few dossiers."

"If it's TV and shown on the news, one of your gate guards might recognize me when they screen it."

"Your guess is as good as mine. But it's late to worry."

"I feel apprehensive. By the way, just after leaving the escalator, I saw your friend Curtis."

"Oh that's neat! What did he have to say?"

"We didn't talk. He disappeared before I could catch-up. He didn't seem to recognize me, but isn't it strange to see him here?"

"Not at all. He's an opera buff," she added, to his surprise. "He doesn't like to miss a new production."

When they got to their seats, she pointed up at the VIP box on the next level and to the right, but it was empty. Shortly before the lights went out, they saw some figures moving in, including the Africans. He could recognize the colourful costumes from before. "I just remembered, there's a President of one of the new African republics in town, with three wives. It must be them. Wow! Did you see how he looks after the ladies?" She said smiling.

"Are all three his wives?" He asked.

"It's what I heard." The African leader took one of the places near the middle. There was an elderly lady seated on the other side of the box. Four men, probably guards, or translators sat behind, three seemed Russian, the fourth African. The lights went out, with the chair in the middle still empty. The second half of the opera was as long, but after the shenanigans during the interval, he was not tempted to sleep. When the lights went on, they looked up towards the VIP box, but saw only the backs of the women leaving. The men were out of sight.

They went to her flat and as she drove through the gate, he instinctively turned his face away, avoiding the usual glance to check if the guard came out of his box. It made no difference. They knew him and silhouette would suffice, identifiable from the link. They had this to her and the car. They had it since the start. They could not have seen the television news. They would enter the same description—only times of arrival and departure would be different. Had the effects of the champagne deteriorated to a hangover? Maybe the mammoth opera wore them out, or was she too, treating this more seriously than either wanted to admit. For whatever reason, they needed sleep. They prepared for the night and took up positions by the bookcase. He put his arms around her and she was soon asleep. He was not just worried, but angry with himself and lay awake, thinking: since the incident with the police, I consciously tried to avoid exposure which might invite attention, but tonight I walked blindly into the view of the camera. A remote ache increased, when he considered how long he must have stood in front of its giant lens. It was thoughtless and it agitated him. As he lay trying to sleep, concern intensified: if they showed the film on television, my face must be visible and they could call me for interrogation. It might happen any time. They would monitor the rushes, to get every possible sighting of the conspicuous head. They might find the report from the earlier questioning and it would drag her in. Maybe the camera wasn't shooting at the precise moment, or I wasn't in the field of vision. Perhaps it was out of focus, or the people at headquarters would overlook the screening and re-screening. As if it were likely!

13

The secret police had many names. In Tsarist times, it was *Okhrana* and in early days of the revolution Red Guard, in Lenin's time, referred to as *Czerezvyczajka,* shortened to *Cheka*. Stalin renamed it OGPU, which at the height of the 1930s purges, was absorbed in the NKVD, confusingly called: 'People's Commissariat for Internal Affairs' more conspicuous for the millions, eliminated or sent to Siberia by Stalin. In World War II, a parallel organization the NKGB was formed to handle state security. Subsequent renaming as MVD and MGB were simply reclassification, as ministries. On Stalin's death, his henchman Beria merged both in the MVD, to consolidate everything under his control. When the post Stalinist leadership sacked and executed him, they transferred responsibility for the secret service to the party, renaming it KGB. Over the next six years, the dreaded MVD was officially run-down, but in practice, functions were transferred to the new organization, whose domain stretched as persistently as the predecessor.

Western visitors treated the KGB with apprehension, as if they had no counterpart. But *Cheka* was an abbreviation for: 'Extraordinary Commission for Combating Counter-Terrorism, Sabotage and Speculation', which is almost the name used by the leader of the 'other side' years later. Was Lenin's vision prophetic, or were the others behind? If my concerns about the secret police in Moscow seem exaggerated, 'he' could not have known at the time, and it was logical for 'him' to feel anxious. As a foreigner, he probably fell within the scope of the KGB (since renamed FSB), crossing paths with their people at the ministry of scientific coordination. He could expect them to monitor him, or investigate issues concerning the firm's business. Interest in his private affairs was less distinct. As internal security, this could be under what earlier was MVD, the vast state-within-state pervading every corner of the Soviet Union. It's uniformed *corps d'élite*, checked, counter-checked and more highly trained than the Red army, was immense. Its tiers of supporters, included the *agent provocateurs*, who spied on the spies and the mercenaries with double jobs, like the prostitutes at the foreigner's bar in the Hotel National. It was responsible for sedition and subversion, running the interrogations and trials of those unfortunate enough to be detained. This diffuse but pervasive body could be building files with the reports from her gate guards, presumably militiamen within its force. These would also contain the furtive bugging and surveillance, which seemed to accompany him through his trips to the city. Now in addition, was his breaking into a security zone, close to visiting officials. Would they consider the earlier questioning with her by the police, as confirmation of whatever grounds for subversion, they might attribute to this trivial *faux pas*?

His visit ran into a second week and he spent the last evening in her flat. Whilst driving there she seemed excited and mentioned she had something to tell him. As soon as they got indoors, she admitted, she couldn't get the incident at the opera out of her mind. It worried her and realizing she could do something to limit risk, decided to approach a professional. She got the name of a security man at the embassy and set a meeting. There was a snag however and before he would see her, she had to be screened. She didn't like it, but as standard procedure, had to permit access to her file.

"I am sorry to hear this. Was it worthwhile? Did you tell him about me?"

"I had no reason. I volunteered nothing about us. I pretended to be in your shoes. I posed a hypothetical question and asked how the secret police might act, had they spotted me, near a big shot on television. He was concerned and wanted details. I told him about the guy in the colourful robes and the three wives. He recalled a State visit by an African leader, with quite some coverage on the news, and phoned a colleague, responsible for monitoring broadcasts, particularly news cuttings. He remembered the visit to the opera, because of the person accompanying them. Can you guess who it was? I mean—the Russian host in the VIP box, whose seat was still empty when the lights went out."

"If it's someone I would know, was he from that ministry I had dealings with, the one linked with the KGB?"

"Forget it! This was someone important. You were close to the top. It was a member of the Presidium. I am surprised you didn't recognize him."

"From where I stood, I saw only the back of his head. But, would I know him?"

"For sure, we would both have realized who it was, had he come into the box before the lights went out. His face is unmistakable."

"There are not so many here that I could identify. Of whom can you be talking?"

"It was Mikoyan."

"God! I wasn't expecting anyone that important."

"My security guy couldn't believe they would allow me as a foreigner, to get that close. It's surprising they hadn't stopped people from going up the escalator. Are you sure you didn't break-into a restricted area?"

"I went up as normal. It was only on leaving the escalator that I got into the crush. Then, I squeezed through the crowd, but saw no sealed-off area. I was trying to find you."

"You got real close to someone powerful."

"It's absurd! He must have been directly in front of where I stood—within a matter of feet. With a gun, the target would have been unmissable. It needed only a single shot and I could have gone down in the history books."

"Sure! It would have made a stir and you would have your mug shot in important newspapers. But you wouldn't survive. The area must have been swarming with bodyguards. There were probably sharpshooters on the floor, or in the roof above." It was all right to make light of it with her. The disclosure was a shock and reprehensible from many angles.

Anastas Ivanovich Mikoyan, an Armenian with a reputation for shrewdness and a fiery tongue, was a survivor. Like Stalin, he trained as a priest. One of the 'Old Bolsheviks', he was already in the Politburo nine years after the revolution. When Khrushchev made his de-Stalinization speech to the closed session of the Twentieth Congress, Mikoyan broke the ice. The following year with Zhukov, he supported Khrushchev to oust the 'anti-party' *troika* from the Presidium. Zhukov lasted barely months, but Mikoyan continued, sometimes as number two. When Brezhnev replaced Khrushchev and Kosygin was prime minister, Mikoyan, still among the selected few—was chairman of the Presidium. The people referred to Mikoyan affectionately as 'father of Soviet ice cream'.

Unusual among Kremlin leaders, Mikoyan spoke some English, perhaps because British troops, supporting White Russians, arrested him in the early days of the revolution. At the time, they executed his elder brother, but somehow he outlived his sentence. He escaped death a second time, when Beria planned to murder him and other leaders, in the post-Stalinist power struggle.

It confirmed his worst fears. With Mikoyan involved, a restricted zone was unquestionable and breaking the barrier, must be a serious offence. He asked what her security man said. "They wouldn't like it. If markings were missed, I could be intruding in a confined space and might be charged for spying. He pointed out that it would be tough to convince them it was accidental. I had to give details and he promised to check if recognizable from news viewings."

"But he doesn't know what I look like."

"You forget we were talking about me! I went to see him a second time, and naturally, he confirmed I was not visible in the section screened. But he said—I could have been observed in the rushes, before they cut the film, and that applies to you."

"What do they think could happen?"

"In his view, they would act swiftly. It's almost a week now and the fact they have done nothing, is a good sign. It's possible you were not as visible as you feared, or haven't been recognized," she said thoughtfully.

"If they charged me for spying, I shall tell them the unexciting truth."

"But how could you prove it? I guess, being close to a top guy, must itself incriminate."

"For them easiest option would be keeping me under observation, until I go tomorrow and not give another visa. If recognized though, they surely wouldn't let me get away without investigation. By the way, did you tell him about the time they questioned us at the building complex?"

"To avoid questions about you, I gave no details. I said it was a parking offence and I was given a warning. Perhaps foolishly, I mentioned that my name and details would be in a report on their file. After making a note of the date and location, he suggested there would be numerous documents from tailings I did not notice, or reports from the gate guards. The parking offence wouldn't alter my status." He asked her what the man was like and with some reluctance she told him: "He is from Louisiana—young, with a crew cut and the sort of face you'd see on a bar stool! Clearly CIA, I guess most are and reportedly a rough crowd, in it for money and kicks. I had to swallow my pride, he wasn't merely cold, but near insulting."

"It's absurd you have to put up with such behaviour from your own embassy!"

"As I said, after you told me about the attacks on your colleagues, the boundaries seem to become less distinct."

"Although politics may change, people don't. Remember, we discussed rules of how nature plays with order? There is a set about energy in the world: whatever happens to its form, or distribution, the sum stays the same. Imagine if applied to the games mankind plays. A drop in intolerance could compensate persecution of minorities. Local decline in avarice would balance poverty somewhere else. Less depravity here might offset barbarism over there and looking on the bright side—the score remains the same."

"Aren't you taking matters too far? I am over it!"

"I can't accept that trying to help me, you face affront from your own side, but if the case—we can expect aggression from anyone, anywhere."

"Yeah like sex, it applies to all, remember . . . all, regardless of creed, capitalists, even communists, but there is an exception, hopefully two. Let's straighten the rug and disprove the theories," she said.

"Agreed and we can rid our minds of newsreels, Soviet ice cream and belligerent security agents, for a while!"

He got through the departure formalities at the airport, without more than the usual delays and frustrations. Sitting on the plane, he thought about their conversation the night before: either they did not notice me and I was in the clear, or they might shut me out in future, refusing the next visa. It is possible they would defer questioning, until I am at the embassy. They could use it to blackmail, offering a deal to spy for them. I heard of such situations. It could put her at risk and if I refuse, it would be the end of work in Russia, an end to the relationship. "Are you alright?" asked an attentive hostess. "You look a bit pale."

"It's nothing a little vodka wouldn't put right," he said.

"I'll get you some at once."

14

Would they send a formal refusal? I was apprehensive when submitting the application. Perhaps they would shroud everything in mystery and indefinitely delay action. In the event, neither supposition proved correct. I got a message from the embassy, saying, I should go there next Friday. It was a week earlier than usual, which seemed to indicate rejection of the application. The fact they asked me to attend in person, suggested they wanted to check my reaction, probably for the blackmail set-up. They might try to frame me in an adverse situation. Ostensibly, she was not involved in the incident at the opera, but the problem was links on the files. Apart from the questioning at the building complex, there would be reports from the gate guards. They could not pressure her the same as families of a Russian abroad, but being resident made threats a possibility. For an American, they would have to adopt another approach. In the worst situation, her embassy could make formal complaints and get her out of Russia. As long as they did not menace her, I could take it. Refusal to cooperate would mean exclusion from the country, end of the relationship, and loss of my assignment, but it would be better to seek transfer to another geographical area than get involved in espionage. Likely outcome still seemed a straight no. There were three more days to wait and in this period, I considered possible scenarios for my visit to the embassy. I thought about calling the company lawyer to ask his advice, but he would be powerless. With no laws to dispute, they would act in whatever direction suited their aims. As the days dragged, I tried to suppress thought of her.

There were several others in the visa section at the embassy. I had to wait my turn, then the man I dealt with in the past, called me. He returned the passport without a word. I slipped it casually in my inside coat pocket, thanked him, shook his hand and left. I didn't check in the hallway, somebody might watch. I walked up the road, around the corner into the park. Once there, I leaned against a lamp post, took out the passport and nervously looked through. I found the three previous visas, but when I turned the page, both following sides were blank. I fumbled on through more blank pages. Almost at the end of this relatively new and half empty passport, I saw another visa. Stunned, I double-checked the dates and there was no doubt. It was the first time I received one in three weeks. I must have been over pessimistic about the news film. For some reason, they could not have spotted the extraneous head, or must have thought it belonged to a Russian body. Maybe the camera's focus was worse than I suspected.

In less than ten days, I would be with her. Excited, I went towards the Round Pond, circled it and walked on over the grass to the area with paths and hedges, where the small statue stands. Retracing my steps, part way towards the pond, I zigzagged backwards and forwards across the park. People looked at me quizzically, I must have had an inane smile on my face. I kept going for thirty minutes, or longer. Finally seeing the monument on the south side, looming through the trees, I composed myself, walked around it and out of the park. Standing in the main road as a double-decker bus roared past, I hailed a taxi asking the driver to take me to the firm. Calvin had left and I went to my office to call Anna. I wanted to take her to dinner at a French restaurant, in a small street, close to where we lived before. I got the booking without difficulty. It was my lucky day.

Walking along the Kings Road the following afternoon, I met Langton, a publisher who lived in the country. He seemed excited and explained that an aunt had died, leaving him enough money to buy a *pied-à-terre* in Belgravia. Wanting to display it, he invited me for a drink and we walked there together. He took me around the two floors—a downstairs with restricted view to the front and upstairs, a living room with windows on opposite sides and a small bedroom overlooking the mews. As his wife was determined to stay in the country, he had spent a few days each week in the new place—there was no space for his books. As we sat upstairs, he outlined plans to publish a study into the reproductive patterns of the anopheles, for release later in the year. Discussing the new life in London, he raised the subject of neighbours. I expected him to laud celebrities in the area, but instead, he told me of their quirks. At the back, a sole window overlooked the small paved garden of a house in the adjacent street and from above, he could see into part of the ground floor living room. While sitting at his desk one evening, he noticed a light and saw a man, who seemed back from an office, igniting the gas fire. Later, the same person reappeared in a dressing gown and sat in a wing chair beside the lit fireplace, masturbating in front of the television. On other nights, the light went on about the same time and the man did as before. Because the line of sight cut-off the upper part of the body, the face was not visible and he did not know who it was. He admitted curiosity however, at what the man watched.

Something else happened across the mews. Opposite was a double garage with large sliding doors, cumbersome to open. The owner drove a Bentley and when he returned in the evenings, Langton would hear the purring of the engine, as he struggled to manoeuvre the large car in the narrow street and back it through the opening, so he could drive out in the morning without reversing. Apart from the brand of car, the man wore immaculate clothing, probably for the City. After closing the doors from inside, nobody left. Then following an interval, the same man would reappear through the access-door, dressed from head to foot in black rubber, pushing a motorbike. With a roar, he would disappear until late in the night. Langton was often woken by the noise of the returning motorbike. From the bedroom window, he would see the rider go inside the garage and after changing to the original clothes, walk away to his house in the neighbourhood. The following morning he would return, dressed for the City, open the stubborn doors and glide away in the Bentley. The procedure was repeated most weekdays that Langton was there.

As if looking through an undersea porthole, Langton could peer inside closed worlds. After the country, where things appeared remote, he experienced the anonymous intimacy of a city. I understood the feeling, as sometimes in the Soviet Union—tangible life seemed separated by a glass partition. I could see inside, but what I saw was out of reach, often prohibited.

15

Travelling to the city, down Leningradski prospekt on arrival from Scheremetjevo airport, the sleek glass-front of the Aeroflot Hotel would stand out against the older buildings of the neighbourhood. Once he was booked there, and the inside view betrayed the grand facade. This was not an official hotel for foreigners, staffed with regular room guards. They were authorised for locals. Late at night the scene was set by disconsolate drinkers, collapsing over vomit covered tables, glasses upturned among broken vodka bottles and bodies, spread-eagled in the forsaken bar and cafeteria. They weren't alone in suffering the vodka.

Foreigners succumbed in the hotel bars, as well as being encouraged by officials to follow the *Nasdroviej* custom for bottoms-up draining of glasses. The soggy flow of intoxication hit the head, minutes before the earth started spinning with an ever-persistent increase in acceleration.

Yes, he avoided the second setting on her American showerhead. He found it aggressive, but this is not the whole truth. It was when alone, while standing under the adjustable fitting behind the white curtain, by himself. There were times, when he was not behind, but outside. Then, she would be inside and he would be watching her. Sliding the metal hooks along the shiny rail, he could ease the opaque material back sufficiently, to observe her body without obstruction, yet not enough for the splashes to escape its protection. I see how he observed her, examining the patterns of the flow, as it slipped across the skin. When the lever was in the normal position, the stream would smooth the dark hair that hung down from the top of her head, falling away—a back-to-front veil. Her image would be mat, silhouette softened by the fine cloud of droplets steadily descending on their way downward. In the other position, the rope-like jets would twist the strands of her hair, pressing them against the nape of her neck. Then the body would be clear, its wrapping of fast-swirling water, glistening before his eyes.

There were occasions, when they would be inside the curtain together, sharing the circular space defined by the droplets, falling evenly around them. With her, the lever became an instrument of diversity. It could induce a feeling of protectiveness. He might press himself close, arching his bulk over her slender back and in the moment before releasing the torrent, lean his head forward above hers to steal its impact. He would let it break against his crown and flatten his hair, as it spilled outwards over his shoulders, whirling between their wet contours in its rush, to collect in the pool gathering at their feet. The lever could also provide a sense of excitement. Sometimes she would shriek as together they exposed themselves to the deluge. With hands reaching around cupping her breasts, he would mould himself to the curves of her body. Limbs swaying together under the stream, he would feel the soft cheeks of her bottom pressed against his groin, as they allowed the punishment to alternate between them, in the midst of its frantic course.

Her striking appearance was beyond dispute, like when Brandon first pointed her out. Her conduct belied it, as if unconscious of the effect she had on others. It posed a risk—she drew attention unawares. Wherever she went, the scarcity of foreigners, shortages and rigid codes of dress, made her stand out, visible from afar. In the anonymous crowd that might notice, many given the chance, would take his place without scruple. Need for caution was a restraint among those he worked with and he had to check the temptation to show off. He thought of what a visitor from the firm's headquarters told him. Ambrose had an unexpected reverence for Randall, not from his professional skills, but from an adroitness with women. Randall had an unusual nickname and when Ambrose heard it mentioned at a local restaurant, by two women, discussing affairs at the next table, his attention was rooted. It was a popular venue decorated with tropical plants, where the extravagant foliage gave visitors cover from view, but did little to curb their voices. Seated alone, waiting for a delayed guest, he could overhear without risk of being seen. What intrigued him was the admiration for their lover's discretion—no phone calls to the house, no remonstrations and above all, no telling. "You can be safe with him," said one. "Absolutely!" echoed the other. "There'd be no disclosure, he wouldn't tell." It sounded a role model. Better keep silent—it is also prudent.

"Have you been to Leningrad?" He asked.

"No I'd like to, but it's difficult to get permission."

"Is it off limits for you too?"

"Yes and no! I can go on an Intourist excursion. They bus you around however, to look at Commie monuments and party buildings. I just want to stroll beside the Neva and go see the Hermitage. I'd like to daydream in the old streets, thinking about Dostoevsky and the *White Nights* and it's not possible!"

"I've discovered the institute for a business I am following, is based there. Their experts make the decisions about planned investments, but don't show at meetings here. I have to do what your friend Curtis suggested. I have to find a way to beat the system and visit."

"If the guys are important, you should go."

"I plan to combine business with pleasure and take an Intourist trip."

"I know people who did. They were transferred from the plane to a bus and not allowed out of sight. That couldn't do much for your work."

"To travel independently, I need a formal authorization and few people can sign one. It probably needs a vice-minister, anything less would be useless."

"Is there no-one at that level you can approach?"

"The import-export people block the way. I haven't been able to meet anyone that senior."

"You mentioned you had earlier meetings."

"That's a point! I met a vice minister in the Ministry for the Five Year Planning a couple of times. He came to London and we helped him. In fact, he owes me a favour."

"Sounds promising, why not go to him? If unable to help, maybe he can put you in touch with someone who can?"

"Clever idea! If it works, how about coming as my assistant?"

"It would be easier to apply to visit the moon. If I were allowed to go, we wouldn't be able to walk around the streets together. We probably wouldn't be in the same hotel and we certainly couldn't sleep together, but I appreciate the invitation," she said leaning over to kiss him, then adding conclusively: "In this country, some things are impossible and others unthinkable."

The vice minister at the Five Year Planning Ministry agreed to a meeting. The office was in a spreading complex and an administrative assistant escorted him. It was a long way. Workers blocked the last corridor, repairing the floor. They had to return to the reception and take another route. The vice minister apologized for the obstruction and explained the new floor would impress visitors. He listened attentively to an account of the business and agreed to sign the request. It was not his job to raise the necessary document. The correct department in the responsible organization had to do this, using the requisite form. If sent to him, properly completed and signed by the responsible department head, he would give his authorization. It took two more visits, to accomplish these steps and have the signatures incorporated. Then he applied for the ticket. "Which tour do you want?" The young girl, languidly manning the Intourist desk asked.

"I don't need a tour. This is an official visit. I need a flight ticket"

"How you get to city from airport? No transport except for tours."

"I don't need transport. I am visiting an institute. They will send a car."

"You leave documents and dollars. We investigate. Come back four days, we say result."

"Too late! I have to travel in three days. I must know if I can go."

"OK come two days. We say nothing. Need look documents. You send papers to office. Seats Leningrad very difficult—we say you two days." Then without warning, Intourist left a message to go to their office. "*Vazmozhno*! We can do it," said the girl behind the desk, issuing the ticket late the evening before. The flight left at five a.m. There was no way to check with the institute. He had to take a chance.

One is used to planes having a horizontal ceiling and almost vertical walls. Apart from a flat floor—this was a tube. There were rows of seats, but not the type expected. They had the shape of 'park benches for two', with metal frames and the rest in canvas. From hooks in the middle and at either side, one could see there were seat belts, but only frayed remnants were visible. Overhead, a few metal shelves were attached to the curving wall. The luggage, wrapped in cloth and tied with string, was on the floor. Piles were stacked behind the last row of seats ahead of a metal grill that spread the entire width of the plane, to segregate the animals. He could hear baa'ing of sheep until the raucous engines started, blotting all else out. He reclined unbelted on his bench waiting for lift-off. Most passengers seemed agricultural workers, many in unfamiliar costumes. He was tired and slept.

Shortly before arrival, he woke-up. The plane taxied, then shut-off the deafening roar of the engines. The front door opened and a uniformed guard appeared, walking down the aisle, calling a name. It sounded like his. When he raised his hand, the guard asked for the passport and beckoned him to follow. It crossed his mind that he might be locked up, until the institute intervened. People waited at the foot of the stairway—was it the secret police? As he passed, one stepped forward and shook his hand. They were from the institute, and drove him to their headquarters in a suburb of the city.

Apart from instances when he could disappear to relieve himself in safe conveniences, from which escape was impossible, he was not out of their sight. The discussions took half of a long day, but results were enough to cover a lunch with more than the normal supply of vodka. Later, he was taken in their car to tour the city, view the sites and sober-up. As parting tour de force, they walked him through a few kilometres of the grand rooms in the Hermitage. When it was time for disposal, his hosts accompanied him to the steps of the plane, to be certain he boarded the flight for Moscow.

"Well I didn't get an opportunity to stroll along the Neva prospekt, but I drove down it. I also saw the Neva. As you said, they wanted to display the communist monuments and State buildings, but we visited a part of the old city and the buildings constructed by the Italian architects of the Tsars. Mind, they drove me past Dostoevsky's house."

"You're ahead of me now. I will invest more effort to get there myself."

"They gave me VIP treatment, didn't allow anyone to leave the plane until I got off. At the foot of the stairway was the welcoming contingent, lined to greet me with waiting car."

"That's real nice! But have no illusion—it was security. They were terrified to lose you. It could cost them their jobs."

"I enjoyed the make-believe, pity you curb my vanity,"

The concept of the mausoleum was the brainchild of Stalin, exploiting Lenin's legacy to screen his megalomanic designs for the evolving state. Of levelling dimensions, death chastens the mighty to match the least significant and nature reverts to earlier moulds. With awe for a leader fading, new forms of allegiance, or treachery, replace those of before. As head of the 'Committee for the Immortalisation of Lenin's Memory', Felix Dzerzhinsky, chief of secret police, implemented Stalin's plans. Initially they considered freezing, then performed trials for embalming. It took seven years, before temporary wooden buildings could be replaced with the granite mausoleum, but apart from wartime evacuation, Lenin's remains stayed in situ. When Stalin's body was admitted, it was set on the left of Lenin's, in a carefully ordered arrangement under the diffused light from above. They lay inert beside one another on the soft material of the catafalques. With authority absent, removal of Stalin's embalmed corpse and eviction from Lenin's side was unstoppable. Buried under the Kremlin walls, it was confined on the outside. People in Moscow warned visitors: ". . . don't sleep in a mausoleum that doesn't belong to you".

"It's time!" She said. He struggled to wake, watching her from the corner of one eye as she nimbly rose from the rug, to disappear into the kitchen. When she had to go to work, the routine was the same. She was first into the bathroom and not from courtesy, as a matter of convenience. It was logical that she should go before him. She was a person able to jump out of bed, or up from the floor and immediately be sharp and alert. On her way, she would start the percolator. In the mornings, they drank coffee and had a few biscuits from the PX. Bread was a luxury—they did not eat it then. As the slow one to wake, he lingered till the last moment. Besides, before getting to his feet, he enjoyed listening to the familiar sound of the shower, or her movements in the kitchen.

One morning, he must have fallen back to sleep. She came to wake him and tell him the coffee was ready. When she returned his kiss, bending down to hug and fondle him, he was overcome. Though concerned about an appointment, the continuous state of yearning and limited time together, took precedence. He remembered struggling to ease her stockings around her shoeless feet, but by then, their lateness was beyond dispute. When they left, he spotted the stockings still lying on the floor. He grabbed them, handing them to her, but there was no time to stop. She pushed them in her handbag and rushing down to the car, said she would wear them at school. As she walked ahead, shoes crunching on the frozen gravel of the courtyard, he could see the bare legs below her coat. When she drove, it excited him to think of the icy air between her thighs. Later, when teasing her for exhibitionism under the gaze of the guard, she suggested it was an unconscious counter-reaction to voyeurism.

That day, he missed the chance to use her shower and had to struggle with that of the hotel. Standing under a trickle of cold water, he asked himself: was it punishment for over-sleeping, or for meddling with time?

16

I do not deny existence of parallel lives. Splitting was my way of dealing with incompatible thoughts, a term used by psychologists for unconscious behaviour. It is what I did so far—the conscious suppression in my mind of the existence of one, when with the other. Because it was not 'unconscious', they might say it was 'denial'. But I already said: 'I do not deny . . . '. I stay with 'splitting'.

The sense of the word matches the circumstances. It portrays the separation between two different worlds and the importance of keeping them apart. What is wrong with this? It was pragmatic. She knew about my wife and children at the start and her silence implied acceptance of the status quo. She was in Moscow under contract and I could not join her permanently. The authorities would not permit it. There would be no visa! Why should the splitting not be in Anna's interest? Some might say: it is deceit and must finish. But deception to protect is more logical than the reverse. Openness was not an option. Anna would insist on divorce and it would harm the children—so I could ease my conscience, under the dubious banner of honesty. Curtis talked about people 'passing the buck'. That's what this would be and splitting was a better choice. 'Some' might say I could stop and give her up. But no one could comprehend my alienation in Moscow without her. Only conceivable alternative to continuation, was removal from the entire scene—quitting the job. Capitulation would mean hardship for the family and disappointment for Calvin, hardly just reward after his support. For her, it would be one more abandonment.

"It's time!" she said. I struggled to wake from the stupor in which I lay. When I had to go to work, practice was the same. I was first in the bathroom and it wasn't a matter of courtesy, it was a matter of matching time demands. I had to leave before anyone else. As I lay, I remembered hearing the alarm, but must have fallen asleep again and had this dream: I had an important appointment with someone. I was sitting in his office and he didn't appear. As I waited, I got increasingly distressed. Eventually, I told a woman working there I could stay no longer and must go. "You must stay until he comes!" she replied. "You will not be allowed to leave, until his signature is on the visitor's pass."

"How long will it be?" I asked.

"He should have come today, but he probably will not arrive till sometime next week."

"Today is Saturday, the office will be closed for the weekend and I will have to leave," I told her with assurance.

"What do you mean?" she asked. "It makes no difference. We have to go, but you cannot leave, the guards will not allow it. It will soon be closing time and afterwards you can remain in peace. There will be nobody in the building to disturb you until Monday morning."

"I won't be able to get anything to eat. There is nothing to do and nowhere to lie down. Besides, I don't know where the WCs are."

"That's your problem! We can do nothing." After saying this, she bent over some papers, absorbed in her own affairs. Almost immediately, a similarly dressed woman came along the corridor, putting her head around the doorway. "We must leave! It's time!" She called to the other.

That was when I woke-up again. "I must have fallen back to sleep. I had an unpleasant dream." I said to Anna, but she didn't hear. She could stay in bed until the children had to get-up and have their breakfast. In spite of returning only the previous evening, I needed to arrive at the office early for a meeting with Calvin. He was going to India and would be away ten days. I walked quietly out of the bedroom, carefully turning the brass knob on the door, so that I could close it silently, before going down the stairs to the bathroom. I looked forward to having the water stream from the shower at full flow, over my head and across my eyes.

On each occasion, the transition happens so fast. Should I feel guilty to relapse into familiar routines with no concern for the other? At present, the 'other' is absent and there is no connection. There can be none—'she', as well as 'him', have ceased for a finite period. Games time plays with distance are persistent. Time has made a reverse turn. It does so without exception.

Still in the dark, I crept out of the house and drove-off. When I arrived at the office, Calvin had been delayed. Was time slowing at this end now and will I have to wait for things to happen here? Were the two worlds becoming less defined, as she suggested? No—they are securely apart and cannot merge. Besides I wasn't struggling for meetings, the appointment was fixed. Calvin arrived at two o'clock. I gathered the papers and went to his office. First, he wanted to know about Leningrad and I gave a verbatim report of what happened there and at meetings in Moscow. We discussed people and positions in the hierarchy. What excited him was the immense scope of the development and the number of localities.

For a moment, Calvin sat thinking then said: "You know when I met the minister, he told me they were going to place contracts for twenty establishments, spread throughout the Soviet Union. If all are the same scheme, it means one firm. Each will be a significant investment. Altogether, it will be the largest deal we handled, bigger than all before, combined!" He got up and coming round to my side of the desk, sat on the edge, bending to peer directly into my eyes, "Are they serious?" He asked. "Do we have a chance for the plans Dobrinski outlined?"

"Now we are talking to specialists. They understand the risk from taking second best. If things go wrong, it won't be their jobs they'll lose, it could be their heads. It was a marked difference from the Moscow people and their preoccupation with trade and politics. Time is the problem. We have to get through within the deadline."

"Tell me the game plan. What must we do, to win?" After reviewing strategies and potential outcomes, he asked me to leave. He needed to talk with America and would call me when through.

I thought of 'her' and her role in this. Calvin could not know how I obtained the new insight about the impact of the institute in Leningrad. I did not disclose that she was the one to encourage me to steer my activities outside the accepted channels of the ministries in Moscow. Calvin did not need to know about her. It was a personal matter. He might not understand.

It was after five and I had promised to take Anna out to dinner. It was better not to be late, the first day back. She knew the importance of my work, but resented the fact that it could interfere with private plans. Anna did not like to think of the firm as provider. At times, she seemed to regard them as rival and maybe, she was right. The subject of my business bored her.

Beaming with satisfaction, Calvin put his head round the door—it must have been a good call with the boss. "Stanford agrees! He wants us to go ahead at full steam. To assist us through the bottleneck, he will put a team on the job to supplement our efforts and Melvin will be in charge. Completion should be no problem, as long as everyone understands what is to be done." I asked whether we should continue our discussion in his office. "That's why I looked in to see you. We're through. I have to rush, because of my trip. Go home now and get-off to a prompt start in the morning! I promised Stanford, we would send a telex outlining requirements. Fix arrangements with Forsyth, agree a split of work and send it by midday. Call Melvin after lunch, as soon as they start. Any questions?" I wished him a good journey. "By the way, you'd better put in for a visa. You will have to follow this closely. Have fun!" He said over his shoulder as he strode down the corridor, carrying a bulging briefcase and a large wrapped Stilton cheese, promised to one of his hopefuls in India. If I left right away, I could be sure to arrive early, see the girls before they went to bed and still be in time to get to Anna's preferred restaurant.

As I drove, I thought about my conversation with Calvin. For the first time, chances in the Soviet Union looked realistic. My provisional assignment appeared to be lasting. Nothing in the country was sure, but at least they were unlikely to pull out abruptly. I could expect my involvement to continue for the present. Priority was for continuity and material benefits could follow later, but prospect of winning contracts larger than before, would stir jealousies. Several might try to oust me from my success, the more so if they found out about her. I realized what an astute move it was, to have kept her secret and resist boasting. In as little as four or five weeks, I would be with her again. The thought induced a sense of elation, but I felt guilty and curbed myself. In present surroundings, such thoughts are contrary to objectives of the splitting and should be suppressed. If splitting is successful, I can behave with Anna in the same way, as if 'she' did not exist. When in Moscow, it has to be the reverse. It is naive to claim that a man cannot love two women at the same time. Think of the Russians and their idol Lenin. When he went to live in Zürich before the revolution, he didn't go with his wife alone—he took along his mistress. It became one of the most fruitful periods of his life and without it, the Revolution might not have occurred. Both women accompanied him through this crucial stage. A more recent example is Khrushchev. His wife, a home-loving person, was rarely in Moscow. She stayed in the country and avoided the spotlight. In the city, Khrushchev enjoyed the company of Tupolev's daughter. In my case, the reality, though unpalatable is that each strengthens need for the other.

I was running into rush-hour traffic. I switched on the radio and started to think about uncontroversial trivialities, like what I should wear. It was almost three weeks since I spent an evening with Anna and friends. It was good to be back. I should not be too diligent in chasing my visa. With the repetitious trips, I must not take home for granted. Now was time to enjoy the family.

17

As the relationship progressed, the nature of the patterns mutated. The earlier configurations of four dimensions and fleeting permanence, transformed to new ones. Static forms replaced those of unrestrained passion and excitement, in which anything novel or unconventional was explored with zest. Absence of motion made the time dimension redundant and no more than three dimensions were required to define the space immediately above the rug, in position and straightened in front of the bookcase after putting out the light. It was as if stills from a projector, supplanted the flickering cinematic images of before. As intimacy matured, habit folded action into predictability. The patterns formed in the darkness from the ordered arrangement of the two bodies, as they lay inert on the soft material, beside one another and close together, portrayed familiarity.

Without fail, she would be directly alongside the bookcase, in a line parallel with its straight white shelves, her legs stretching away from the window, in the middle of the left half of the rug. He lay on her left, technically at the centre of the right section, but in practice at its extremity and near the midpoint. They would be on their backs and if he turned his head towards the bookcase, he would see her profile picked-out by the diffused light from the un-curtained window above and behind them. He would slide over to feel the warmth of her left thigh, naked and pressed against him, as he lay still in the dark.

Apprehension that ideologies on the opposite sides were getting less distinct prompted disagreement. His initial hostility to their system, made him overlook progress but after the improvements to his business, he had to acknowledge exaggeration. She maintained that as a man, he was not capable of recognizing that emancipation of women in the Soviet Union set an example to the rest of the world. Coping with conservative demarcations where she was raised, the education-for-all and seeming lack of discrimination that followed the revolution, were 'close to her heart'. She admitted gullibility in earlier aspirations of 'post revolutionary' equality, but he alleged, the shortfall had more to do with the actors—masters at swapping their parts, but unable to change themselves. She accepted that among the lead performers, Stalin and Khrushchev were both opposed to change in 'no uncertain terms'. He recounted that confidential political reports subscribed to by the firm, showed a doomsday scenario for circumstances in the so-called free world, with predictions of starvation, drought and destruction, in critical regions by the last decades of the century. She questioned, how man-made problems could reach such proportions, when animals and insects had endured longer on earth without destroying the environment. He argued that other species accept nature's laws, without rewriting them to confute disorder as 'order'. Restoration needed immense financial resources and incontrovertible action to overcome opponents to birth control. She questioned, why Western newspapers did not mention such critical developments and suggested it would be illusory to expect funding and political support in her country, for non-profit activities that opposed religious bastions. If the situation was real, the Soviets were more likely to exploit it, to extend communism in the affected continents. (We did not know that Communist China would be sole country to introduce a single child policy). Both agreed that regardless of ideology, neither side could win a fight with nature. In his view, return to the status quo had to be reckoned with. A trusting person, she was ready to give others the benefit of the doubt. In the estranged situation, he believed no one but her. A particular participant irritated him—the security man, involved by her to help him. It was *fait accompli* and he kept quiet.

To avoid the *Gastronom,* they treated bread as luxury. The PX where she got everything else didn't sell local products. Russian treats, such as: champagne, vodka and caviar were available at affordable prices from *GUM,* next to Red Square and he could walk there from his usual hotels. Perhaps influenced by the mausoleum, this showcase department store induced a feeling of enshrinement. There was often a crowd, which could be watched from wrought-iron observation bridges on the first floor, as they meandered through the intricate pattern of lanes and cross alleys below. Like a museum, people looked, rather than bought. When bread was important, a *Gastronom* visit was unavoidable. Typical of everyday city activities, this involved joining a queue. Getting to the counter before supplies ran out, was not the end, but the beginning. Anything ordered had to be paid for from a second queue, where cashiers used the abacus, skilfully flicking wooden balls, backwards and forwards along metal wires. A hand-written receipt was pass for a third queue, where unwrapped goods could be collected in a paper bag brought optimistically for the purpose, but anyone needing more, faced repetition in other departments. Party stalwarts of a communism that stretched half-way around the world, might claim that the *Gastronom* structured for specialization was model for today's globalized corporations—different shops, selling intrinsically the same goods.

Foolishly, he took her one evening to the foreigner's bar at the National for a bet, to see if they could detect the KGB agents, milling among the unsuspecting Western visitors. The inevitable 'America, America . . . ' was playing over the loudspeakers, the bar's signature tune for the capitalist world, it was supposed to represent. There were about twenty people, sitting at small tables, or standing around. The men looked bored, or pretended to be amused. He noticed a couple of Russian women talking to each other. As they entered, he felt a gentle tug on his arm. "I don't want to stay," she whispered. "Let's go to my place!" As they went, he enquired what upset her. "I saw someone I don't want to meet. It was the guy with the crew cut and moustache, perhaps you noticed him over on the far side? It's the security man from Louisiana at the embassy. I don't think he saw me and it's better we don't meet there." He didn't notice the man she described, but it was a reason to leave and he didn't glance back.

He was to meet a local business contact at the Ukraine. The reception, with high ceiling and columns had a daunting air. Arranged around the area were the check-in desk and amenities, with two back-to-back rows of armchairs in the centre. It was rather full and apart from those sitting, a number were standing, or strolling in the open space. After fifteen minutes, pursuing his usual pastime of watching people, he realized from barely perceptible signs, some knew each other but did not want this recognized. From a mental register of those sending and receiving, he could isolate at least ten, who were hunters in a chase—and no foxhunt. As object of the appointment did not arrive, he stayed to follow the covert game play out, narrowing selection to three near the newspaper stand. Before he could isolate a quarry, the drama climaxed with a scuffle. Whoever was chased, disappeared through the front entrance, with ten or so agents behind. By the time he was himself at the door, he saw them bundling the quarry into the first of three cars, lined-up below the wide stone steps that lead up to the hotel. The rest jumped into the remaining two vehicles and all three raced-off down ulica Ukrainskij, in the direction of Tarasa nabereznaja along the riverbank. As they turned the corner, he lost them. Sickened by what he saw and with knowledge that a person who earlier was a couple of feet away, might no more be seen or heard of, he went back and sat to collect his thoughts. Glancing around the room, which now seemed deserted, he noticed Curtis, sitting further down. He went over and called to him: "Hello Curtis!" He got up and approached answering: "Hi! Londoner!" Then, lowering his voice, asked: "You staying in this hotel?"

"No. I am here to meet somebody, but he didn't show. Fancy a drink?"

"Thanks, but I'll take a rain check. I need to prepare for a meeting. How's the little beauty? Have you seen her since the Baku?"

"I saw her recently," he said coolly, hoping to ward-off prying questions.

"If you see her again, don't mention you saw me here. OK?"

"If you say so!"

"I'll explain later, when I have more time. I must get back to my homework. Have a nice evening!" Curtis said, before turning and moving to a different chair at the opposite end of the row. Needing to walk, he left the hotel. He would stop a taxi in the street.

Next day, they were standing together in her kitchen, while she finished heating a soup. He told her what he witnessed at the Ukraine, but didn't mention Curtis. "I assume it was an arrest."

"Make your own guess! I doubt he'll be around this part again. If you hadn't sat so long, you might not suspect—most visitors wouldn't notice."

"If eliminated, do they shoot them?"

"It could be Siberia," she said removing the saucepan and turning-off the gas. "You know, the odd thing is—there is no death sentence in the penal code. The State invokes it as 'a measure of social defence'."

"It must have had broad interpretation in Stalin's time."

"Unlimited, I guess!"

Stalin was on record, extolling his belief in 'the power of the human will'. When it came to his 'will' and the numbers of persons killed, tortured, imprisoned, or disappearing under it, records were broken. It was not just the trials and purges of the thirties, it continued up to the 'Doctors' Plot' in his last year. Stalin's death was reported as from a heart attack, though some suspected he was murdered. A story printed in a foreign newspaper falls somewhere in between, suggesting: 'The heart attack was induced by a fit of rage, brought on by a stormy encounter with Voroshilov, then elder statesman of the Presidium, in connection with this last odious case. Nine among the country's most prominent doctors several of them Jewish, were arrested two months earlier. They were charged with trying to poison members of the Presidium, for whom they were house physicians.

The claim was fictitious, but Stalin used it. He gave instructions on how the case be run—insisting one be put in chains and another, 'beaten'. He curtly told the minister of state security: "If you do not obtain confessions, we will 'shorten you by a head'." To discredit the Jewish intelligentsia, Stalin drew up plans to deport some of them to Siberia.'

The disclosure in the foreign press went on: 'When Molotov and Kaganovic were too timid to speak up at a meeting of the Presidium, Voroshilov got enraged and slammed his party card on the table before Stalin, threatening: "If such a step is taken, I would be ashamed to remain a member of our party." Stalin purple with rage shouted back: "It is I who will decide whether or not you keep your card!" In the ensuing scuffle, he collapsed on the floor and while he lay prostrate, his daughter Svetlana forced her way in and threw herself on top of him. Stalin opened one eye, but could not speak. Beria dropped to his knees, hysterically kissing the leaders hands. After arrival of doctors, he was removed to his chambers, but did not regain consciousness.'

A former American Ambassador wrote of Stalin: "His brown eyes are exceedingly kind and gentle. A child would like to sit on his knee." A certain member of the Swiss communist party might agree. As a boy, his Russian-speaking mother took him for a holiday in the Crimea. Walking in a country lane, the boy got tired. Seeing a large car approaching from the distance, his mother waved it to halt. The uniformed driver talked to someone inside, stopped and got out. He opened the rear door and ushered them into the back. The boy and his mother were astonished to find themselves seated opposite a man with a heavy face, large moustache and wearing the legendary tunic shirt with the Russian collar. It was Stalin. Their host made a few friendly comments to his mother and when they left, leaned forward to give the boy a fatherly pat.

Sometimes as she slept, she would roll over to face the bookcase. She would then be lying away from him on her right side, legs bent and projecting towards the space where earlier the gramophone was playing.

By raising himself with his right elbow supported on the floor, he would slide his body towards hers, until he could feel the warmth of her hips and her back, pressed against his belly and chest. In this pattern, his head would be nestled in the nape of her neck. He would contrast the smooth skin where it rested against his left cheek, with the texture of the rug pressed against the right. At the same time, his left leg would have slipped into the void created by her bent legs, so he could feel her along her left thigh, to the point where the contour of her leg swelled at the calf. In that position, his right leg stretched under the left, would have slid across the surface of the rug to feel her toes against his. He was not certain whether they were those of her left foot, or of her right.

18

The patterns together were limited by the confines of her flat—in the way a frame defines the borders of a painting. The rug could be construed, an empty canvas and the pattern, the graphic representation of the bodies on it. There were differences between these and were they works of art, they might not have fitted in a single exhibition. First patterns were expressive, the forms and figures infused with wild dramatic gestures, those that followed of strictly minimal designs, the shapes concealed by the darkness and almost invisible, against the outline of the rug. He recalled pictures seen at the studio of an artist he had visited. On one occasion, the painter showed him a painting in which the entire canvas was covered with a single tint in perfect uniformity, undisturbed even by brush marks. As if to crown the centre of the monochromatic composition, a single incision was cut with great precision, resembling a wound. Tension of the canvas stretched on its frame, made the cloth twist and curl inwards to form its own unique contours. In the immediate vicinity, the single colour was infused with chiaroscuro, by deflection of the light. The shadows and reflections stressed the power and magnetism of the penetration, at the centre of the otherwise minimalist piece.

In the middle of the night with the room in darkness, lit only through the un-drawn curtains of the window at the back of her flat, he thought of this picture. In the diffused light, the unblemished evenly tinted body, merged with the plain umber colour of the rug, stretched beneath her as a canvas on the floor. Then, accentuating the life encapsulated in the static image before him, it was the power and magnetism of her sex that crowned the centre.

There is intrinsic wisdom behind the saying 'Never volunteer!' It's what she did unwittingly with her security man, because of his faux pas at the opera. She didn't volunteer services, but she exposed eligibility to practised professional eyes and invited dangers that were absent, had she stayed out-of-sight. Ostensibly, it was a security screening, but to her contact, she bared credentials that could serve them for a variety of purposes. He could recognize her strength of character and staying power. He would see she was not a 'wasp' with backing from a powerful family, who might raise questions. She was a safe candidate. The actor was on stage and there was no going back.

"Did you see him?" she asked. She had driven through the gate and was parking as usual. This time the guard followed them to approach within a few paces of the car, glaring. "Let's talk inside it's safer." She continued in the lift: "They seem to take more interest in us. The last two or three times, they moved further from the sentry box, but not as close as this!" She opened the security lock on the front door and they walked through the narrow hallway, to stand a moment near the bookcase. "I need a coffee," she said, going to the kitchen. He sat down on the carpet and went over the facts. What could have prompted the new attention? I asked myself. In the past security, problems arose from our mistakes. At the building complex, a resident called the police, because we behaved suspiciously and although worried, nothing happened. When filmed at the opera, it was through my carelessness. I thought it would end my visits, but again I was wrong. This time I could not point to a mistake by either of us and deterioration of the guards' behaviour seemed inexplicable. It was uncanny that this should occur, when things were going well. There must be a motive behind the curiosity. Apart from her routine contact with them, she dealt with Americans and seemed insulated from Russians. I asked myself, what was different that could upset them. One issue was, contact with the security man, made without my knowledge. It should have no influence on the guards, but if the only fresh factor, we must ask:

Could there be a hidden link? People in that métier are not social workers, nor are they picked for fun. Those inhabiting the no-man's land on either side—must be inured to unseemly duties and cannot afford to squander opportunities. In the gamut of clandestine pursuits be it: tip-offs, leaked information, plots, or 'plants' to trap potential victims, like others they face career pressures and have to earn bonuses to support families.

He joined her in the kitchen. "I noticed yesterday morning," he said. "When we went out of the gate, the guard ran behind and stood in the middle of the street, hands up shielding his eyes, watching us until you turned the corner and were out of sight. He was checking the direction you took. They used to stay near the sentry box and observe us from the distance. Why do they show this amount of attention? Surely, it can't be the stockings!"

She laughed: "What nonsense! It was bad enough having them log us in and out, but then they were consistent." After pouring the coffee, she took it into the other room and they sat on the carpet.

"Do you think it has anything to do with your security man?"

"Why do you say that?"

"Because he is a new factor. People in that game face fuzzy demands and could be in contact with the other side. He might inadvertently use your name or particulars for something unrelated."

"I don't like you saying this, but I remember something else and I'm sure it shows your assertions are misdirected." She paused. "Shortly after you went back at the end of the last trip, the guard came up as I parked and asked to see the vehicle documents. I waited in the driver's seat and he went back to the sentry box to search for whatever he was after. Then, he returned to ask for my personal documents and disappeared a second time to his cabin. This had not happened before and I was upset, because he was slow. When he came back, he went to the passenger side, opened the door and leaned across, to pass me the documents. I thought I saw him pick-up something between doorframe and passenger seat. As I was looking through the documents at the time to check nothing was missing, I did not challenge him. Is it possible something fell out of your pocket during that visit?"

He was confused. "I don't believe so. Had I lost something, I would have realized. What was it like?"

"I couldn't see. Whatever he removed was small, hidden in his hand, but I am sure I saw the arm go behind the seat." He wondered: should I keep away for a while, to see if they revert to previous moulds. We could meet in restaurants, or in concerts, for however long it takes. It would be an end to lovemaking and who knows how long we have together. Instead, he said it was crucial to understand why the guards altered their patterns and she responded pensively: "I suppose it is."

He hoped she was not becoming a victim. It should not be possible—she claimed to be a free spirit and her adventurous nature, endorsed it. She didn't approve of those, who victimized themselves and professed it was important to defend oneself against exploitation, but he learned that the role pattern could be subconscious. He thought about a woman he fancied at a party: I wanted to spend the night with her and she refused, saying she didn't know me. It was not important, I countered, what mattered was how a person felt and she was the right type for me. If we went to bed, it could lead to a relationship. She replied it was the other way around. She had been to bed with a number of men, and the problem came next morning. After insincere compliments and promises to call, she would not hear from them again. I assured her it could not be so with me, particularly concerning a person as attractive. After continuing to press through the evening, she gave in to persistence. On the way to her flat, she reminded me that I was going to be the exception. More interested in the lovemaking, I didn't think about my assurances until the morning. When I awoke and saw her beside me, I remembered how I came to be there and thought about my promise. I felt, taken advantage of—burdened by the expectation to be different. I would let her down, same as the others. Why should I not be free to act as I chose, if they were? I got out of bed, took my clothes to the bathroom and dressed. When ready, I woke her, kissed her and wrote down a phone number—I knew I would not use.

One Friday night, he cancelled plans with her for a last minute invitation from a business associate—Ivanov, boss of an organization he dealt with. His card listed him Vice President. He and two others would have dinner at his hotel. Refusal was out of the question. After arrival, Ivanov sat on the far side of the table with the department head beside him. The third, a younger person, sat next to him—opposite them. He was introduced by name, but gave no card. Before ordering, they asked for vodka and when the bottle arrived, Ivanov complained, it was not properly chilled. The waiter brought as replacement, a decanter in a bucket of ice and he noticed that the glasses on that side of the table were filled from this decanter, whereas the others were filled from the bottle. They talked, they ate and had more toasts, each following at ever decreasing intervals, with the *Nasdroviej* accompanied by 'bottoms-up'. They had to wait for the courses, but refilling of the vodka was immediate. The evening passed uneventfully, until the young man next to him, got to his feet and staggered across the room, swaying noticeably. On his way to a door at the far end, he almost lost his balance, knocking clumsily into other tables. When the man did not return, he felt uneasy. He drank as much and realized that the decanter probably contained water. He settled the bill, took leave of the guests and headed to his room. As he opened the door, he noticed rotation of the walls and before reaching the bathroom, passed out. He woke intermittently and murky tap water, unsuitable for drinking—was the sole succour and less noxious than the poison in his head. Next morning rotation stopped, but extreme nausea made standing difficult. It was Saturday and he recalled with dismay his four appointments. Worst part would be the lifts.

He remembered the call he didn't make the night before. "I meant to phone you when it was over, but passed-out. The night was terrible, I feel weak but have a list of meetings and hope to get through by four o'clock." She would collect him at the usual place and asked him to contact her by three, if unable to make it. He walked down to reception and took a taxi to the ministry of foreign trade building. The first meeting was on the second floor. He walked up the stairs and survived by leaning across the arm of the office chair, supporting his head on one hand. Afterwards, he couldn't find the stairs. A door in front was closed, but someone opened it and he could follow him to the street. With half an hour to spare before the next meeting on the tenth floor, he went to an *Apteka* and bought a yellow potion which he drained-down. Resting on a bench and propped by the medicine, he felt strong enough to return. He got to the next meeting fifteen minutes late and in the following hour, salvaged appointments won laboriously the previous Monday. Nobody commented on his state, from some he sensed a hint of sympathy.

"Have you heard Shostakovich's fourth symphony?" She asked. It was a surprise, as normally they listened to baroque or earlier music. After Bach's cantatas, or Palestrina, Shostakovich could be a jolt. "I heard some string quartets, but don't remember hearing a symphony," he admitted. Before she knew he would be in town, she invited someone in the building—a music enthusiast with a collection of most of Shostakovich's works, to come with a friend and bring the records of the fourth. He was apprehensive, as since the start they were alone in her flat. She assured him her visitors could be trusted. The neighbour worked in the administration department of her embassy. She planned to get snacks at the PX and he promised to get drinks from GUM. Whether from guilt or fear, when the bell rang, the sudden unfamiliar commotion, prompted fantasies of guards striding down the hallway and bursting into the room. He felt as if waking and not knowing where he was and must have looked stunned, when she introduced the guests. The girl from downstairs, Maryellen was friendly. She had been in Moscow the longest and after complaining about conditions, was going home in a couple of weeks. Her partner Armand was a linguist on temporary assignment to his embassy, as translator. Maryellen had studied music and whenever possible, used her time in the city to visit concerts. She was an admirer of Shostakovich and always hoped to see him conducting, or among an audience. Once, she thought she spotted him at the conservatoire, but it was a look-alike.

Music from her gramophone was accompaniment to conversation, or lovemaking, but this time they were going to just listen. She propped the pillows against the bookcase and divider wall, while he filled glasses with champagne. They stretched-out directly on the carpet, bodies arranged diagonally—in two open 'V's with shoulders together, leaning against the props, glasses at their sides. The work revealed surprising polarities and he understood why she wanted him to hear it. There were tense parts that menaced and she had to turn the volume high to get full effect with her gramophone, particularly the dramatic opening of the first movement. At one point, he thought the floor shook, but it was the neighbour upstairs banging. It was more than an hour, but he kept his arm around her shoulders and except when she replaced records, they stayed motionless. When finished Maryellen said: "No-one is sure whether the voluminous opening theme, is a tribute to Russian communism, or an echo of the underlying threat."

"It was completed in 1936, but he withdrew it after the final rehearsal, upset by the attack which followed his *Lady Macbeth of the District of Mtsensk*," explained Armand. "The opera ran to packed houses, until Stalin walked out of a performance. The official criticism that followed was headlined: 'Chaos instead of Music'. The Secretary of the Composers Union said: 'it showed a propensity for the world of degenerate repulsive pathological phenomena'—or words to that effect."

"He was also scared by Stalin's liquidation of his friend Tukhachevsky," added Maryellen. "This piece got buried until 1961, almost 8 years after Stalin's death and 25 from the aborted premiere. Poor man, he had to write the fifth to calm the party critics, announcing it: 'A Soviet composer's response to just criticism'."

"I thought he was well accepted. He is alive isn't he?" he asked.

"Supposedly! They say he is living incognito in Moscow. He probably did not get over the fear and anxiety of that period. If alive, he must feel hunted. It would explain why no-one has seen him," added Armand. "In 1948 they stripped him of his Professorships. Then he had reason to feel victimized, as well as scared." He told them that he saw what could have been the last appearance of Stravinsky and how the frail composer almost lost his balance going down the steps from the podium. "What a bizarre twist! People would have blamed the KGB," said Armand ironically. "It would have been an international incident—a believable one." Maryellen explained, it was a shock to hear Stravinsky's name, which was not mentioned in the Soviet Union—if he walked down a Moscow street, passers-by would ignore him, as if he did not exist.

When they had gone, she spread the rug on the carpet, but the evening had cast a shadow over the immunity represented by the flat. The music and remarks on the composer's plight focused attention on their insecurities.

Shostakovich was not alone in fearing for his life. Khrushchev would have lost his, had Serov not sneaked him a warning, about Beria's plan to murder him and other members of the Presidium. Then, there would have been no chance to make the de-Stalinization speech. A favorite remark of Nikita Sergeyevich Khrushchev, First Secretary of the Central Committee of the Communist Party of the Soviet Union, as he was termed from 1957 till removal in 1964, was: 'If you think that peace means giving up socialism, you can wait until the shrimp learns to whistle.' It showed his candid attitude to change.

For Stalin, change was an affront. In his de-Stalinization speech, Khrushchev recounted how he tried to persuade him to adopt a different strategy and avoid one of the highest losses of Red Army soldiers in the war. He telephoned Marshall Vasilevsky, begging him to take a map to Stalin, but the leader refused to hear any arguments to alter his plans. When Khrushchev tried to call him personally, Stalin refused to leave his chair, and ordered: "Let everything remain as it is!"

As chairman of the committee for the arrangements of Stalin's funeral, Khrushchev must have authorized admission of the body to the mausoleum and it was he, who later ordered its removal.

In the dark, when she awoke from sleep, she would roll towards him and once again be lying on her back. As if he had moved away she would reach-out, checking he was there. She would slide across until their bodies touched, and would then be close to the centre of the rug. For some time he would remain motionless, preserving the stillness. Then patiently, he would ease his left leg on top of hers, until positioned along a line that ran from her groin down the non-existent gap between her closed legs. His left arm would slip over the flat tight skin of her belly, so that encompassing her right breast within his hand—he could feel the nipple against the fleshy section below his thumb, at the centre of his palm. His head would be located adjacent to hers—noses aligned like sides of a parallelogram. He would be conscious of the smoothness and regularity of her breathing, aware from its warmth that the air had penetrated her more deeply than he. Sometimes, the little finger of his left hand would be lying along the curved line, where the swelling contour of the breast, joined the flat surface of her side.

19

I spent the afternoon at the offices in the outskirts, where the British part of the firm was located. I hadn't seen Brandon for a while, and put my head round the door to greet him. He responded warmly saying, his wife was out for the evening and that I should stop for a drink at his house. He would enjoy the chance to talk about something current. I told him, I took Anna to the airport that morning, and could only leave on Friday to join her. As the children were with the au pair, there was no immediate rush. He said he was ready to leave and I could follow him on his way. The house was completely quiet and he mentioned that his wife had taken the children to her sister's for a couple of nights. Pouring me one of his usual mixes, with twice the normal amount of gin, we went to the living area and sat down, facing one another across the room. "What's going on in Moscow? I've heard nothing since the convention," he asked. "Are you still spending time hanging around waiting for something to happen? My God, I cannot forget the restaurants and the endless delays! What do you do when you are alone?"

"Take a book along. The situation is the same—you have to tolerate it, or pack up and move elsewhere."

"But it can't all be bad, I remember a stunning dark girl in a red dress, you must remember her. It surprised me to see her there. Did you run into her again by any chance?"

"I remember the one, but you are right, it was unusual. She must have been visiting from some Western country," I lied. I would have liked to tell him. In a sense I owed it to him, as he pointed her out to me. He would promise to keep it to himself, 'just between the two of us.' I couldn't take the risk, it would surely reach Calvin, and one of the wives will make certain it gets back to Anna. Brandon himself was the subject of a new source of gossip, and I suspected he wanted to talk about this. He started straight away. "Has anyone mentioned me and Sonia to you in London, or while you were here?" he asked.

"Calvin mentioned last Friday you were in trouble with Thornton about her. Is it true?"

"What did he say?"

"That you developed a new pattern for the boardroom—getting in at dawn, to make-up lost time.

"Did he give details?"

"He said Thornton walked in last Thursday morning and caught you two, in flagrante on the conference table."

"The bastard! It's what I expected. You can't trust him! Look, he appeared early that day and there was no one else around. He told Sonia to go home and we had it out together in his office. We made a deal—if in future I kept it off the premises, he would keep it to himself."

"Maybe he told Allen in confidence, their rapport is unhealthily close. I believe Calvin mentioned that Allen told him. He made me swear, I would not pass it on."

"I don't care so much about who knows in the firm. I'm terrified that if the story spreads, it's only a matter of time before it gets to Glenda. Many people here would be delighted to do me the favour. She's threatened me with divorce before. God knows what she'll do this time. But your glass is empty. Let me pour you another."

I asked how it started with Sonia. He told me it was driving her home in his car after the last Christmas party. "She's a hot bloodied Italian and I'd fancied her since she started here." He explained that afterwards the car was crucial for continuation. Sonia shared her flat with a sister, so they could not go there and it was expensive to keep using hotels. During the winter he could park anywhere in the surrounding countryside but with the light evenings, it became difficult and several times, they were disturbed by passers-by. He recounted a couple of 'nightmare scares', as he put it. The first was when both heard footsteps circling the car.

Before they could protect themselves, they saw a face pressed against the windscreen and eyes peering through the side windows. It was two uniformed policemen, who stopped to investigate the vehicle, which appeared deserted, parked without lights on the hard shoulder. When they asked for his driving licence, Brandon feared letters to the house, which Glenda could open, but they let him off with a warning. After the fright, they met less often and went farther afield. The second 'scare' occurred when he planned an outing to a special nature spot that he wanted Sonia to experience. She brought a pick-nick and enough blankets to cover themselves. Before it got dark, they were lying together partly clothed under one of these, when they heard voices and footsteps approaching. There was no time to dress and they had to lie humiliated, while thirty or more people filed past. It was a local rural protection group, having a Midsummer Night fancy dress party. Wearing grotesque costumes, they giggled and ogled from behind the protection of their masks. By the time the last had passed, the distraught Sonia vowed: it must be hotels—from then.

This pressured Brandon to consider Sonia's rash suggestion, to use the boardroom alongside her office. She had a key, so they could get-in anytime and lock the main door from inside. In the mornings, no one was around before nine, and Brandon reckoned they were safe, if out by eight. Thornton had insomnia that night or a fight with his wife. It was seven o'clock, when he breezed in. It must have given him his excitement for the day, but in his petty manner, he insinuated they scratched the surface. Brandon conceded it was remotely possible, as one day Sonia wore a belt with metal fittings. "For God's sake, the firm can afford to get it re-polished," he moaned. I asked how he planned to contain the talk. "I'll speak to Thornton once more tomorrow. I'll have to threaten him. Sonia can make his life difficult. He's been after her for months. She can make a formal complaint for sexual harassment. He tried several times to get her to stay late, to help reclassify the confidential files." I asked what I could do to help. "Do me a favour and talk to Calvin. Perhaps you could let him know about Thornton's broken pledge. Calvin's a good sort and when he knows, he'll keep it to himself. Let me fill your glass, one for the road."

"No more for now thanks, I need to be going. The au pair promised to leave some food out and if I don't get back soon, it will be uneatable."

"I didn't grasp what you said before about Anna, going away and leaving you and the children. You mean she left you alone with a young au pair? Some people have all the luck!"

"I am not alone with her, the children are there. Anna wanted to get a tan and I can only take next week off, so she went ahead."

"Glenda won't consider having an au pair, she regards it—unfair competition. A friend of hers discovered that her husband was sneaking home during lunch break. She caught him and the au pair, copulating in her own bed and dragged him through a horrendous divorce. Now, he's a ruined man."

"Anna knows I am not the type for such excesses."

"Given the right circumstances, I don't think anybody can be relied on. Is she sexy?"

"She looks like a school mistress."

"Sounds dangerous! For God's sake, don't leave evidence that can be used in court."

"Appreciate your advice Brandon. Good luck with Thornton and I will await the next instalment. Thanks and love to Glenda."

"Let me know the result with Calvin—time is pressing. Drive safely!"

I felt light headed after the drinks. Luckily, it was outside rush hour and traffic sparse. I went back more slowly than usual and as I drove, contemplated Brandon's insinuations. He seemed envious of me, going back to a house with a young au pair and I assumed that most men would think the same way. I felt no particular attraction to Heidi, but his remarks and the drink unsettled me. Was I a prude? Many men would say—take what opportunities you get. But it seemed like a trap, and one set by Anna. I did not suggest, she go away before me and she could not have missed the inference. With the alcohol, I did not feel like further self-investigation. Instead my thoughts veered to Moscow, she made 'him' complete—sensibility and sensuality combined, I surmised. Lovemaking seemed second nature—nothing forced or constricted. Why should I want more? Need I feel abnormal, if I decline a taste of misconduct, however fleetingly exciting? I must devise an alibi, or a plan until Friday that permits defence against compromise. For this evening, it was late and confused, I was too tired to care. I decided to get the food, eat it and go to bed, before I could run into trouble. It was past 9.30 and I went to the kitchen, where I found the meal left in the oven. I took it with me into the living room, closed the door, switched on the television with the volume low and sat in the chair beside the fireplace. When halfway through, I heard steps. As the children would be long in bed and asleep, I knew it must be Heidi. She came in saying: "Oh you're back! You find the dinner OK? Mind if I watch TV?" She was wearing a long dressing gown and went to the sofa on the other side of the room. As she sat down it slipped open, revealing one of the 'baby doll' short nightdresses and a considerable amount of leg. "You are late. You must have had a hard day in the office," she remarked.

"Yes, I am tired. After eating this, I will go to bed."

"Can I get you some coffee?"

"Thanks, that would be nice," I replied.

She got-up, primly wrapping the long dressing gown around her. "I can take-up the coffee and leave it for you in the bathroom," she added going-off towards the kitchen.

"Then I won't wait. I'll say Goodnight!"

"Goodnight!" she called back.

When I got to the bedroom, I lay on the bed until I heard footsteps on the stairs and could assume she was in her room. I then went down to the bathroom. I could see the light burning. Heidi probably put it on, when she left the coffee. I went in looking for a mug filled with the hot black liquid, but did not see it. My attention was taken by something else. She was there, standing in front of the washbasin, her back towards me, dressing gown and panties removed. I heard splashing of water. She must have been washing her face, and her leaning forward, drew the hem of the short nightdress upwards at the back. The bared bottom protruded defiantly from below the almost transparent material. The white skin and the youthful flesh, curving seductively out on either side, dissonantly contrasted with the shadows of the cleft in between. "Hello!" she said without turning. "Don't mind me!" And she bent down over the basin, further parting the scissure, wantonly exposed under my eyes. The deep furrow led downwards to an area of darkness, where the fullness of the cheeks shut out the light and where black pubic hair could just be discerned. There was something raw and healthy about her body. She obviously knew which weapon to draw, and was ready to use it. Though young, she couldn't lack experience. Under normal circumstances, I might have backed away and avoided danger. However, my alcohol-softened state lowered resistance. I watched my right hand, as it powerlessly moved forward, seeking out the warm flesh and mapping the sensual contours under the fingertips. For a while she didn't move, she must have enjoyed being touched and observed. Then suddenly she spun around. She had small rather flat breasts, which seemed singularly high on her chest. Her spectacles and hair drawn high in a ponytail, made her look studious. I felt an arm behind my back, as she pulled me to her. A hot clammy mouth enclosed mine and a tongue thrust hard between my closed lips. One hand groped inside my dressing gown, as the other drew my right hand to her warm crotch. It sensed bristling hair then wetness. As she pulled me closer, one of my fingers was aware of a small piece of string slightly projecting from within. "It's not comfortable here, but you probably won't feel good in your bed. Why don't you come up to my room?" she proposed.

"Good idea!" I replied. "Why don't you go ahead?"

When she left, I drank down the coffee, which was no longer as hot. It was now my turn to lean over the washbasin. I opened the cold tap and scooped the water eagerly over my face. I dried my hands and face carefully, hung up the towel and switched out the light. I tiptoed up the stairs, pausing at the door, then opened it quietly, closing it behind me. After sliding the bolt across, I got into the bed. I set the clock an hour earlier than usual, turned out the light and pulled the blankets over my head. It had been a near one. Was it because of Anna and thoughts of spoiling our nest? Or was it because I remembered Moscow and thought of her? Maybe it was nothing like that. Perhaps it was because I didn't like the blood. It's possible that was all that stopped me.

The next night she would go to school. Asking a neighbour to look after the children until I got back, I spent the evening in their house and then took them home. We watched television and after putting the kids to bed, I was careful to be out of the way myself, before Heidi returned. On the Thursday, I got back deliberately late, after everyone was sure to be asleep. On Friday, I was leaving, taking an afternoon flight to Athens for an overnight stay, before catching the boat the next morning. I called the children from the office to say good-bye and drove directly to the airport.

20

In their segregated world, time stopped when parting and clock-hands moved when together again. While he was away, the physical gap was uncommonly wide and on returning, it was understandable, if it appeared narrower than reality. Was this why they felt close, or was it the risks and uncertainty? Continuation of the relationship remained stubbornly, subject to circumstances beyond their control. It was always possible—the present stay would be the last. Her future in the country lay in the hands of government officials. At any moment, they might transfer her, outside the reach of his travel. Although prospects for the firm improved, continuity of his involvement remained provisional and private visits were forbidden. Intimacy seemed profound, yet values cannot be the same. Levels of nearness, in respect of the barrier present between two persons differ. He accepted that the divergence, the space between separate beings, which destines each to exist alone, could not entirely be taken away, but it seemed thinner with her.

To his surprise, she saw her security man another time. He was away on leave and in spite of earlier unpleasantness—she waited for him to come back, to avoid a new security clearance and release of her personal data to a second person. When she told him about the guard coming out into the street, trying to see the direction she was driving, he said it was unusual. He reminded her their duty was to monitor the visitors, not residents.

"That's how they were before."

"I know, but he seemed intrigued by the increased attention they show in me. He said, it revealed an interest from their side and he requested supporting details—which documents were examined and how much time on each."

"Did he give a reason, or explain what could be behind it?"

"He claimed I could have crossed one of them by showing insufficient respect and he warned that party rank of the one concerned, was crucial. In his view, it was my fault. I probably provoked the one who checked my papers and this was unwise. If a similar incident occurs again, he wants me to inform him."

"Is he being straight? He seems to take their side."

"He made no effort to be pleasant, but may have a point about avoiding contention." She planned to follow his recommendation, adhere to the rules and avoid argument. She told him that during the times he was away, she would keep watch on them, to check deviations, good or bad.

"It's unjust that we must worry about guards and what they may or may not do. On the 'other side', no one would understand our concern."

"You're right. They could not imagine what it means for us, unless here."

"I want to write about this. I keep notes in a diary for later," she added.

"You keep a diary?" He asked, with some apprehension.

"Not a real diary—a workbook of jottings about impressions, moods and feelings. I didn't mean, I write about us. I wouldn't put down anything that could interest our friends out there. It should be safe in the flat, but if I carried it outside, they could apprehend me and take it from me." When he asked, if they stopped her before, she assured him: only the once—with him at the building complex.

They went to visit the University. She stopped close to the main building—another Moscow style skyscraper and the peripheral location magnified the nonconformity. Strolling through the grounds, they had to work their way through a crowd to return to where she parked. In the throng, he noticed a number of Africans and when they were inside the car, he mentioned it. She told him, some countries of the continent were encouraged to send students to study in the city, with a promise of higher education, to increase Soviet influence in that part of the world. When in Moscow, allowances were meagre and they were left to fend for themselves. "Despite the ideology," she said, "there must have been prejudice. With accommodation tight and insufficient knowledge of the language, life was difficult, there was rioting. Sadly, the authorities tried to hush it up, arresting some and sending many back." Her explanation suggested that her hopes might have been affected.

"I just finished a fascinating book by Genet," she said.

"I heard about the *Balcony*, is this another?"

"*Our Lady of the Flowers*. He wrote it in prison and it's rich with surreal imagery. I brought it back last time I was home, but didn't start immediately. I did not realize how powerful it would be. You should read it."

"I will, but I'm partway through *The Magic Mountain* and surprised how it mirrors aspects of life here."

"I didn't know that Thomas Mann was in Russia."

"Probably he was not, but he writes about timelessness. In the sanatorium, everybody becomes obsessed by the unbroken uniformity. Events follow each other according to pattern. Patients become preoccupied by the minutiae of their daily lives—the regularity and slow unfolding of time."

"The comparison would not have occurred to me, I read it long before I came here, but I see what you mean, we have got used to immutability, waiting and other time related factors. With the regulation here, the detail of our lives takes on a new dimension, an importance of its own."

"More significant is isolation. If you recall, the sanatorium was a restricted space. Apart from lying on the balconies, patients rarely left the building. They were insulated from everything outside. Our life is cut-off in a similar way. When we are 'between the boulevards' nothing else appears to exist."

"That's true! We experience the small annular sector, familiar to us and the rest of this country is unreal. The 'other' world seems as faraway as the past. It is that way through the year—one vacation to the next."

"You remember the part, where Castorp goes for a walk in the mountains with Settembrini. They get lost in a place that was out of bounds to patients and as alluring as the vast space around us, that we only see on maps. It must have been equally exasperating to them, to know it is there, yet not approachable."

"You could be right."

"Interesting! When we met, you talked about your posting as like a stay in a sanatorium."

"Did I really? It's a strange comparison. Did I really say that?"

"I remember it distinctly."

"If I said that, it was to do with a need for recuperation. I had to recover from what I went through."

"I believe you explained it that way."

"It makes me want to read the novel again. Why don't you bring yours along next trip? I can read it from new perspectives. Timelessness and isolation are part of life here." While speaking, she got to her feet and disappeared behind the bookcase into the kitchen and on returning, picked-out a book from one of the lower shelves. She sat down again next to him on the floor. It was the Genet volume. He browsed through a few pages at random and made a mental note, to add it to his list.

"It looks promising," he said. "But tell me, when you get new ones, do you put them in order on the shelves?"

"It's not worth it. Additions here are limited. It's hard to find books in English and by plane, they are heavy. To put them through the bag, there are limitations. I must read those I have a second time, or borrow when I can."

"What I mean is—it would ensure there has been no tampering. If you rearranged them from time to time, it would guarantee that nothing foreign was admitted."

"You can't still be worrying about being watched! No one can get past the locks. But for your benefit, I'll set a roster of inspection," she reacted with mock fawning.

He put his arms around her and stayed motionless. "On the subject of present reading, do you remember the passages, about the 'Good Russian Table' and Clawdia Cauchat?" He asked

"Of course! You mean about, how he views her neck? They are as romantic as anything I read."

"It made me think of you, the first time at the Aragwi. I know the Russian table was on the left and didn't precisely match descriptions in the book, but the distance was similar and it was the view I had of you first. When I turned, I saw the back of your neck. Your hair half concealed the nape, but it was a part of you, I observed first. It was before you turned yourself and noticed I was looking at you."

A Canadian journalist got in trouble. They arrested him for questioning. When they wore him down, his embassy had to extricate him from the country. Colourful rumours circulated around the foreigner's enclave, disclosing practices used in the courts and prisons. She passed some to him. As well as keeping inmates in darkness and silence, they devised ways to prevent them meeting, or seeing one another. Guards escorting a prisoner to and from interrogations, usually at night, would signal at various stations on the way. When answered, they made him hide in an alcove, or face the wall, so another could pass unseen. The sign used by the escorts was a 'smacking of the lips', and when she told him this, he found it amusing. Ice cream sellers did this to attract attention from cinema audiences in Cairo and to transplant it to the corridors of the Lubyanka, seemed ludicrous. It became a joke between them, and afterwards when someone came out of the bathroom or kitchen, the other might hide and make this noise. Under their rules, challenger must avoid detection and challenged close both eyes. Winners extracted penalties, usually consisting of miming titles of books, or plays, for the loser to guess. The winner had to name a category and give a clue. These might be: play—'ice block', for *The Iceman Cometh;* or fiction—'Lubyanka', for *Crime and Punishment;* or non-fiction—'Soviet ice cream' for *The Collected Speeches of Anastas Mikoyan.* To add sophistication to their stratagems, they might add riders that reversed results for say, an uneven number of signals, or a loser caught unawares. It was insensitive to make fun of something abhorrent for those involved, but for them—it was a game. Just as the well off, seldom show sympathy for the needy, so they found it hard to see themselves in the plight of prisoners. As foreigners, they assumed they would be left alone, if adhering to the rules. A modicum of concern lingered however—the legal system was disturbing and contrary. When they arrested someone, they did not say why, they interrogated first, to determine the charge. Many were willing or coercible, to act as witnesses for the secret police and the interrogator could disregard evidence in favour of an accused. Being there all the time, her risk was in theory higher, but she had the embassy to extricate her, if needed. With his firm remote and uninformed, he could count on no support and in practice faced more risk than she. This was why she helped him, when in trouble.

It was not possible to visit restaurants every time they met and with limited alternatives, they spent much of the time together in her flat. The limitations prompted ingenuity. They sought deeper satisfaction than 'lip-smacking' and like children playing, invented another game: *'Kommissar & Prisoner'.* The pantomime imbued fantasies. With their relationship in its current phase of 'familiarity', there was benefit from enlivening, what had become predictable. They exchanged roles, but in practice that of *Kommissar,* went to whoever suggested the logic for a charge. Her creativity was well suited. She would invent cases, which were apt and topical, often from what transpired in previous months. She was assertive in this role, unmatched in her questioning, or the ruses employed. She might try to break his resistance, or trick him to a confession that would make her angry. His customary role as prisoner was demanding, requiring relentless fending-off and attentiveness to avoid a single crack, or weakness, in the arguments. It was known that discharge of the captive was left to the *Kommissar* alone, yet with him as prisoner, a session rarely lasted more than an hour. Her sharp mind would not miss his first mistake and then, unless he could find a novel pretext to justify prolongation, it was the end of the case. After a verdict, there were refreshments, as before an imagined ceremony. There was no violence and punishments could be symbolic. When they got excited, penalties were more daring, sometimes exposing subliminal yearnings, but exercised with gusto and a touch of theatricality. To prolong sensual impact, penalties were at times left in suspension. They had fun at these games. Playing them, made each protagonist in their fantasies, to ward off dangers from outside.

When at night sleep evaded him, he could lie for intervals as long as his earlier periods of waiting, but was not bored or conscious of the time as it passed. She would usually be lying on her left side and he on his right, facing her. As she slept, he might extend his left hand to gently touch the skin of her left thigh, with fingers suspended lightly over the warm surface. Raising his wrist, he could steer the lower portion of his hand upwards and to the right. In the area between the base of the little finger, and the narrowing at the wrist, he would be able to discern the curve of the *Mons Veneris*, through the ends of her pubic hair, brushing capriciously against the outer layer of his skin. The lightest of contact was sufficient, to send signals racing through the fingers, along the arm and up to the brain. Like with a crystal set radio, as patient practice showed years earlier—the nimbler the touch of the cat's whisker against the exposed exterior of the detector, the stronger the waves and impressions transferred. Now he was making contact not with a single wire-thin sensor, but with hundreds, each as animated as the other. The stimulation was reassuring.

21

Arriving on the island next day, I found Anna was there to meet the boat. She was relaxed and after the days on the beach, already looked brown. She wanted to know how the children were. She did not mention Heidi, that is not until later, when we were in bed lying side-by-side. We had our arms around each other and were about to make love. "What did you get-up to with Heidi, while I was away?" She said it rather saucily. When I asked what she meant, she continued: "Oh come on! I bet you seduced her—you two, alone in the house together. I want to know what happened." I told her—it was not me, who seduced her, but she who tried to seduce me. When she wanted details, I naively described what took place: my drinks with Brandon, how she came down while I watched television, the Baby Dolls, how she offered to leave coffee in the bathroom and what I found there. "So you groped her. Did you kiss her at the same time? Did she feel you? Did you have an erection? Did she put her hand inside your dressing gown?" She persisted. I said we didn't get that far. She suggested I go to her room, but I chose to go to bed. "I bet you did and in bed with her. Did it excite you? Tell me! I want to know how you felt. I know you would not turn down an opportunity like that. You should be man enough to admit it."

"I already said I didn't take-up the invitation. But if you don't want to believe me, you can fantasize what excites you most," I added, proceeding to make love to her. It was good that night. She seemed to enjoy it.

When I awoke, I was surprised to find myself alone. Anna must have got up earlier, and gone to the restaurant. It was after nine and as I went downstairs, I wondered whether there was a connection, with what I volunteered about Heidi. The woman serving breakfast, said: "She had hers. She went out." I looked for her at the beach, but she wasn't there. She must have walked to the village. I wandered around searching likely places. Not far from the hotel, the road divided and I turned to the right towards the harbour, then on as far as the main jetty. Everyone I asked looked blank, or shook their head at my description. I had a stand-up coffee at a bar and retraced my steps. When I got back to the fork, I didn't go to the hotel—I went right in the direction of other beaches. The road ran alongside one, before continuing to more remote locations further down the shore. Opposite was a row of buildings with shops, and going into the first, I obtained another negative response. Continuing to the last, a woman was locking-up about to leave and I thought she didn't understand my question. She stood in silence, staring at me. Then in perfect English, told me she saw someone with fair-hair, walking past several hours earlier. She was Greek—tanned and with thick shoulder length hair, brushed straight back. She wore a plain, ankle-length dress, with a string of stones around her neck. When she asked bluntly, who I was looking for, I said, to my surprise: "My wife has left me, she ran-off,"

"She will come to no harm here. My house is that way, we can walk together and I can help you find her." I was glad to have the company. Elektra told me she was from Athens and bought a house on the island, for the summer months. From running the small antiques and trinkets shop, she knew the place well. When we got to where she lived, we found no trace of Anna and no leads from the various locals questioned on the way. Sensing my anxiety, she said: "It's hot, you need a drink. Why don't you rest in my garden and I will fetch you one." Pointing to a chair by a small table, in the shade of a fig tree, she disappeared into the house. She returned with a bottle of ouzo, glasses on a tray, water and a plate of large black olives. We sat in a paved area at the side of the house, surrounded by flowering oleanders that screened us from the nearby road. Beyond, on the other side of some rocks, lay the sea, and I noticed glints from its brilliant blue, shining between the leaves. She was confident and attractive. Though Moscow was far, the dark hair and tan reminded me of 'her'. Apart from the age difference, there was a remote similarity. The ouzo made me feel relaxed and I remarked: "I admire your tan." She pointed to the roof, "There is a small terrace, where I can lie without being observed. I worship the sun. Why else should I come here from Athens?" For a moment he imagined, what it might be like to lie with her on her sunny roof, but began to feel guilty and said: "I must continue my search." "You can find me in the shop. I am there after six and usually till nine, sometimes ten," she called after me.

By the time I got back to the hotel, it was almost two o'clock. I noticed the key had gone and I went up to the room. Anna was packing her suitcase and I could see she had been crying. I asked her what she was doing. "I am going back. I don't want to stay here with a womaniser."

"What do you mean? I thought you enjoyed last night. What happened?"

"It was pretence. I wanted to know what took place between you and that slut."

"I told you. Because I was somewhat drunk, I felt like touching what was displayed, but only that one occasion—the first evening. There is nothing else to tell. You know it all!"

"Not very imaginative! The moment my back is turned, you can't wait to have it off with the au pair."

"This is ridiculous! It was unfortunate that I had Brandon's drinks, otherwise I would have kept my hands to myself."

"I don't believe it. She was thrown out at the last place, because she seduced the husband. I should have realized you couldn't be trusted. You're not going to see her again. I am going to sack her the moment I get back. I'll have her packed and out of the house within the hour."

"You did not tell me what happened with the previous family. If she had a record, why did you hire her?"

"She was available to start at once and seemed suitable for the work."

"But if you knew what occurred before—you should have told me. Whatever made you leave her alone with me? I didn't ask you to come here ahead. It was your idea."

"I wanted a tan and thought this couldn't happen with you."

"It didn't! But if she had her way, it would have. You tried to frame me."

"Where do you take this from? You seem indoctrinated by cold war practices after your ever-longer absences away, behind the iron curtain. First, you suspect Heidi of spying on you, now you are becoming paranoid!"

"Why don't we talk sensibly? Let's go downstairs and have a drink."

"I don't need one. I have to go back to the travel office, to see what flight they found for me."

With no supporting witness, there was no way to prove to Anna that I did not go to Heidi's room. Maybe she would calm down by the evening. In the meantime, if we went our separate ways, the futile rowing would stop. She couldn't travel that day, the boat already left. I had barely a week of vacation and it was absurd to waste it fighting. Still siesta time, I wandered down to the beach, where I was able to lie undisturbed on the sand and think. It was a paradox that had I acted more warmly to Heidi, she would be on my side and Anna could not sustain her allegation. My abstemious response to Heidi's invitation turned her a hostile witness and put the two in opposition to me—sealing the case. With Anna judge and Heidi sole witness, she will say what Anna wants. Whether I accepted the invitation, or rejected it, is irrelevant—verdict will be the same. In retrospect, I was snared the moment I entered the house. I should have stopped Anna from going to Greece ahead of me, but I had no reason, I didn't know what she knew about Heidi. Now, I was entangled and thinking of Brandon's insidious warning, became disheartened. If Anna can establish I slept with Heidi the first night, she can claim I did so on all three. If the initial charge were proved, it can be trumped-up to a serious affair with grounds for divorce and grotesque possibilities. Anna might go through her diary, trying to prove that for weeks, I met Heidi for sex—at the house, or some secret meeting place. On evenings I worked late she could allege, Heidi came to my office and accuse me of a long running affair. In a court, if Heidi gave supporting evidence, I would have no chance. It could destroy the family and lawyers would consume our assets. The more I reflected on the situation, the more frightening it became and from one simple mistake: agreeing for Anna to leave me, 'to get a tan'. My only hope was that she might become worried about damage to the children.

As I continued lying on the sand, I contemplated the precariousness of my life in Moscow. If word came out, there would be real cause for jealousy. If Anna acts out over something that did not occur, it was alarming to consider what could happen, if she found out about 'her'. If only I could do like Rainer and persuade the two, to accept each other, as he did with his threesomes. Rainer was German living in London, working as freelance theatre critic. He wasn't content unless he could live with two women. When he found a new girl friend, he would introduce her to the remaining one and there would be a gradual process, during which he would somehow persuade them to accept each other. After a week or two, the new woman would move in and they would establish a *ménage à trois*. The threesomes lasted for months, sometimes a year or more. Eventually, one would complain and leave. Then he would find another and repeat the pattern. I watched him at a party. As we arrived, he pointed to someone on the far side of the room, saying: "She looks astute." A moment later, he was chatting to her and they disappeared together. It wasn't as if he were handsome. What a fantasy it would be—no more division of time and no more splitting. Rainer inferred there was nothing original about the idea, telling me he used the protagonist from the play *Stella* by Goethe, as model. According to Rainer: Goethe professed that for a 'man in love', life changes for the better—luck improves, perplexities can be understood and supreme obstacles seem easy to surmount. Autobiographical, he wrote the play shortly after an intense affair with Lilly Schöneman, whose character and expressions are incorporated in the role. The protagonist temporarily separated from his wife, was already living with *Stella*. When the two women meet, they 'hit-it-off' at once and readily agree to live as a threesome. They share the husband and continue happily thereafter. Rainer boasted that he was more realistic, as Goethe overlooked the vital step of acclimatization, but I could not share this optimism. In my circumstances, no matter how much time I allowed, if together, my 'two' were bound to quarrel and I had to ensure they did not meet. It could have been good for the children, as in the play, the husband had a daughter and Rainer asserted that the wife's praise of his mistress's competence as tutor, illustrated maturity. 'She' was professionally qualified and things American captivate them, but would she agree to live in London? After the Soviet Union, all is possible yet they were sharing me already—with a difference. It was not I, who fixed the allocations. How did Rainer manage it? A pity, I had not questioned him more closely.

There was a footnote to this and Rainer later admitted that the play ran into difficulties that closely paralleled what happened to Shostakovich with his opera *Lady Macbeth of the District of Mtsensk*. Goethe was attacked by the church—theatre should render virtue enticing, vice abominable, et cetera, and with similar results. Both works were taken out of production and then buried for more than 20 years, until reworked. In his rewrite, Shostakovich softened his work and gave it a new name. Goethe kept the same title, but was persuaded by Schiller to replace the utopian ending with a 'true-to-life' version, in which the mistress poisons herself, the man is ruined (shooting himself), and the wife lives-on to enjoy the spoils.

When I got back to the hotel, Anna was talking with the receptionist. She said she couldn't alter the flight—it would require a new ticket. She decided to stay and we made a pact not to discuss Heidi, until we were home. I realized how fortunate it was I planned my return to include a stopover on behalf of the firm. I wouldn't need to witness the showdown.

Next morning, I needed to walk and not wanting to run into Elektra, went in the direction of the harbour. After wandering around and looking at the boats tied-up to the jetty, I went to the café and ordered a drink at the bar. Almost at once, I noticed Electra sitting at a table in the back and she called me to join her. When she asked if I found my wife, I told her about the cause of the crisis. When mentioning fear of divorce, she comforted me saying, it would surely not come to that but if it did, a trip to Athens would take my mind off problems. She gave me her phone number and address. While walking back together, she mentioned a new restaurant on the island that allowed plate throwing, same as in Athens. She explained how to get there and arriving at the fork, we parted. As I walked to the hotel, I thought: I went to the port to avoid Elektra, yet saw her again—the day after the first.

I took Anna to the restaurant Elektra mentioned. The plate throwing reduced the tensions. She threw quite a number during the evening and when we returned to our room, things seemed almost normal. She kept her word and did not mention Heidi that is, until I came home after the sacking. Then, she held to her version—maintaining she got a confession. She did not build the charge I feared. It left me deliberating, why did she leave us alone after knowing Heidi's record and could there be a connection to what happened with her family in France?

22

Questions were not asked, nor letters sent that could compromise others. The disengagement and delineated polarities of the two worlds, made times together seem compartmentalized. It was as if walls, shut out thought and perception that were extraneous, to disconnect all from the 'other' side. Proust wrote of time's dulling of the senses and awareness of 'remembered feelings', brought back by taste, or smell. In this city, there was no recalling from outside, the 'tastes' and 'smells' were different. In their cubicled domain, distance was the substitute for time, which separated not past from present, but the contrasting lives between which, each journey transposed another's present, temporarily to the past. In relieving the isolation that segregates each person, from parting at birth to extinction at death, intimacy initiated a need that was on the inside, shared from within. It became impossible to deny, a craving that was insatiable—an indispensable object of necessity.

Definition of necessity comprises the inevitability of a consequent, when the ground is given. Did not the repetitive chance meetings, matched affinities and special bond, provide this? In terms of logic, it was the character of that, whose contradiction is not conceivable. Now, driven onward by the indistinctness of the future, the necessity was to be consumed to the full and lived for the moment.

When they took books from her shelves, they did not read them aloud, but referred to points of interest, or contention. The exception was when they played the matches game from *Last Year at Marienbad*, where not knowing the rules, she was repetitively the loser. A different scenario evolved when she brought back the script of a play, seen at a fringe theatre in Greenwich Village. It was based on a classical story of a princess, who leaves two slaves to look after her palace during absence on a trip. She thought the young writer wrote it as parody of Genet's work. The subject was a spark for fantasy: clue in a paper chase, leading to the tempestuous patterns of before. The play was not followed, except for roles—his as Sosarme a eunuch, sometimes playing the part of Elvira, and hers as Elvira a female slave, sometimes playing the role of princess. They improvised—unconstrained by rules.

An atrium. A set of shelves with some books scattered at random. A brown rug spread on the floor. Several chairs and a cupboard. A window at the back looks over some buildings. To the left a doorway leads to two rooms. In one, food is prepared, the other contains a bath. It is dark outside.

Elvira is near the window. She leans against the wall. Sosarme crouches on the rug, in front of the shelves. Both appear disgruntled. They wear intimate apparel and too much make-up.

ELVIRA. Pay attention Sosarme, I sense we are watched and listened to. It's someone outside. Someone is keeping a record of our movements. They can make reports on us.

A pause. Sosarme holding a flesh coloured brassiere in his hands, strokes it across his breast.

SOSARME (*flinging away the brassiere with a sudden roar*). There are eyes in those buildings. I know it.

ELVIRA (*moving forward on stage, away from the window*). It's easy to be afraid.

SOSARME (*inscrutably*). Don't panic, Elvira! We cannot afford to relent, but there is ample time for precautionary measures.

The play gave the opportunity to reverse roles. In her eyes, he was in the 'position of power', ostensibly controlling the times for his comings and goings. In fact, 'he' was not in control, but merely emissary of whoever threw the dice. Nevertheless, when not together there was nothing she could do, except acquiesce—or break-free and quit. With awareness of these roles in the under-currency of the relationship, they could exchange parts, like in their game, but unequivocally for a single night.

ELVIRA. Stop trying to dominate me.

SOSARME (*annoyed and leaning above Elvira*). I urge your Highness's pardon. I've never tried to dominate you. I want your Highness to have pleasure.

In the version played, instead of dressing her up, he had to undress her and give her a bath. In the time, he knew her, he did not see her take a bath, she used the shower. (She was American, and most did.) The bath could add new perspectives (an oriental scenario, for example). As he started to run the water, he opened cupboards looking for oils, foams, or perfumes, anything that could enhance the images.

SOSARME (*pained*). I am getting everything ready for your Highness's bath. (He drew the word out lingering on the sound of the vowel).

ELVIRA (*firmly*). Prepare my belongings and set them in display. The long flowing bathrobe and lots of essence. I want my best eyeliner.

SOSARME (*opening the door of the cupboard and clumsily sliding the clothing along a noisy rail*). I want your Highness to put on the white robe. I long to see the coarse towelling pressed against the sensuous curves of your Highness's fulsome bosom.

Her breasts were delicate, flawless in their shape. The cross section could be described by a semi-circle, cut horizontally at its centre. The convex curve of the lower quadrant delineating their fullness and firmness, while the reversed concave upper portion, flowed gracefully upwards from the nipple to the chest.

ELVIRA (*freeing herself and wrapping the excess of the material around her bare legs*). Don't be presumptuous. I don't like you seizing me in that foul manner.

SOSARME Stand still.

ELVIRA (*mocking*). Do you enjoy seeing me without attire? I hope you appreciate that I am a beauty. Yet, to be royal is agonizing.

SOSARME (*with a calm smile*). Highness! Whatever shall be your desire Highness! We can start at once.

The curtain must have dropped. Perhaps the audience went home. He could hear her voice. "Wake up honey! Wake-up. We are late." When he opened his eyes, he saw she was dressed." This should help," she added, handing him a cup of black coffee. He drank it cautiously, still half asleep. He dressed and they went out to the car.

He used the metro only when he went to the North. It was a feature of the city that was lavish. It could afford to be, built with prison labour from Stalin's camps. Tunnels were large with stations, ornamented by grand panels, glorifying the rising of the proletariat. The journey was almost as quick as a taxi, and the five *Kopeck* fare covered the whole system. When he went to that part of town after staying with her, she would make a detour and drop him on her way to school. Unless she was in a hurry, she parked in a quiet spot in Akademika ulica and they sat chatting in the car, until time for her to leave. It was a unique fixture, for the particular area, delaying their parting, as if each extra moment were won and farewells faint reflections of those when he left the country, with the consolation of being together later the same day. These stolen moments in the car were shared with the newly built Ostankino television tower. The country's tallest structure would soar over them, as if watching through whatever telescopes were concealed inside. In that spot, they felt anonymous, ignoring it. Otherwise, after nights together in her flat, she would drop him near his hotel, or round the corner from an office, he was visiting. In the centre, lingering unnecessarily inside, or beside a parked car, could attract attention. There, he would get out, say goodbye and leave.

He talked to her about a Russian couple employed long term on his last trip, to make contact with organizations, unknown to the firm. The responsible institute formally approved the arrangement. This time, he could not reach the pair and someone told him they were not available. He did not accept that politics could have anything to do with it. When she asked if they fraternised, he mentioned giving small gifts and being invited to their flat. "I hope you didn't go?" she remarked with a smile. He said the others went without him, as he spent the evening with her. "Considering the overcrowding, it's hard to take foreigners home without being seen. They could have been followed, or reported by a neighbour. You remember what happened, when we went to the complex in the North of the city."

"I hope our people didn't get them into trouble."

"Most likely, their office transferred them to another job. It seems there's no remission for breaking rules!"

"On the subject of rules, what happens in the play—the one about the slaves? I forgot how it ends."

"Tragically, Elvira quits—opts out."

"But Sosarme, appeared the dominant one. I am surprised Elvira takes that step."

"There seems confusion between appearance and reality in the play. You are right about Sosarme, he is continually boasting action, but bungles each step—even his attempts to murder the centurion. It's the reverse with Elvira. She is supposedly the gentle one, but in fact the more courageous."

"I admit I saw no clue."

"There were a couple of hints, but we went through rather fast. You probably didn't notice."

Sometimes as they lay alongside one another half asleep, half awake in the dark, she would give him a sign, a movement, an unspoken code. Then supporting himself from the floor, he raised his body barely enough to slip without sound across her left side. His two legs, pointing away from the window and between hers, would be in contact with the surface of the rug, exposed between her open thighs. Sensation was magnified by the silence and obscurity, with skin against skin, tumescence within softness, warmth enclosing warmth. The most imperceptible of movements were intensified many-fold in their minds, as if impressions focused and assimilated the energy and motion from earlier patterns. Only a difference in the frequency of her breathing was discernable. Was there sometimes the sound of a gasp? Perhaps, but nothing that might disturb the calm, as silently and almost without motion bodies fused for a brief sense of oneness and abated, to the tranquillity, which characterized the nights in the darkness together. If he raised himself to look into her face, only the faintest of outline would be visible. But he could shut his eyes and see her image as he saw it, when he turned halfway around in his chair to look at her the first time.

23

The dull feeling of sickness was a new experience. He did not remember this before. If worry was its cause, did it relate to her, or was it about himself? Concern at contending with her loss was not new. It almost became fact after the opera incident. The relationship could have ended suddenly and irrevocably at that point, but impact was different. There was disquiet, feelings of sadness, perhaps a tinge of fear, but not this gnawing feeling that pervaded the body. It seemed to stretch through the hands, to the ends of the fingertips, which appeared on the verge of tremor. Was it worry that consumed him? He did not like to admit this, but perhaps it was jealousy! If so, why now? When he was away from the city, she could meet whoever she fancied and replace him anytime. How about the special bond! From the other side, distance mellowed sensibilities. Sometimes, he might think there was someone else, but not this feeling of sickness. At this moment, the picture is sharp, well defined. He senses and visualizes her as part of the immediate. Together or apart, both are on this side now—no separation, no blur.

He did not recall feeling that way, when Anna admitted her affair with Spencer. They met at the children's school. Although men often did the morning drop-off, it was usually the women, who were free for afternoon collections. They planned to go away, and Anna would have left me for good. Spencer was bound by theatre schedules and on more than one occasion, I discovered him at home with Anna. They had the perfect alibi. He could say with bland innocence, he just dropped our two, or she would claim, he was fetching his, after she brought them back. While I was traveling, Anna and he had unlimited opportunities and most evenings could count on my absence until seven. The children imposed limits, but there was the au pair to ferry them to a safe distance.

I should have had reason to be jealous of Spencer, yet at no time, were there grounds for suspicion. I did not once see them close and I knew he had Clare. Anna did not tell me they were on the point of splitting. From the way she talked about his brilliance, sensitivity and success as actor, I realized he fascinated her, but after some notable productions, it was reasonable to consider her fan, not lover. It was the children, who upset their plan to go away permanently. He had one not yet at school and they could not agree how to divide the five. They thought of trying to match me with Clare. Then it could have been a straight wife swap, with mutually agreed allocations. When Anna told me about the affair, I did not have feelings of sickness, but there was a shift in time and place. You could say—it was late for jealousy. Spencer and Clare were then separated and he was moving away from London. It seemed out of range.

Those in espionage employ 'drop-offs' and 'pick-ups', as part of their trade. They did not need 'drop-offs', but had their own use for the term 'pick-up'. It was only possible to enter the gates to her building, with her and by car. He did not risk walking through the gates and she strictly warned him, against trying on his own. To visit the flat, they had to meet elsewhere, or arrange for her to collect him. In hotels authorized for foreigners, each corridor was barred by stocky female 'room guards' parading as hotel staff, employed by the secret police. They held the keys for round the clock control of entry, or exit and female visitors were forbidden. Meeting at the reception was dangerous and would be reported. Rendezvous in the streets, called for ingenuity to cope with problems from delay: her waiting in the parked vehicle, or him in the open. After dark, a person sitting in a car was less conspicuous than a foreigner standing on a lit pavement. To limit the risk, he would appear at the agreed time, or within a few minutes margin. Preferred pick-up was a small cul-de-sac, unremarkable and not directly overlooked. It was off Belinskogo ulica, conveniently located for the National and other hotels he used. Typically she would say: 'Make it 6.30 at the usual place'. As alternate, when the first was over used or they might have suspicion, was a location near Kishovskij Sredni pereulok, roughly mid-way between her embassy and his hotel locations, referred to as the 'other place'. When they went to opera, concerts or restaurants, they could meet in the seats, or at the table.

With the limited traffic and central location of her flat, her punctuality was high. The incident when she was forty minutes late because the car would not start, was unique and other times, delay was rare. Not surprisingly, on the day in question, when she had not arrived after meandering in the vicinity for fourteen minutes, he was concerned. Had he made an error? Did she say: 'See you at 6.30 at the usual place?' Or perhaps: 'See you at 7.30?' That must be the reason, he reassured himself walking away down Ogarova ulica, to make a wide detour through nearby streets, for twenty-three minutes in one direction and then back to the meeting point. Another circular walk of seven minutes duration yielded no better result. He felt a pang at the base of his stomach. She expressed anxiety over the secret police, but it was not credible they would take her in. If in the CIA, perhaps! It crossed his mind at the time he met Curtis, but dismissed the thought as not possible—he would have noticed giveaways. The new patterns of the guards at her gate were disturbing, but if angered by her behaviour, the Soviets could not hold her without grounds. As an American citizen, she qualified for protection from the most powerful of the Western embassies. More credible could be an accident. Was she in hospital? He returned to his hotel and in case he made a mistake about the day, asked the operator to call her number, but to no avail. If there was an explanation, he assumed someone would try to reach him. In his despondent state, he was in no mood to sit-out the monotonous delays in the hotel restaurant. He was not hungry, and would have a better chance receiving a call in the room. That evening took him back to the patterns of earlier visits to the city, spending hours alone in a hotel room, waiting for a telephone call that might not come. After spells of reading, dozing-off, getting-in-and-out-of bed, or intermittent bouts of pacing-up-and-down the room, he wrestled through a long night.

Next day, he called the school. She was not available. He spoke instead to a friendly American woman in administration, who reassuringly told him: "I haven't seen her around today. Maybe she'll be in later." Before ringing-off she added: "Come to think of it, I didn't see her yesterday. That's unusual. I guess she's sick. Why don't you call again in a day or so?" When he called her flat, the phone just rang. He tried several times, at spread-out intervals, in case she went out, or in case the operator did not dial the right number. The result was consistent. In the time he knew her, she had no accident when using the car. Her driving was impeccable. Besides, in spite of lacking communications in the city, if injured, or in the worst case killed, it was unthinkable that the authorities, would not advise her embassy. The more he thought about this the more unbelievable it became, but to be sure, he phoned the school a second time. He explained to the woman he spoke to earlier that he was a private acquaintance and as he repetitively called her home, she could not be sick and concerned about an accident, wanted to know if the school would be notified. "Oh my goodness! I am sure nothing like that could have happened. But to be certain, I'll call the department at the embassy. Try me in an hour." He didn't have a chance until lunchtime. Finally, he got hold of her, just before leaving for an afternoon meeting. "There couldn't have been an accident. It couldn't be anything like that," she assured him. "In such a case, the embassy would have been advised long ago. However, I believe I can throw light on the matter. I spoke to another teacher here, who believes she took a short vacation. Why don't you call in a couple of days? I am sure she'll be back by then." It should have been a relief to know there was no accident. It should have put his mind at rest, but it didn't. The 'pit in his stomach' got worse. He was preoccupied by what the secretary at the school had said. Her remark, explained the gnawing in his stomach, which could no longer be ignored. It was not plausible to go on vacation, after fixing an appointment with him. She was not callous and too well coordinated, to do it in error. Desperate for reassurance, he reminded himself—for them it was different. Their life together was under a spell, entwined by recurring coincidences. In the real world however, there is no monopoly of emotions and things can happen fast. At their first meeting at the Metropole, she accepted his invitation for the following day. It was not possible that a woman as attractive did not have a current relationship. Someone else, must have been dropped for him and if once, why not a second time? Now with someone new, she could be overcome, same as when they met. Unexpected factors may have upset equilibrium and the special bond.

He had to keep an afternoon appointment and when back, there was nothing to alleviate his anxieties. They engulfed him, shutting-out everything else. He had only to think of the uncertain future he had to offer her, or how dependent he made her, on his comings and goings. The facts were plain—how could he blame her, if she decided to quit? He had dragged her into an untenable situation and it was logical for anyone in her position, to get out of the trap. The dejection, to which these thoughts brought him, increased the loathing for his room. With nowhere to go, anything seemed better than staying in the hotel. He had to get outside and started walking—aimlessly. It was later that evening, he decided, he would observe her flat.

24

Her apartment was on the fourth floor of a five-story building. It was at the back, with no window facing the street at the front. Outlook from the casement in the main room was into a closed area at the rear, defined by a similar line of terraced houses immediately behind. There was another small opening in the kitchen, little more than a ventilation duct, high in the wall, with no line of sight to the outside and giving no opportunity for looking in. Although view from the main room was mostly enclosed by the structures along the parallel street, on one occasion he noticed a car passing in the distance. The blocks were not the same height. The line of vision over a flat roofed building of only two stories, seemed to intersect a space in another line of houses, where whatever was there, got demolished, or collapsed. The car must have been in a street perpendicular to the one, which ran on the other side of the blocks, facing her window. If he could see a vehicle in that street, it must be possible to see her window, from the pavement at the same location. He resolved to find the precise spot and make observations from there.

To avoid being noticed by the guard at her gate, he planned a detour. He took a taxi to the Puschkin Museum in Volchonka ulica continuing on foot down the same street to Kropotinskaya ploshad. From there, he didn't go up Metrojevskaja ulica, for fear that from this point, he might still be in view, when passing the intersection with her street. Instead, he made a deviation by going along Kropotinskaja ulica and cutting across to Metrojevskaja ulica further down. The resultant direction of his approach confused his precise whereabouts and he was walking for some time, before he could be sure he was in the parallel street at the rear. Looking ahead, he noted another road crossing further down and to the right. Proceeding along this intersection, he could see the empty block wired off with fencing, through which he must have observed the moving car. When correctly positioned, he surveyed possible lines of sight. At first, he was bewildered, having not seen her building from that angle. It was hard to recognize anything in the unfamiliar panorama. He had to work out bearings, by individually identifying each street, the sites and the rows of houses, then trace his way to where he felt her building must be. Eventually, he identified it with reasonable certainty. After examining each window visible in the elevation, he was able not only to identify the casement in the main room, but also the small ventilation outlet of the kitchen.

The flat appeared in darkness. His watch showed twenty minutes after eight. Had she entered with another visitor, it would be too early to switch off the light. He assumed they must still be out. He decided to come back to the same observation point at hourly intervals, so as not to miss the finite time between their return and the putting out the light. The first two hours and many miles of walking, to smother the time proved futile—the window remained darkened. He felt tired and more depressed than before. Now after half past ten, it dawned on him, her likely companion would be someone having a flat of his own, probably a resident diplomat. He realized that to keep watch longer was pointless and went back to the hotel.

Next morning he was distracted by a busy programme, but came back to the hotel at lunchtime. Going to his room, the floor guard told him about a call. "*Telephon, Gospodin. Niet!*" she muttered. He assumed she meant there was a call, but no message left—maybe a business contact. He needed desperately to relieve himself and rushed directly into the bathroom. A moment later, the ringing phone interrupted him. He halted clumsily to reach the phone in haste, before the line was cut. It was her.

"Hi, glad you're back. Tried to reach you this morning, but you were out," she said, as if out of breath.

"What happened? Where have you been?" He asked.

"I've been away. Let's not talk now. I'll tell you when I see you. Can we meet today, when you are through?"

"I have two appointments this afternoon. The second may drag. I can be free by six thirty," he replied.

"Right! To be safe, lets make it seven at the usual place."

"I have to leave tomorrow and I want to see you!" He said before putting the telephone back. Now he knew he would meet her. If the news was unpleasant, they could at least talk. He went back to the bathroom, then down to the restaurant. He ordered lunch with all the courses.

A few minutes before the agreed time, he was at the pick-up. Almost exactly at seven, he saw the car approach from Belinskogo ulica. She turned and parked at the usual spot. Clambering into the passenger seat, he noted she looked tired and seemed anxious. He tried to embrace her, but she pulled away. "Not here," she said: "Someone may be peeping. We'll go to my place." She started the engine and drove along the familiar route. The guard must have checked him through the gate, shortly before a quarter past seven. On seeing him, it crossed his mind that the subtraction might be easier. I could be checked out this same evening after an hour or so, with no need for the tick in the other column.

Once in the flat, she didn't dim the lights, or set-up the gramophone. In front of the bookcase, the carpet was bare. There was no sign of the rug. "I need a drink," she said bringing two glasses and putting them down on the floor. He noticed a couple of books that seemed new—the first a slim volume *House of Incest* by Anais Nin, the second a play by Arthur Miller *The Death of a Salesman*. As he read the titles, he heard her draw a cork. She returned with a bottle and filled the glasses. "New books?" He asked, but she told him, a friend sent them from the States. She sat down in front of the bookcase, leaning back against it. He sat deliberately apart, at right angles to her, supporting himself against the division wall. He could observe her from this position. He braced himself. "I have been away," she started. "I was a guest."

"What do you mean?" He asked. The choice of words was intriguing. His first thought—she was softening discomfort she might feel, by suggesting the initiative had not been hers. She got an invitation. In the infinitesimal delay, before she continued, my imagination generated three scenarios. First, forthright action—she would end it now. Second, playing for time—she would say it was platonic, meant nothing and we should continue undisturbed—that is until later, after indecision could be clarified. Third, the optimistic outcome—it was a failure. Display of images is instantaneous, but the analytic processing needs time. Before he could take first position about a likely winner from the alternatives, the reality of her next words abruptly altered the calculation. "The guys in uniform took me in. They stopped me in the car." That was it! Dumbfounded, he went over to where she sat. He crouched, gently pulling her to him, his hands on her shoulders. He kissed her, his lips flaccid and lightly pressed against hers, without passion—an action of relief. To hell with the police, why were they not my prime suspect from the start? I was ashamed of my reluctance to consider the possibility. It was like a collector after a break-in, finding his favorite work hanging in its rightful place. I had no right for claims on her. After the continuous generosity she demonstrated, how could I have showed so little confidence—assume she would, on whim, exchange me for another? He moved to sit alongside, easing her towards him, to feel her directly against his hip and along his thigh. "The militiamen forced me to stop, saying my lights were up. 'So what!' I told them. Then they read the riot act. According to regulations, it's illegal to drive in the city, with the lights full. They got into the car and sat for hours, talking on their intercom. Finally, about two in the morning, they made me leave it and drove me away in one of their closed vans. It had heavy mesh between two guys, who sat up-front, and me with another two in the back, I suppose to guard me, in case I became fresh. It was no match—they were armed and sat real tight, pressing me between them. I thought they were going to force me on the floor, but the vehicle stopped and I was unloaded at one of the local stations. My God! What a place!"

He questioned her amazed: "Why did this happen? What is this about?"

"For sure, it can't be the lights. After so much time and questioning, I don't know," she replied. She sat for a moment expressionless, then looking at her glass, continued: "Tell you what, I don't know now—I cannot figure it out. Actually, I got a shock when they let me go home. It was a sudden switch in strategy. They made it clear they are going to charge me for drunken driving. It could be scare-tactics, to pressure me. Hard to say." He kept his arm around her while she finished the drink, holding her close as they leaned against the bookcase. Rigid spines of books jabbed into their backs and the carpeted floor seemed hard, ungiving. Could it be real, this recovery of closeness, which a few hours earlier seemed to have drifted out of reach? They were on the inside now. "You know the procedures here, the interminable waiting, the piles of dossiers, the endless questioning, the forms and filling-up of forms. This time, there was absence of any foreseeable limit. At one point I attempted to kid myself, I was auditioning for a play, or practicing a game. I had to face a stream of people coming and going in every possible costume: the long greatcoats, the grey, then khaki uniform, the heavy leather coats, the black leather motor-cyclist suits, not to mention the array of different badges, stripes and emblems of rank. As it went on, I tried to figure out what my role could be. Then, the questioning would start from the beginning with another set of forms. I had to complete many and sign them. The first time, I objected because I didn't understand. I told them brazenly I must show it to my embassy. It was only a matter of time however—time for the exhaustion to set-in. After a while, it didn't seem to matter, I would sign anything, just to get out.

"The second day was real strange. At sometime they transferred me by car to another place not far from the first. After more waiting and form filling, they took me to a building that was presumably a centre for interrogation. A more senior guy sat behind a desk with masses of their buff coloured files. They made me sit at another table and there was a continuous succession of stagehands, who came and left at various times. Here, the questioning became more direct, concerning particular suspects on their files. They showed me photographs of about twenty, mostly male and all but two, African. At one point, they tried to force me to admit a relationship with a guy, who seems head of an underground movement for students from developing countries. They showed me pictures of him in bed with a woman, who they claimed was me. It was surreal! In both pictures, the man's head and shoulders concealed the woman's face, but I could tell from the visible parts of the body—there was no likeness. I have the greatest sympathy for the students and their lot, but have no connection. They put me in this situation, from the way I look. They went backwards and forwards, questioning me on precise details, of buildings and addresses I don't know, and dates when I was supposed to have been at the places. Regardless of their source, it's a frame-up, or else gross misidentification and once they get a fixation they are hard to budge. They know, if they ask the same question enough times and hold a person long enough, most will admit, or confess to whatever it is, they seek." He was perturbed when she added abruptly: "Let me tell you the games we played, are far from the real thing!"

"We were dumb!" He said, then stayed silent, as she continued: "You could not imagine, what it means for a woman, to contend with the banter of the militia. They may not realize that I understood their insinuations, which would be the more offensive, if intended for my ears. I didn't elaborate on what happened in the van. The prospect of a prison term is a nightmare. From the time they stopped me in the car, until the time they let me go this morning, it was more than fifty-nine hours. I couldn't wash, or go to bed for three days. Last night, they allowed me to lie down in a cell, with just a padded bench and a slop bucket. I heard the key turn in the lock and thought I'd not get out. I was dead tired and almost asleep on my feet, but there was this light, shining on me from above the door." He realized the aspirations of finding a more tolerant society, under another political system, hoping that life under socialism would be humane and less discriminatory must be fading. The harassment and racial innuendos by the police were a sobering sequel to her expectations. He understood how disillusioned she must feel. He was quick to assume recovery of his favorite work hanging in its rightful place, but did not notice the crack. He could not deny her right to leave, but he was angry. In a matter of weeks, she could be transferring out and he would be on his own again, to face the emptiness of the earlier times. It seemed certain and her words confirmed it: "I could not survive such madness. I have to get out. The whole system disillusions me. The people are as reckless as everywhere else." He remembered how she quoted Shostakovich: 'It's the vileness of the world that ruins love'. This time, ideals were ruined, but he couldn't argue. Instead of: 'I told you so!' He merely said: "Thank God, they let you out when they did!"

After a pause during which no one spoke, he asked where they kept her. Initially the places were downtown, but the last day, they took her to see someone in the periphery. The office was in a building with fields around. It took hours to get there and then the man was away. Asked if she saw him in the end, she responded: "He showed up, sometime yesterday afternoon—seemingly a Colonel, intelligent and a touch classier than the others. They left me alone with him. At first, he showed respect, but you know how he addressed me? *"Krassavitsa"*. It means 'beautiful' then rambling somewhat, I'm sure I made out the words, 'I can keep you out of the cold'. It sounded as if he was propositioning me, but I couldn't be certain I understood his Russian correctly and acted dumb."

"To hell with him! They can't treat you that way."

"There was no witness and you can guess how much weight my words would have against his. If I crossed him, it would be open confrontation."

"Did he threaten you, when you ignored his remarks?"

"He continued matter-of-fact. But I could make-out enough, to know as a minimum, they will charge me for drunken driving. It's absurd, as I had only one drink. They did not make a breath test and they didn't take a urine sample either. He said too much time elapsed and tests were unnecessary—there were enough witnesses to testify, my driving with full lights showed I was drunk."

"And what was his role in this pantomime?"

"Of the people I met, he seemed the most senior. Maybe he wasn't internal security, but from the KGB. My being a foreigner may involve them. It was weird he should be located in a building so far from everywhere else. I can't speculate, but he told me, a charge will be prepared and the case come-up in three to four months. If the court finds me guilty, there will be a prison term. When I asked if I could pay a fine instead, he mentioned an astronomical figure in dollars."

"But why would the Russians stop you for a minor traffic violation that normally warrants a warning? The story about the lights can only be a ruse and stopping you, must have been planned. It cannot be connected to the incident at the opera—it's too long ago. Maybe there is a link to reports from the gate guards, or perhaps the people in your embassy?"

"It could be anything. But as regards my people, there is something disturbing. This special guy told me, a 'countryman of mine' to use his words, was among the passers-by, who recognized me and certified my identification. His evidence included the statement: 'He was shocked to see my condition.' It was no one from the embassy—a businessman with sound connections, someone they could rely on. He wouldn't name the person, but it could only be Curtis."

"I knew he couldn't be trusted. What was he doing there?"

"I know you dislike him, but don't forget the time he helped you. I can't understand his involvement. It is a real surprise to learn he would discredit me."

"How closely do you know him?"

"Oh for Heavens sake! I imagine what you're thinking. I bumped into him at parties, or embassy functions. There was nothing between us, he was a friend, or at least I thought he was. He asked me out to dinner and took me to the opera twice. I was at his flat, but for parties."

"Was he at yours?"

"Once at a small celebration. He brought a girl friend, a Lithuanian, who lived a long time in America. They came and left together."

"After the evening you introduced him to me, I was convinced he must be CIA. It sounds crazy, but maybe he works for the other side, or works for both. It's unlikely he was informant—there must be thousands in the no-man's land between the two sides."

"If he saw me the other night, why didn't he show himself? Why didn't he help me with the police? If he testified for them against me, he's a snake!"

"If involved for them, they would keep his name out. Maybe it's invention. He probably wasn't there—it would be too much of a coincidence. He must be on their list. How often did you see him since the time at the restaurant?"

"I only remember a single occasion, at one of the regular embassy events. There were many people and when I saw him, he was busy and we just waved at each other. I was surprised to hear he was still around. Certainly, he is no longer resident. You remember when we dropped him that evening, he was staying in a hotel."

"At the Metropole, I remember. Look, however insidious, he couldn't have manipulated the incident, his function can only be a minor role for one side or the other. Did this Colonel volunteer additional information?"

"He gave no leads. I arranged a meeting with the embassy this morning. I will see a more senior man in security next week. I don't plan to mention your name—it could cause trouble. They are sure to meddle and ask questions. I'll have to tell you next time. Do you know when it will be?"

"I have grounds to request a follow-on visit immediately and will push for six weeks. I cannot rely on getting the visa in less than four weeks, and need a week on either side," he said, thinking, it could be my last opportunity to see her before she leaves.

"Try to keep to it."

"Look, you must eat something. Let me take you out."

"If you don't mind, I would prefer to remain here, but you must be starving!"

"I'm OK. I took the hotel lunch after you called."

"Ever since they stopped me I couldn't reach you. Had they allowed me to use a phone, I could not call you, it would have been insane. I was convinced you would be gone by the time I was released. Now, I just want to be alongside and stay close. If you're leaving tomorrow, it's the last chance."

"This turn of events appals me, I should have taken your place." Later she brought the rug and put out the light. They lay in each other's arms, until she fell asleep. He was awake most of the night. As she lay alongside, he listened to her breathing, conscious of her closeness. He was aware—their time together could be limited.

He was uneasy about leaving her in such circumstances, but there was no recourse open. He had to travel next day—his visa was non-extendible. Until her case was settled, she could not leave the country. Only solace was his promise to return in six weeks. Some rudimentary coded expressions were worked-out, for exchange of basic information from an unidentifiable callbox, over bugged telephone lines.

25

We had dinner with the Lowthers. There were two couples that we met before. It was an amusing evening and though bawdy at times, the conversation was animated. We stayed until after midnight. When we got back to the house, Anna walked down the hall towards the stairs. I reached forward and held her arm to stop her, suggesting we sit awhile before going upstairs. I offered to get a drink, so we could relax. "Oh come-on! It's after one and we've been drinking the whole evening. Don't you think it's time we went to bed?" She protested. Going to the sofa and drawing her next to me, I put my arm around her shoulders and kissed her: "I'd like to stay here a moment and unwind." I felt compelled to make love to her, stretched-out on the carpet in front of the fireplace, in view of the bookcase and directly under the gaze of the 'spectator with cigar', who sat fully clothed in a wing chair, while a naked couple embraced in the background. It was a large drawing, bought from a young American painter, living in London. It hung diagonally across from the fireplace and at right angles to the door. The man's expressionless stare would focus on the spot, where I would like us to be lying. "It was a pleasant evening and it can be a special night. I want to make love to you down here," I implored. "Look, we can remove our clothes, stretch out on the carpet and expose ourselves to his view. With the undrawn curtains, we can imagine ourselves watched through the rear window, from the roofs behind."

"They would need a telescope. How much did you drink tonight and what other kinky ideas are you going to suggest?"

"I drank the same as the others. Everyone is in bed at the top of the house. No-one will hear, or disturb us," I tried to reassure her.

"Why must we behave like juveniles, it's not comfortable on the floor. It's unhealthy to want to be observed, you were not an exhibitionist before. This is not the Soviet Union, nor my kind of excitement!" She rose from the sofa and stood a moment, before walking through the doorway and continuing up the stairs. I heard the bedroom door close and her footsteps through the ceiling, as she walked around. Disappointed, I stayed sitting where I was. Was it a betrayal to suggest that? I should not be thinking of 'her', but I couldn't resist glancing out of the window to see if the roofs behind were visible against the night sky. Most people would describe our love life as good. We'd been married ten years and when I was not travelling, we made love with what seemed a normal frequency. We didn't flirt openly with others. Even during Anna's affair with Spencer, she behaved discreetly. We appeared to satisfy each other in our lovemaking. I could not describe her, an unwilling partner and could not say she unreasonably turned me down, under the right conditions. I mean: when together in bed, particularly before going to sleep, or in the morning before we got up. Unusual surroundings deterred her. It would be unthinkable to make love on the kitchen sink, or in the bath, and although making love in the back seat, or even cramped in the front, seems accepted use of a car—it could not occur. It's not that she might not like it—she would not agree. She would remind me, we didn't need it. Unconventional items were left blank on our menu.

Anna's father went missing during the war and when I first met her, she rarely talked of her stepfather. He was French and I knew that at one time, he became rich and lived in a chateau near Montpelier. With three children from an earlier marriage, he seemed a colourful personality, popular with women and prone to liaisons on the side. As only child, she had a close relationship with the mother, and her sudden death when Anna was eleven, proved traumatic. I sensed an antipathy to the stepfather, but did not know the cause. She mentioned it to me unexpectedly, when discussing his financial woes and problems with a third wife. It happened at the chateau. She opened a door to one of many reception rooms of the vast house, in the middle of the afternoon and there it was, in front of her. The stepfather, rear to the door, trousers around his ankles, was making love to her mother's closest friend, who lay back on a sofa, dress partly removed and legs spread at either side of him. What made the spectacle particularly shocking to the child was that she had come to stay for the funeral. It was barely two weeks since the mother was buried in the local churchyard. What she witnessed could possibly account for the apparently restrained attitude, later adopted to sex. It might have been the source of differentiation, between what could be considered proper, or unacceptable. A hint of something unconventional was likely associated with this embedded memory. I realized it would be difficult to alter.

I went up and found she was still awake. I undressed in the dark and got into bed from my accustomed side. I moved across and took her into my arms. She was warm and receptive. I turned my body, so I was on top. It was normally that way for us.

26

As winter approached the greyness and melancholy of the city intensified. Roads would soon be interspersed with dirty mounds of frozen snow, lining the tarmac and piled around. Gorky Street will once more be a sea of fur-hat muffled heads, bobbing up and down above wrapped figures, on their way outwards and inwards hunched against the biting wind, struggling along pavements blanketed with snow, some icy or ragged as arctic seas. One among them would be different, bare head exposed unprotected, hair blown in the frosty air, where temperatures can drop to thirty below during the bitter months—a visitor from abroad. At vestibules of buildings, matronly women staffing coat check-ins might gesticulate with disapproval, at defiance of their harsh Russian climate. Better keep chill times short and walk a little faster.

The coded telephone messages were scant help. He did reach her on three occasions, but the lines were worse than expected. Apart from faintness and distortion, there was a disquieting echo, probably caused by the bugging. An oscillating volume of competing background crackle, periodically drowned out speech. Her voice was unrecognizable. First call was cut in mid sentence and reconnection was not possible. The operator announced—delay would be indefinite. Subsequent attempts, merely gave confirmation, using the coded phrases 'no news' or 'case still pending'. Almost keeping his promise, he got back in less than two months, clocked-in by the guard at 7.32 p.m. and impatient to learn what took place over the weeks of separation. Nothing was finalized. She held meetings with the new security man, an older person with wider experience than the first. "He avoided the brash talk of the Southerner." But she was upset they forced her to go through the clearance procedure again and there were now two of them with access to her personal material. He was concerned when it was one, but not wanting to dishearten her, said nothing. Behind the scenes discussions confirmed that the charge about the lights had been a ruse, used by the police to demonstrate she was drunk. Because there was no witness to corroborate her story, the Russians proposed, she plead guilty without contesting the charge. Daunted by her earlier experience, indeterminate sentence, risk of abuse, she refused. She insisted that the embassy have the case rescinded.

When she left him to go to the bathroom, he thought over her position: I did not understand why the embassy was not more forceful. They brought her to Moscow and were responsible to fend for her. They knew the case was trumped-up and that she had no record of drinking, let alone drunken driving and as last resort should transfer her out of the country. When she got back, she gave him the disturbing news that the Russians rejected diplomatic immunity, as the school did not qualify. She slipped between regulations and seemed to have no more protection than he. The embassy was ready to ship her out before the trial, but without immunity, she needed an exit visa, which was blocked by the charge. Strictly, she could be held in the country, until the case was heard and sentence served. Penalties for most offences were defined in Russia, but 'driving under the influence' depended on concentration in the blood. She had one glass of wine that day and it seemed the police deliberately omitted samples, to leave blood count open for the court. Her security man warned, the judge could pick a presumed level to match the witnesses, who would repeat what the police tell them. Although sentence appears to be between three months and a year, no one in the embassy could say for sure. The embassy could insist on regular visits, but she would be in confinement with no possibility for him to see her during the term. This situation was inexplicable and he asked why her embassy could not buy an exit-visa, as with the Canadian journalist. The new man was working on this and she confirmed that he had informal talks with the Colonel, mentioned earlier. She explained there was a special 'abrogation' provision for prosperous countries, allowing them to have a charge annulled before it goes to court and receive an exit visa, against payment of a penalty. The sum was significant, paid in hard currency to a nominated bank account, in her case the 'Staff and Social Fund' of one of the local police divisions. The parties agreed to use the procedure, but implementation was delayed by the penalty amount, which has to be proportional to the sentence. The two sides had to agree what this would have been, if the case were not rescinded.

There were a couple of factors, working in her favour, she told me. First, it was necessary to pay the penalty in full, seven days before the date the court sits and this deadline avoided procrastination. Second, absence of alternative, compelled the Russians to be realistic about terms and agree in time, to avoid loss of foreign currency. This could be crucial as reserves were critically low. Meantime, the Russians wanted more, while the Americans stood firm for prestige. Because of the magnitude of the penalty, her government might insist on a contribution, but payment could be spread over 10 years.

She explained that in the worst-case, if her people missed the deadline, the abrogation would lapse and could not be used again for her case. Then, she would be back in the original situation—court appearance on a set date, threat of imprisonment, unpredictable sentencing. But as the embassy had given her an undertaking that the application would be followed to successful conclusion, this doomsday scenario could not take place.

"That is good news! Such an assurance from your government must be definitive," he interrupted—relieved that finally her people seemed to treat the matter seriously. She told him how her security man joked: not wishing to chasten her, the dollars meant more to the Russians, than having her pretty face around in jail for a few months. It was shameful to leave her in suspense, through the bargaining, but he realized that the deadline eliminated risk of something going wrong at the last moment and said: "It is a relief that settlement takes place a week before start of the trial."

"Absolutely! At the worst, I have to accept early termination of my contract and reimburse my government with part of the cost. But my security guy has set stringent conditions. I am not allowed to talk with anyone about moving, until the deal is settled, even those in personnel. Although security is part of the embassy, it's an independent organisation with their own rules. No one at the school has the faintest suspicion that I might be leaving. Some may have heard that I was in trouble with the police, but assume the case was dropped. I haven't yet told those at home that I might be reappearing in the States."

"You mean that when the deal is settled, they will be surprised to hear you are returning?"

"That's the way it is, and you should acknowledge, how privileged you are. You have exclusive advance information."

"I am honoured," He smiled.

"But you have to understand, it is vital not to disclose a word. They made me sign a confidentiality agreement that forbids my talking with anyone inside the embassy or outside until the contract with the other side is signed. The reason is that another deal was upset through an information leak. Because only they can help me out of this mess, I must do as they say. The agreement was five typed pages. I am not only restricted before the deal, but afterwards. All I am permitted to say to others is that the Russians did not charge me. The good news is—the current guy has hinted that if I follow their instructions, I might be able to stay on."

"I thought it was not possible. Great!"

"Officially, it is so. This is something he hinted, but cannot guarantee now. Once the exit visa is issued, there might be a way to modify its date, so I can remain to complete my contract. But after what I have been through, I am not sure, I would want to."

"Otherwise, when would you expect to leave?"

"The exit visa has a thirty day validity, which they argue is sufficient to make arrangements for job transfer, travel and shipment of gear. I wouldn't want to risk less than 10 days margin inside the limit, so I would plan to get clear around two weeks from the issue date. I have no idea what I will do at home, except take vacation. The only job I could qualify for, is a posting with our sister school in Athens. I sent my documents to get on their list, but cannot formally apply, until the case is concluded. The job would suit me and is an option."

He asked what she heard from the new man about Curtis and she told him, he wanted the complete story, grilling her on how they met, how often she saw him, every detail. Checking their records, he told her that Curtis had already left and was back in the States. After sending someone to question him there, she learned he tried to reach her, but was prevented by the police, who insisted he give a statement. When informed that she behaved in a drunken manner, he expressed dismay. He assured them she was not a drinker and as a one-off occasion, should be excused. Being late, he could not stay and was certain the police would let her go. Apparently, the authorities gave Curtis a mild dressing-down, telling him he should not have signed anything that incriminates another American citizen. They said he was lax and should have talked directly with her, to make his own judgment about the statement. Curtis argued it was not possible, as they would not give him access. The character reference was an attempt to help, but he could not be sure what the police wrote, and they must have misled him. He is ready to sign a qualifying statement prepared by his local police, but it had no validity in a Moscow court, the Russians would maintain, it was signed under duress in a capitalist country. In theory, Curtis could be induced to sign something in Moscow, but he had no plan to visit, and would not return before the case comes up. The initial interest in Curtis suggested they had him under suspicion and their uncommitted follow-up was disappointing.

It was worrying that her security man seemed to have no lead, on why the police stopped her in the first place. He admitted there must be a reason and suggested 'mistaken identity' from anonymous reports, sent to the secret police by countless do-gooders. To pick her up for drunken driving, at a time when she hadn't been drinking however, suggested something more fundamental, yet he was unable to identify a motive. She was as uninformed as before. The security man questioned her at length, on anything she did that could have attracted their attention. At that point, she felt obliged to mention the meetings with the previous security man, but he would not discuss this, claiming: it had no relevance to the present case and was unimportant. This surprised her—the other man must work in the same department. Fortunately, the guards had in the meantime left her alone and no one had dragged her from a hotel lobby. "I'm keeping my fingers crossed and hoping the best terms can be worked out within 6 or 7 weeks," she said. After a moment's reflection, she smiled: "It's enough! I know it's serious, but we cannot allow 'what's coming' to compromise 'what is now'. Let's forget it for a while."

The following morning the guard made a notation that he left the building at 7.56 a.m. They had arranged the pick-up for that evening at 6.30 p.m. at the 'usual place'. They agreed on a restaurant and she booked it in his presence.

He went to the pick-up and only when he saw no sign of her, did he remember that they were to meet at the table. The restaurant was in Kalinina prospekt on the west side of the city, just inside the second ring boulevard. He got hold of a taxi and was soon on his way. Realising she would already be at the table, he pushed past the people waiting at the doorway, telling the doorman he was joining someone inside. She was not there and their name was not on the list, but they were full and the man, who handled the booking, was off-duty. After the usual drama with dollars, he got a small table, at the back. By then, it was ten to eight and she was not there. He remembered her mentioning, she might have to go outside the city during the day. Perhaps she was stuck in a traffic jam. At half past eight the waiter came to tell him, he must order or give up the table. He offered more dollars to use the telephone, but it was occupied. While eating the first course alone, he was beckoned to the phone. When there was no answer from her number, he asked the waiter to take the plates away, fetch the bill and call a taxi. As he got to the hotel, he noted it was just before ten and there was still no reply from her number. The new absence was unaccountable, but he was sure there would be an explanation. Though tired, he decided to wait for her call, certain she would phone when she got home. He prepared for the next morning's discussions, but didn't get far. Concern and frustrations of the evening had worn him out. He fell asleep and had a singularly vivid dream: It was summer and I was visiting an uncle, who lived in a mansion, perched on a steep hill overlooking the sea. Below, was a town stretching along a shoreline that faded, away to the west. As we sat inside the house, I noticed the darkening sky was tinged with a glow, which wasn't the setting sun. Leaning out of a window, I saw a plume of billowing smoke, coming from a building on the seafront that seemed to be on fire. When I drew this to the attention of my uncle, he said it was a street with interesting old buildings and speculated about which was burning. Next, we were driving down to check first-hand. We parked elsewhere, because like after a match, the streets around were milling with spectators. Going on foot, we reached a small terrace that included the protected houses. It was directly opposite the sea, projecting into the promenade. As we stood on the pavement in front of the burning house, my uncle told me it was a risky place to live in. "The danger is not from fire, but from water!" He added. "During storms, waves break against the parapet wall, swamping the road and sending torrents of spray over the buildings, sometimes flooding the basements." The fire was not in one of the older houses, it was next door in a corner building—a large and relatively new block of flats, which my uncle, who was an architect, described as '. . . this cheap monstrosity put-up twenty or thirty years earlier.' He seemed pleased, it was burning, gleefully rubbing his hands together, as flames lapped the window frames and started to break through the roof. Fire engines were parked in the small streets in front and at the side, with ladders propped against the walls. As I watched, my vision zoomed-in and the firemen appeared unrealistically large. I could see them, arms wide, lifting enormous sections of masonry and passing them to outstretched hands of others, perched on rungs below. My uncle gazed unperturbed, as if knowing that all was as it should be. Above the burble of unintelligible voices from people in the crowd, a large heavy-set man was shouting with his hands cupped around his mouth: "Look, they are trying to take the building down, before it is destroyed by the flames." My uncle seemed angered by the man and leaning towards me, muttered in my ear that he was not right—they were trying to control it, to prevent it from spreading to the sound ones alongside. Nothing seemed illogical about the enormous sections of brickwork, fifteen to twenty feet across, and weighing several tons, that the firemen were lifting, as if sheaves of wheat at a harvesting. The front facade and the side, visible from where I stood, were both being taken-apart in the same way. I stayed where I was, anxious to know how much of the building they could dismantle, before the inferno took control. I remember noticing they had removed at least half of the six or seven stories, and that sections stacked on the ground, reached an equivalent height. I turned around to look for my uncle, but he must have wandered-off and disappeared. I began to worry, how I would get back to the house.

He woke-up. It was not the inconsistency of the subject, which disquieted him. Many dreams are unsettling, but the intensity was unique. The precision severed boundaries between fantasy and reality. Absurd images of giant helmet-clad firemen, balancing at the end of flimsy ladders, remained in his thoughts. The picture of enormous gloved hands, gripping whole sections of brickwork, complete with windows and frames, seemed indelible. For a while he lay with eyes closed, convinced he was elsewhere. He wanted to get up and look out of the window, to see if the fire was still burning. When opening his eyes and seeing the hotel room, it was a few minutes, before he recognized he was in Moscow. He must have fallen asleep, sprawled fully clothed on the bed, and when he looked at his watch, it was ten minutes before midnight. He staggered to his feet, fumbling out of his clothes and in between the covers, without fully waking. After switching the light off, he re-enacted what happened in the dream, curious at how it might have ended, had he not awoken. He lay still in the dark, hoping for the images to continue in chapters through the night, but it was not the case, and when he slept, it was dreamless.

He came to with a start. It was already morning and as he answered the telephone, he could see daylight penetrating around the heavy curtains. "Whatever happened to you?" A voice demanded.

Confused and trying to get his bearings, he asked: "What happened to the fire, did they put it out?"

"Are you alright—is something the matter?" Now he recognized her. She was on the phone.

"I'm sorry! I was dreaming about a fire and didn't know where I was. What time is it?"

"A few minutes before seven."

"I'm OK now. Did anything happen to you last night?"

"There must have been a mix-up, but I remembered you said, you planned to go north this morning. Why don't we meet and I can drive you there. It's a chance to talk."

"For heavens sake, you are right! I have a meeting at nine, by the trade fair grounds."

"I can collect you at eight, the usual place."

"Great! I'll see you there."

"Last night was a double disappointment. I wanted to ask you something, but let's talk later. See you shortly," she added before ringing-off.

He got up immediately, but felt uncomfortable. It was the first time he could remember the fusion between dream and reality, lingering as long. The visit to his uncle and the fire seemed real and he could visualize firemen lifting the large sections of brickwork. Walking towards the pick-up, he wondered what it was she wanted to ask. It must be something recent. Perhaps the embassy had agreed the amount to be paid. She hinted it was an astronomic sum in dollars. Although she suggested her contribution could be by instalments over ten years, maybe the first was too much and she needs help. She arrived on time, he heard a clock start its chime, as the car appeared around the corner. While she drove north, they talked about the evening before and their irritation that one of the few evenings together was lost. "You were with me when I made the booking," she said. "We agreed to meet at the table and I was there. I thought your business must have gone on late. I called your hotel a couple of times from the restaurant, but there was no reply from the room."

"I'm sorry! Mistakenly I went to the pick-up and when I reached the restaurant, almost an hour late, you had left. There was a blunder on the reservation and I had to fight to get a table. I sat alone for more than an hour. It was just ten, when I got back to my room," he explained.

"But where did you go?" She asked amazed.

"To where you booked—the Arbat."

"That's strange! You were with me when I called. It was the Ararat."

"Where is that? I haven't heard of it."

"On Neglinnaya ulica, just north of the Metropole. You could have walked from your hotel. It's famous for Armenian cuisine. I can't believe you don't know it."

"Maybe I heard the name, but I was not there. I was sure, you said Arbat. It seemed logical. We were there together—at least three times."

"It's crazy! How could it happen?"

"I called you from the hotel at ten and you weren't home."

"I waited till the last minute. I ordered for you and was sure you would show. There was nothing to do, but sit tight and hope that you would arrive. I didn't get home until just before midnight. Then I phoned, but you weren't in the room."

"I was there at the time."

"The operator said there was no reply. She seemed to take delight in saying it. Maybe she didn't connect."

"But wait! This dream was interrupted, ten minutes before midnight. I did not hear the phone, but maybe your call woke me."

"Could be!"

"What a waste! But I must tell you about the dream. I was in this strange mansion, on a hill overlooking the sea . . ." He recounted to her the whole sequence, up to the point he woke-up. "Why this one?" She wondered, he couldn't respond, they had arrived. She didn't go to Akademika ulica, but stopped by the park containing the trade fair buildings. "Let's take a stroll through the gardens," she suggested. There was no snow on the ground, but it was a crisp morning and as they walked, mist from their breath hung in the cold air. There were few people and nobody within earshot. "I have been teasing myself what it is you wanted to ask," he said to give her an opening.

"Oh! Something nice! It's something exciting!"

"I cannot wait!" "A friend has offered me a dacha. It's outside Moscow. You remember the time we were discussing 'The Magic Mountain' and you compared it to our life here? You talked about Settembrini and the vast space around us that we see on maps, but cannot visit. This isn't that remote, but it gives a glimpse, of what is outside the city—an unspoiled spot surrounded by woods, one-minute speck on the map in the vast landscape. I wanted to take you there before, but it was not free at the times you were here. Can you get away?"

"It's tempting, it really is! But this is one of my short visits. I am supposed to travel back on Sunday, and for Saturday I set a couple of meetings."

"That's a pity! Is there no way to postpone?"

"I don't know. I'd have to make phone calls. I won't be able to try before this afternoon. Can you give me till then to check?"

"Sure! I will be home by six. But if you postpone, try to move the Saturday meetings. It would be better to start before Midday. If we leave in the afternoon, much of the way will be in the dark."

"What about a permit? It must be off-limits for me."

"It's borderline—outside the city, but within the administration district. The last part is on country roads and there are no checkpoints. It's worth the risk, we will be somewhere new." They walked between brittle winter flowerbeds, to where she parked. He watched the car, as she drove around the corner out of sight, mindful of the difference since the first time. Then, he was the one inviting, now the invitation was from her.

27

A weekend in the country with her would be enticing, could fill voids from life in the city. In spite of days and nights spent in her flat, not once had they stayed away together in a different environment. It is hard for a relationship to flourish from the familiar. Could he deny her a single weekend away? To make it possible, he must delay his return. Schedules of visits were determined independently, through plans established beyond his control. He will have to interfere in allocations of time between the two worlds, quit his passive role as emissary and throw the dice himself.

If playing the omnipotent and interfering in something as rudimentary, as distribution of time to match 'a weekend in the country', resistance can be expected. I knew about games nature plays against change restoring conditions of before. Whether by natural laws, or fate, scope to re-establish status quo is broad. I need not look far, to see the possibilities. If result were refusal of the next visa, benefit would be null. For the splitting, consequences could be critical. Its success was crucial for continuity and did not depend on me alone—a single report from the authorities could expose my precarious position. On earlier visits, the patterns of the city displayed immutability, yet they could revert at any moment. The relationship was an object of chance and if the run of luck were disturbed, the shift in balance could be irreversible. To accept her invitation for the weekend, I would have to claim that unforeseen commitments forced me to extend my stay. Whether through improper information, or by misrepresentation of the facts, intent would be to mislead. For the first time, I will have to lie.

If anyone were to ask her guards, they might question, how a single lie could be of weight against prolonged and blatant infidelity. From their vantage point at the gate, it would seem protracted. Patterns mutated, but the relationship had continued over months, interrupted only by the gaps between the visits. For them and those with access to the dossiers, the brazen behaviour was beyond dispute, yet judgments can be the inverse. In one respect, splitting was deliberate suppression of facts and information. Viewed another way, it was protection of 'others' from issues that could harm. The dilemma was impossible to resolve. Like an impeachment, verdict had to be 'according to circumstances'. It depended on deposition of facts and judges might be from either side.

Significance of his actions derived from effects. Acceptance of her invitation and delayed return would mean 'others' must unwittingly, alter plans. Refusal would mean disappointing her and denial of an opportunity together, supposedly unrepeatable. When he thought of two uninterrupted days of tempestuous lovemaking in a setting that was entirely unfamiliar, he felt aroused. But though excited by the prospect, it meant breaking a precept, regarded sacrosanct. An earlier precedent when I almost challenged the 'rules of time' evoked a *déjà vu*, an affair that started when I was on the ship and the girl in question was just deserted by her partner. In summer, we made trips to a secluded, protected beach. We went in the evenings and when late could swim naked in the dark water. We did not think about time, it seemed in abundance. When she drove me back, we sat in her car kissing and petting. I longed to make love to her, but there were limits. "I don't want to now—maybe tomorrow." On the night of embarkation, she stopped near the dock to spend remaining moments together. I realized something was different, when she allowed me to remove her underpants. It seemed foolish to meddle when time was restricted but after weeks of longing, my ardour was unstoppable. Near the climax, my eyes noticed a clock-face through the rear window. It was an hour later than I thought—departure was in ten minutes. Pre-coital urge, replaced by post-climactic realism jolted me to an obedient servant of time. "It's leaving!" I cried, hastily withdrawing, tugging at my trousers and smoothing down her skirt. I said goodbye and ran. As I sprinted down the jetty, the guard phoned. The ship had sailed, but after the call, a boat crew took me to board mid-channel. I got the ship but lost the girl, who did not forgive. After countless opportunities without deadline, I was puzzled why, aware of the restraint—she chose that evening to make love. Was she re-enacting a pattern of desertion? It was a match with time, a warning in whatever guise.

Was there a choice? The present was more demanding than the future. Intimacy had become a necessity, whose 'contradiction was inconceivable'. How could he refuse, when their future together, seemed limited and under threat? He called the airline to rebook his reservation and phoned her a little after six. "I postponed the flight for Tuesday. We can go."

"Great!" she said. "What about the Saturday appointments?"

"I altered the later one for Monday. Unsuccessful with the other, I made it earlier. I can be back by 9.15. Is that OK?"

"I am thrilled." she replied. "And what do you plan tonight?"

"I am through for the day. Let me take you to a restaurant—this time, together!"

"It's a nice idea, but I must prepare for the trip. Why don't you grab something at the hotel and get an early night. It will help you survive the journey in the cramped seats." After a pause she added: "A warning! Whatever happens, don't check out of the hotel. Bring only enough clothes to keep warm. Leave everything else in the room!"

"OK, 10.00 a.m. at the usual place."

"For safety, let's make it 10.30 at the other place. It's early enough and you'll have more leeway."

"10.30 at the other place."

It was a long journey. To head out, she drove diagonally across the familiar part of the city, over the river and down Volgogradskij prospekt. As they passed the outer ring road he was in new territory, transferring to what for him was 'outer space'. As they went further from the centre, the smaller roads twisted and surfaces deteriorated. After a while, he lost orientation and became oblivious of his whereabouts. The last stretch was on unmade roads and it started snowing before they reached the woods. She turned into a lane that ran directly between trees and continued deep into a forest before unexpectedly, leading to a clearing where she stopped the car. The snow was already settling. "Isn't she a beauty?" she said, pointing to a small wooden house, resting on low pillars that raised the whole construction half a meter above the ground. Open tread steps led to a covered veranda stretching along the front, incorporating doorway and porch. Under a steep sloping roof, the dacha was entirely of timber except for a bulging stone structure, surmounted by a small rusted chimney at the rear. Old closed shutters concealed the windows. On the opposite side of the glade, about fifty yards away, were two other small houses, the larger, partly of stone, had smoke surging from its chimney. Otherwise, there was no sign of life. The lane they arrived along, appeared to continue into the forest, but got narrower on the far side.

Inside, the dacha consisted of a single room, with a large stone fireplace at the end. There was a kind of alcove for cooking and washing, various storerooms and a bulky wooden staircase leading to an attic store. Filled with character, the house was quaint, but as if unused and unheated for several weeks, pervaded throughout by the biting chill of damp. There was an old Samovar on the table and he asked if it worked. "Sure! It'll take time though. I'll get it going, when the fire is burning." She looked through the various stores and found some dry logs, but not enough for their stay. He put several in the fireplace using the tinder and matches she brought, to get it started. She lit the oil lamp and set-up the Samovar to boil. Sensing his concern about the cold, she reassured him: "In an hour or so, it'll be another place. We'll be able to take-off our coats and be comfortable." She suggested he bring more wood, before it got dark and he went outside to inspect the pile, already partially covered by snow and wet. He dragged out some logs, carrying them into the house, stacking them near the fireplace to dry.

She went to check about buying local dishes from a neighbour, who lived in the next house and he watched her, as she walked across the clearing. If the snow continued, the pile of timber would be buried by morning. It was the last chance and he fetched more, to be sure it would cover the weekend. When she got back she smiled, telling him they were in luck and could take the PX cans back unopened. The prepared dishes would be ready in less than an hour. On arrival, the cold was penetrating, but as with the fur hats, the wood construction protected the dacha against a harsh exterior. Glow from the fire increased and the atmosphere mellowed. When the Samovar was working, she filled cups with tea and they sipped it, warming their hands. He got two glasses from the kitchen and opened the bottle of vodka, then feeling himself thaw, took-off his coat.

Outside, it turned dark and the snow was relentless, thicker than before. When it was time to collect the cooked food, he wanted to help but she suggested he stay out of sight. "It's safer! I don't know with whom she may talk. What the eye doesn't see," she said on her way. To keep the dishes warm, he propped an iron grill on the side of the fireplace, and dragged the table close to the fire, putting chairs around one end. A few minutes later, the front door burst open. "Hey! It's getting real cosy," she cried excitedly. "That's plucky, close to the fire. I must shake my coat. Can you take this from me? It's snowing like Hell and seems set to continue through the night. Just wait till morning, it'll be a sight!" After spreading her coat over a chair, she went to the alcove to fetch plates, cutlery and larger glasses. The battered plates with their cracks, chips and odd assortment of patterns, blended innocently with the faded disorder of the room. "It's time for the wine," he said, opening the bottle and filling the glasses. "Cheers! Here's to our weekend!" She toasted, leaning over to give him a kiss. "Nasdroviej! It's going to be exciting!" He said, clinking their glasses, then holding her close in a long embrace.

"Come! Let's have this while it's hot," she said, sitting down at the rickety table and ladling out the borsch. She floated the sour cream gently on the dark, reddish brown liquid, that put to shame the watery broth they got under that name in the city.

"Do you remember, when I invited you the first time, I said it would be 'different' for me? It was an understatement!"

"It's nice you say that, the feeling was mutual. But at the time, you labelled yourself—disconcerted."

"Right, I felt estranged and was ready to quit—if it wasn't for meeting you, I would not still be coming to Moscow."

"It is a comfort to know that whatever happens, we can look with pleasure on our times together. It has been an important stage of my life. I could not possibly want you to get that way again."

"And why should I?"

"Have you not noticed that our roles, or the parts we play, have reversed? I mean—when we met, I was reassured and you were unsettled. What you earlier described as being at the 'boundaries of impossibility' is going well and you feel at home in this country. Through my uncertain status, I have as much justification to call myself disconcerted now, as you had then."

"It's hard to dispute."

"Not fair though! Things have to change for me."

"But, change is a mirage."

"That's what Curtis said."

"He was talking about the party—I'm referring to life in general. We have to think positively and as he said, 'beat the system'."

"Maybe it's not possible!"

"Nothing is impossible, it's just harder, to quote that Curtis again."

"I hope you're not being ironic."

"Quite the reverse. Think about what happened to me. I almost gave-up, but we met and my life here became meaningful. This happened abruptly, without notice and it could be the same for you. Something positive can materialize, just when matters seem most hopeless, or amiss."

"You did not have to cope with the uncertainty I face now."

"I felt lost, overwhelmed by the problems I encountered. Look, you have the most powerful government in the world, behind you. Your problem is insignificant for them and the situation can turn-around any day. They must succeed—for them failure is not an option!"

"Fine! Let's put my little nightmare to bed, at least for the present. It should not meddle."

"We should drink to the time we met and not forget what followed. This weekend can be a vantage point."

"A milestone, recognizable from two directions," she grinned as she served the chicken *tabaca* and I sliced the Russian bread, for which she must have stood in line for an hour, that very morning in the *Gastronom*. "And this menu is a distinctive start," I added. It was a double benefit to get the cooked food. Apart from providing the neighbour with needy cash, it avoided messing with the oven, which operated with oil and took a while to get running. Every so often, it faded completely and had to be started from the beginning—not like her cooker in Moscow. "You said it! There I have no problem—it lights with the first match."

"But matches can be tricky, particularly the last."

"Am I likely to forget?" she said feigning a scowl.

"Is it possible that your guards get dishes like these, when they take their notebooks home?"

"We can't see their good sides, but they probably have wives to cherish them."

"How about the one, who checked your papers. Could he have someone to love him?"

"If he treated her as roughly as he treated me, she would have left—for sure."

"Maybe, it explains the curt behaviour."

"*Touché!*" she smiled.

When they finished eating, she took the dishes to the alcove, calling back: "I'll take care of these, please look after the fire—we depend on it." He selected a couple of dry logs and carefully balanced them in place. Interspersed with the clatter of plates, was the hesitant sound of trickling water and he noticed how different it was from the sound he was used to from her Moscow kitchen.

"Look what I found!" She called eagerly, holding-up two chipped eggcups. "Too bad it isn't Easter!"

"We can use them at breakfast."

"Who said there were eggs? It'll have to be next time."

"They would do for the vodka."

"Too late!" She replied, bringing the washed glasses to refill. They rarely drank vodka, but it reinforced courage to undress. The Samovar was still alight and she poured more tea. Sitting side-by-side directly opposite the flames, he put his arm around her, comforted by the warmth.

Whether it was the vodka, they felt sufficiently malleable to deal with the bed, dragging the large wooden frame, near the fire. There were old heavy blankets in the attic, like those used by Army recruits and they spread one over the base, then arranged the white sheet and rug, brought from her flat, with various sizes of blankets in layers and their overcoats on top. As in her flat, they stripped to the skin. She climbed between sheet and rug, he following gingerly, to avoid disturbance of the precarious balance. Gripped in a close embrace and feeling odd under, instead of on the rug, they basked briefly in the cosiness of their own warmth. The bed was out-of-range of the radiation and cold currents circulated over the floor. Slightest movement was enough for them to invade, then chill, whatever components of their bodies were in their way. After vainly struggling to close the gaps, they got to their feet and stood arm-in-arm directly before the flames. Now, spared from searing draughts, they risked scalding their limbs, wantonly exposing themselves to the savage blaze. Taking an iron poker, propped on a ledge, he speared incandescent logs, which roared in retaliation. In these moments, he could turn his head and follow the patterns from the glare, as flickering reflections on her face and on her breasts. The familiar tint of her skin was reddened and flecked with shades of orange in the darkened room lit only by the fire.

Later, they put on underclothing and shirts before climbing under the covers, to try the makeshift bed a second time. She lay facing him on her right side, instead of the left and he realized the bed was the inverse of 'under the bookcase'. Exhausted from hours of driving, she was quickly asleep and he watched her motionless, face dimly visible from the now subdued glow. With arms at his side, he stretched out the fingers of his left hand, for the warm softness of her thigh. An inanimate numbness of tights extended the further he reached. He missed the feel of her bare skin pressed against his and longed to return to her flat. He became drowsy and I had a fantasy of naked women from Victorian paintings, the milky skin curving over bellies to disappear sexless, between marble thighs. Fatigue from the journey, or the vodka, put him in a deep slumber.

Sunlight broke in through one of the small windows, when he awoke next morning. She was dressed, boiling water for the coffee. "Today, we can go walking. I have something you must see," she called beaming. The excitement and unconventionality of the place belonged to the daytime. Looking out from the doorway, the sky was bright. The snow had stopped, but must have continued through the night. Drifts were stacked high against the walls and the columns holding the house above the ground, had disappeared from sight. Position of the road could only be determined from the gap between the trees. Boundless layers of white coated all around. Pines revealed no trace of the green needles camouflaged beneath. Birches and deciduous trees appeared ragged, branches picked-out in entangled, quizzical forms. After breakfast, they put on their thickest clothes, boots and scarves. A heavy old coat left hanging inside the front door, seemed more suitable for a prolonged stay outdoors. She didn't know whose it was, but he put it on with an old fur hat, left in a cupboard. "You finally have one!" She smiled, his head almost disappearing, when she pulled the flaps down. Awed by the prospect of restarting the fire, he put on as many logs, as would balance on top, hopeful it would stay alight till their return.

Taking the lane to the left, they walked brashly through the white blanket, conscious of four lines of clearly identifiable footprints trailing them. The chill in the house and fatigue from the journey, sobered the newness, but in daylight after a night's rest, novelty was exhilarating. Compared with the loudness of Moscow, the stillness, interrupted by isolated bird noises, was near invasive. The unbroken fresh surfaces seemed the more spectacular after the doleful streets of the city, but most noticeable was the air. Not only were they freed from the city's pollution, but the trees performed their natural resuscitation. As they progressed along the lane, the clearing above their heads was the only breach in woods, appearing to extend without frontier. Looking sideways through the maze of trunks, the spaces merged in a deepening blackness, which reawakened feelings of being watched. The silent darkness fading either side, induced a sense of unease, not so different from that in the city. Could unseen eyes be peering through the mysterious backdrops? Since setting out along the track, they saw no one and during the drive the day before, there was no sign they were followed. Sending observers to watch over an empty forest, seemed hardly justifiable, yet until it started to thin, as they approached daylight at the perimeter, concern lingered. Coming into the open, they found themselves on a friendly bluff from where the landscape sloped towards level country. Fields undulated slightly, disrupted only by isolated houses and farm buildings ahead. By then, they had walked about four miles. She moved away to lie flat in the snow, then stood leaving an imprint of her body. No other footprints or tracks were visible ahead. As far as the eye could see—and beyond, all was white. "Just look at that. Didn't I say it was another world?"

"I have seen nothing comparable," he said in wonder.

"It's Russia!"

"I can see why Dostoevsky wrote: 'Russia—a whim of nature . . .' More than a whim, it's an obsession."

28

The vastness of the landscape that lay beyond the woodland could be inferred. This boundless space part real, part in the mind stretched unbroken out of sight, through the Steppes and onwards into Siberia. Size didn't lose its meaning and contrast between the minuteness of the dark figures, accidental brush marks against the white canvas, drew parallels with what was ahead. For a moment, gazing silently into the imagined distance, time was curbed, the light waves fastened permanently before the eyes, a photograph snapped in the mind by a shutter movement of 1/1000th of a second. It was an instant, as when their eyes first met. New images could steep there as in a dark room, the tray of fixative patiently rocked forwards and sideways, to protect the developing forms from perils outside. Detachment removed the future briefly out of reach. In coming weeks, uncompromising restraints can still exact a new sense of time, but in this seclusion, the city seemed remote, his other world, a fiction, story of someone else's life. As with cascading reflections of mirrors, unreality multiplied. With the focusing wheel of binoculars turned in the false direction, the future seemed blurred and indistinct.

They walked down from the bluff towards the houses. It was a small farming village and she knew a place where they could eat. It didn't look official—seemingly, an unauthorized private venture. Although the building was the largest of the cluster, the room allotted to the restaurant was small, with white-painted walls and a low ceiling. There were only four tables and they took the smallest opposite the door. A group of locals, probably agricultural workers, occupied the second and the other two were empty. She sat in the corner, he opposite her, with his back to the room. When a cheery, plump woman, serving, enquired what they wanted, she spoke in Russian. The freshly cooked dishes were as authentic as those from the night before and barely did they finish the first, when the next appeared. They should have felt at ease in the informal setting, but self-conscious of the effect of their foreign language, talked sparingly and in low tones. He was aware how different it was from the city and as if reading his thoughts, she remarked: "Time has another impact."

Unexpectedly, she leaned across to whisper, warning that two men sat down at the table behind with a girl, who stared at him as if she knew him. He waited a moment before turning. In the chair behind his left shoulder, she was in conversation with the man on the far side and he couldn't see her face. Then when she turned to talk to the second man, he saw the profile—typically Russian with high cheekbones and eyes that were a pronounced, unusual shade of greenish blue. Her blond curls were swept back off the face and hung loosely to shoulder length. He had not seen her before. The new additions, clearly not locals, could be from the city and the closeness of their table, further strained the atmosphere. Now, apart from risk of being recognized as foreigners, was the possibility that people from Moscow might identify their language, or even understand it. They became uneasy and decided to leave after the main course. It took longer than expected, as for a while the woman serving did not reappear. At the first opportunity, they paid to leave, but by the time he got to his feet and turned-around, he saw to his surprise that the people who caused their concern, had already left.

When they were clear of the building and safely out of earshot, he told her: "I did not recognise the girl, but I have the impression I saw one of the men somewhere. It's strange that they left before us—they couldn't have eaten in the time. Do you think we were followed?" She said she did not watch closely.

The weather improved and the sky was almost cloudless. Reflection from bright frozen surfaces intensified the light and the openness suggested a sense of freedom. As they were heading back towards the dacha, after walking aimlessly between the snow-covered fields, he again referred to their neighbours in the restaurant, saying: "I realize where I saw the man. Remember, I had to leave you one evening for dinner with two business contacts. It was the night I consumed a lot of vodka. He was the unexpected third, who sat next to me until noticeably drunk—he staggered across the room and disappeared. With no card, I don't remember the name he used. I assumed he worked for one of the other two, but it is conceivable he was a security man, sent to monitor them. Today, he gave no sign of recognition, so I hope he was so drunk the last time, he doesn't remember me."

"I have not seen any of the three before, but if he is the person you describe, the coincidence of seeing him here is puzzling," she said. "It's hard to judge, but perhaps we were followed!" They didn't talk again about the episode, but it put a pall on the exuberance with which the day started.

By the time they were back in the wood, the light was beginning to fade and as they walked along the road leading to the clearing, the sense of unease intensified. In the waning light, blackness between the tree trunks on each side was more pronounced. Walking arm in arm in the semi-darkness, she started the following conversation: "You say that things cannot change, yet the fact that you were able to come here seems to indicate, they can. You altered the balance."

"Yes, but I had to interfere with time and there are risks."

"Could this become a pattern, perhaps lead to something new?"

"How different, if it could!" As he spoke, I thought of the man just seen in the restaurant. Whether in security or linked to Ivanov, it was ominous. I listened unmoved as he continued: "You know the limits. I thought it was agreed—tacitly at least."

"It was. I wanted to know, if the positions in the square may have altered." She said calmly.

"I will do anything viable, but this step does not seem possible, at least for now."

"I see!"

"You know this has nothing to do with what you mean to me. It's like with your current predicament, we have to hope circumstances will differ, or new situations arise." It was a painful subject, but he respected her for raising it. They continued in silence for the last few minutes of the way, made-out only by the luminescent snow and the contrasting shapes of tree-trunks lining the route. When they reached the dacha, it was already dark. The fire was almost out and he tried to put life into it, while she ordered dishes from the neighbour. When back, she told him, she did not feel well. He put his arms around her, asking what was the matter. She complained of a headache, dizziness and was worried about the early start in the morning. He thought: I hope our conversation on the way back, did not perturb her. Perhaps the long walk and driving the day before were too demanding.

The food was hot and they ate it straight away. Afterwards, he suggested that she go to bed and leave him to clear up and prepare for the return journey. She gave him the car key and he loaded the unused cans of provisions and their clothes, to save time next morning. She said she felt chilled and would wear clothes to stay warm. "I'll join you shortly. Sleep well my darling!"

She was soon asleep, on the unaccustomed side. He sat beside her and as on the night before watched her face, this time barely visible in the light of the fire, dimmed by the extra logs. Periodically, a flame broke out, brightening the room, then he saw her clearly, until the glow subsided. He undressed and got in next to her. Listening to her breathing, he thought about the absent lovemaking: in just one day, I would be with her again in the warm familiarity of the flat. He tried to cheer himself, remembering how it would feel to hold her unencumbered in his arms. Briefly lifting the blankets and glancing at her motionless figure, which looked ashen, wrapped in her underclothes, I had a fantasy of a baby's doll, its unmarred surface devoid of aperture, or indentation. For no clear reason, it mutated to a memory from years before of a pallid body, on a neatly covered divan—the image was persistent. When asleep, he had a dream: She was lying on her back in a narrow room with walls that had been painted black. There was a velvet partition between us and when I tried to remove it, she didn't seem to notice. It was thick like a theatre curtain and when I pulled, it got longer. I could feel the material tearing in my hands. I heard the clapping of an audience. Though the noise was loud, she lay motionless and didn't move her eyes.

He awoke. The metal gong of the battered alarm clock was clamouring. It seemed dead of night, but it was four a.m. and they had to leave at once. They washed in the unheated water and hastily dressed. He put the blankets away, sprinkled water on the dying embers, folded the rug with the sheet, putting them behind their seats and they left. He didn't tell her about his dream, but he thought about it. At the time, I assumed that the figure behind the partition was 'she'. What bewildered me later was realization that the hair framing the face seemed fair. As I went over each aspect of the sequence, the more certain I became, that the person was blond and that it must be Anna. I questioned why I should dream about my wife, when she was far from my thoughts. Sitting in the car, I dissected the dream in my mind, seeking clues that might corroborate my exaggerated fear of retribution for interference with time.

Part of the way, he slept and didn't notice the journey. Suddenly, he heard her voice telling him they were in the centre. She dropped him near the hotel, saying she was sorry to disappoint him and he assumed she referred to being unwell. When kissing her goodbye, he was surprised how tired and drawn she looked. He wanted to agree the pick-up for the evening, but she suggested he phone when free. Hurrying for the meeting, he promised to call between six and seven. He rushed into the hotel, up to his room, to shower, shave, dress and sort his papers for the ministry. He got there at half past ten.

29

The vice minister stood from his desk and before introducing others present, stepped over to ceremoniously shake his hand. Holding his head aloft, not once glancing at his visitor and with no pause for the translator who, humiliated, summarized at the end, he embarked on a short speech. The speech confirmed that he had agreed a brief Saturday appointment, to review the subject in hand. Thoughtful postponement by his guest to a whole-day Monday meeting, permitted participation by the institute director. He and his team travelled from Leningrad, during the day-off on Sunday. They had arrived in the ministry building and waited on another floor. The constructive gesture for intervention with time, had provided a unique opportunity to progress their important project towards the goals of the Party. After morning discussions, the vice minister awaited all concerned to review the interim result at a buffet lunch. He instructed his secretary to take the guest to the meeting room. A well-built, striking woman with a somewhat stern look, she walked stiffly a few paces ahead. It was a long way, down wide corridors and up broad flights of stairs. The metal plates of her high-heeled shoes rang-out, as each foot moved forward on the un-giving concrete floors. Her uniform skirt constrained a powerful bottom that with each step, moved covertly from side to side as blatantly as the security agents at the convention. Like a trainbearer, he kept his distance, maintaining the display in his sight. Might members at party meetings be aroused, as she stepped on the rostrum to deliver speeches? Impressions merged in his head, confused with those of the truncated speech, just witnessed.

Without warning, a wide door swung open. The room was larger than before. People sat at either side of a long table and from where he stood, he counted twenty heads. By the time, the familiar faces from the trading organization arrived, there were more than thirty in the room. After rounds of political banalities, it was turn of the institute director to make a speech. His monologue embraced the entire modernization planned for the industry, stretching from the borders of Poland to the outer reaches of Mongolia and covering no less than nine of the sixteen autonomous republics. He extolled the comprehensiveness—no tampering with isolated factories, but addition of twenty new ones, each integral and complete. This echoed an earlier conversation with Calvin, when he spoke of that number, but it was the first time the figure was mentioned at a meeting. The contract would be massive and during interruptions between translations, he could make guesses about bonus, groping with the noughts of the potential dollar sum. It must be significantly, beyond what Calvin might have conceived. There would be resentments in the firm.

When the translator resumed, he noticed odd word combinations like: unchallengeable decision-making, exhaustive investigation of international economic advancement, sweeping technological adaptation. After another interval of Russian, he noticed terms like: unprecedented action, significant steps of scientific progress, fulfilment of goals of the applicable Five Year Plan . . . not forgetting throughout—benefits to the Soviet Federated Socialist Republic. Although they must have dissected the firm's documentation, questions remained and to help circumvent delay and meet the deadline, undercover contacts at the London embassy would be available for discreet use of diplomatic mail. At lunch, the vice minister with his impenetrable face lit by the hint of a smile, was almost amicable. Afterwards delegates from opposing sides scrutinised progress and open questions were disposed of without the expected disputes. For the first time, completion of the business seemed in reach. Contrast with early visits in Moscow was stark and that day, working hours passed fleetingly.

He was back in the hotel to phone at 6 p.m., excited to tell her the progress, to which she contributed. She should be proud of her help and happy to know that he will be back when needed and in case she stays on, his visits would continue.

There was a delay before the operator returned his call. As if back in the earlier times—another person unavailable, someone else rejecting an appointment or promising to call back later. The faint and indistinct voice on the line was hers and she was telling him they could not meet. "We have to!" He insisted.

"I can't drive the car."

"I will send a taxi and we can meet in a restaurant."

"I'm too weak to get downstairs."

"After alteration of my ticket for the weekend, the visa is running out. I must leave tomorrow morning."

"I understand," she replied. "But I am ill and must sleep."

"It is vital to meet. I have important news. Meanwhile, I shall make a last attempt to delay my flight. I will call at nine and hope that you'll feel stronger."

"You can try," she said before hanging-up.

He was sure it was impossible to extend the visa. The ministry had closed for the day. Only remaining hope was Intourist. He went down to enquire at their office next door. There was a girl on duty, busy with several people standing at the counter. He sat down and decided to wait. While waiting, he scrutinized the girl. She had blond hair, swept back off her face and falling loosely behind her head. She appeared familiar. He looked more closely at her eyes—a distinctive shade of green blue. "Could it be?" He asked himself. When glancing up as he came in, she gave no hint of recognition. The more he peered, particularly at her eyes, the more he was convinced it was the girl, sitting behind him in the country restaurant the day before. He decided to disclose no clue. When the others left, he got to his feet and went to the desk. The girl raised her head, looked at him directly and smiled. Was it a sign? He smiled back, but kept to his formal enquiry about delaying the flight. She examined the ticket and reminded him, he had altered it to postpone return by two days. She said she must see his passport.

Since his real motive was about the visa, he couldn't avoid showing it. Leafing through page-by-page, she took her time and he was concerned his nervousness might raise suspicion. There was a long pause while she examined the visa. "No possible! Visa run-out tomorrow." Then, after a moment of thought, she continued, fixing him with her eyes: "Can no stay Moscow longer!"

"I need to stay. Can't it be extended?" He asked.

"Visa run-out tomorrow. Tomorrow too late to stretch," she said conclusively. When he questioned her again, she warmed a touch, explaining it was difficult and took time to get the papers signed. Then she dashed his hopes, suggesting the visa was probably not adjustable. "Next time, you ask visa for enough days. Stretch difficult. You ask more next time!" She exclaimed, looking coquettishly at him. Was there a suggestion behind the words? They were her last. He picked-up the documents and left.

If it was the same girl, and he was sure it was, he asked himself what she was doing in that isolated village. Why did she look at him in the restaurant? Did she know him from before? Who were the people she was with, particularly the second man and why were they in that remote location? Aside from these questions, why did he see her the next day? He would not know the answers, unless they met on a later visit. But, her words confirmed—he could not delay departure.

The day started well. The business was going ahead. Despite current worries, his visits would continue, certainly until her transfer. He could give her his word that he would return before the case comes-up and promise support. If in the end, they allow her to stay to complete the contract and she decides to do so, she would be assured that his visits would not stop. It was important to let her know how her help influenced the firm's success and thank her. They should be celebrating, yet for the first time, they were not together on his last night in the city. The sickness was an unexpected blow. Did she catch a chill in the cold air of the dacha? Was it to do with her period? Perhaps the whole weekend, including the hours of driving, were too much. Could it be connected with his response to her question on the future? Seeing the man with Ivanov unsettled him. He was blunt, forthright, but it was not a subject for discussion over a bugged telephone. Anywhere else, he could go to her flat and talk face-to-face. Here, if not possible to meet, he must wait for the next visit.

Elation at success faded. Without sharing it with her, it lost significance. He started his report—the only way to fill time till nine.

"How do you feel?" He asked expectantly.

"The same," she replied, voice weak as before.

"I have good news about your help. Results look promising. I wanted to celebrate and thank you."

"It needs to be next time!"

"I have to leave tomorrow. Intourist told me, I cannot extend my visa."

"Seems unavoidable," she said.

What is it? I thought, is she ill, or is it something else? Does she recognize the hopelessness of our situation? "It is essential to see you before I leave!" He pleaded. "We haven't discussed the next time—the dates to match resolution of your case, issue of the exit visa."

"Make it like this time, then matters should be decided. My move may take a week or so. Try to get back in seven weeks."

"Count on it! But I must see you now, before I leave!" He begged.

"You know, it's not possible. You can't get through the gate, past the guard. He won't let you." There was a pause before she added: "Don't try, it'll make things worse! Take care!"

Ever since working in the Soviet Union, there was latent anxiety of arrest. Now he felt imprisoned, not on the inside, but locked outside. The bars were keeping him out. Instead of removing the barrier that separated them as they lay alongside in the dacha and making love in the intimacy of her flat, he was shut out. It was anachronism that he could be evicted from what had been home, since their meeting.

The gateway and her guards had transformed their arena, to a place of detention. The Moscovites chiding came back to him: 'don't sleep in a mausoleum that doesn't belong to you.' If applied to the present, it was I, who was removed. Am I condemned to remain on the outside? Could it be a last step, before she is moved out herself? Angered by the omnipotence of the system and the sense of his insignificance, he recalled her words: "In this country, some things are impossible and others unthinkable." Shimmering reflections from their 'weekend in the country' felt remote. He sensed an isolation, hard to comprehend. The closer he studied the set, the more distraught he became. He could not go and shout outside her building, they would arrest him and it will add to her distress. Being loser twice, he could not call again, but must wait till morning.

With nowhere to go except the hotel, he continued his report—writing and rewriting compulsively, kept-on by fear or emptiness, when pausing. He sat at the small desk in the dim joyless room and didn't go to bed. By dawn, he was slumped over the table—like the vodka drinkers and as disconsolate.

The hotel's wake-up call was late, but he phoned, optimistic, that the new day would offer a new script. There was no answer. Was she waiting for the ringing to stop, too ill to lift the receiver? Had someone taken her to hospital? He had to leave and decided to phone once more when checking-in. All airports have public telephones, but he had not noticed one there. "Can you please show me where I can phone?" He enquired from a girl at the desk. "No time! You late!" she shouted at him. "You go emigration now. Customs waiting you in baggage." He couldn't go anywhere, because he had to contend with inevitable lines. He slipped outside, to where he noticed a payphone in a corridor, then tried in vain to make it work. Coins would not fit in the slot. He looked for help, but no one understood. Finally, a young airline attendant speaking some English rescued him. "Telephone? To Moscow? You need special pieces," he explained, offering to fetch some. He waited and waited. Finally, when the man returned with tokens and manipulated the machine, he dialled and listened, but there was only silence. Grabbing the hand piece, the young man put it to his ear. "*Niet. Kaput*" he said. He had to deal with the luggage, or it would not be cleared. Afterwards, was only the departure room. As he got there hopes were raised, discovering a wall-mounted telephone—just one and in use. He waited impatiently, watching the user shout down the mouthpiece and later slam it onto the support with a curse. He realized it would not work. He had to go for the last check and board his plane to the other world.

30

At the airport, Anna's first words suggested that the delay must be promising for the firm and I took it as veiled criticism. As we walked to the car park I kept silent, concerned about 'her' and what might have happened. But I was prompted to the immediate, by Anna's voice telling me that it was a stroke of luck, I postponed my return and I realized she was not complaining. After splitting with Clare, Spencer bought a property in the country and moving there, planned a housewarming. As Clare was giving a goodbye party for her friends, they combined the two. We were invited to see the house. They suggested we bring the children and stay the weekend to experience the idyllic country life, but she had to decline, because of collecting me on the Sunday. When she got my message, she called Spencer and said she and the children would come without me. I reacted curtly, reminding her that it was supposed to be over—she was not going to see him anymore. We walked in silence to where she left the car. She went to the driver's side. I sat without a word, while she drove. When on the main road, I remarked provocatively that I was sure she had a good time. "A fairy-tale! It's unreal there. After the big city, it's a different world. Where he lives is deep country. The house is in a small lane and the only traffic is cows, driven back in the evenings to a nearby farm." Unable to resist, she volunteered the details: "To get the grass cut, he hired a worker, who turned-up with a scythe. Spencer said it reminded him of Tolstoy and *Anna Karenina*. To get there you have to drive through a ford, I didn't know they still existed. The building is five hundred years old, beams everywhere, bathroom included. He lives in chaos and it's dilapidated, but for the party, a fire was roaring in the enormous inglenook fireplace. On Sunday, we went walking down the lane to where there's a bridge over the river, then followed one of its banks. The country air was amazing and we didn't see a soul the whole way." I told her I was glad she enjoyed herself and asked if Spencer was still working in London. She claimed he was freelance and planned to operate from home. Then, she admitted that he had to travel up for meetings with the theatre companies. Defensively, she changed the subject: "What did you do at the weekend. You must have had time on your hands."

"I needed to prepare for a meeting with a vice minister."

"You can't have worked the whole weekend."

"There's not much else to do." I responded to divert her.

"You've probably found someone to help you through at times like that. I bet you've spotted a saucy Russian girlfriend to keep you busy."

"You don't understand life there, if I speak unofficially to a Russian, they could be interrogated or arrested. I am bugged and trailed most of the time. It's the opposite of Spencer's idyllic countryside," I added sarcastically.

"Well I have news to get your mind off Spencer. A Mr. Davidson, someone you don't know, called repeatedly saying he must talk to you the moment you get back. It sounds as if he wants to offer you a job. When he heard about the delay, he promised to send a letter to brief you. The letter's arrived. It's sitting with your other correspondence in the hall."

I stayed quiet, thinking about my situation and what might be ahead for 'her'. Then Anna started to tell me about a shower fitting, I had bought earlier. "The children were fascinated with it when you brought it back from the States, but at first the plumbers said they couldn't fit it, because it had American threads. I finally found one who could. He went to great lengths to explain, how the shower has, what he calls, a 'female' fitting. He knew exactly where to get the missing piece. He called it a 'union'. He said that with it, he could mate the American female, to an English male fitting. Once he got the coupling, it took him no time to get it 'up and running'."

"I'm glad they find it fun."

"Now, baths are out—they only want showers and not just the two. Katie keeps bringing friends back from school, to show it off."

"What is it that amuses them?"

"It's the lever and what happens, when you turn it. You know those funny protrusions that stick out from the bottom, one of Natalie's friends said it's like soldiers coming out on a parade ground. Now, when someone turns the handle, Natalie goes running down stairs screaming: 'the soldiers are out'."

"It's a good shower and a clever design," I said.

"No one will dispute that, but how did you get the idea to buy it?"

"I saw one at a friend's. I believe it was in the new house Ambrose and his wife moved into."

"I thought you stayed in hotels when you travel."

"I spent an evening with them."

"I bet they don't have showers like that in the Soviet Union."

"You can't imagine what they provide in hotels there."

When we got to the house, I could see the unopened letter down the hall. I picked it up and went into the sitting room. This could be a relief from worry. The letter outlined a new opportunity—chance to run a company with promotional prospects and different directions of travel, which could be important, were she to move out of Russia. "It is about a job," I said to Anna. "He's a headhunter, so it means nothing at the moment. I will phone in the morning to check if it is serious."

"Think of the sacrifices you've made for the present lot. No firm shows gratitude. In the end, all they give you is a gold watch."

This time, the distance did not seem to work. The splitting did not function, as it had before. With the unanswered questions, I could not switch her out. Here I was, back in the other world and although distance dulled the senses, I could not get her out of my mind.

Next morning I stayed late to call from home. It was better to avoid the office. Doors would be open and others manage to overhear, what was not intended for them. Davidson wasn't in, but a proficient secretary promised to ring as soon as he arrived. When the call came through, he sketched an outline of the job: "The company is a leader in new areas of expertise, recently acquired by a group with impressive financial resources. Prospects are excellent, but they were badly run in the past and I'm engaged to find a new managing director. The parent company is an established group headquartered in London and will welcome someone with your background. Your resume should impress them. If interested, you will be well placed."

"Where do they operate?"

"Some work is at home, but most has been overseas for the petroleum firms."

"Do they work in Russia? They have an important oil industry."

"I don't know about that. These people work for the majors, and you know where they are—Middle East, Latin America, South East Asia."

"Naturally!"

"Why don't you come and have lunch? We can explore it further. Can you make it next week?" He asked.

I would meet him the following Tuesday. I wasn't thinking of moving, but interested to see what they offered. The new directions of travel could be a benefit, 'she' may go to America in a couple of months and mentioned a possible assignment in Athens. I could stop-off on the way out, or the way back.

As soon as I got to the office, Calvin called me in. "How can we thank you for this sacrifice! It was a stroke of genius to delay your return," he told me radiant. "If you hadn't rescheduled your appointment, it would have been too late for us to meet their deadline." He was eager to know, how discussions went with the vice minister. I explained that since the visit to the institute attitudes were different. Many faces were the same, but it was like performing with another cast.

"There are a couple of factors that work in our favour," Calvin proclaimed, more enthusiastic than ever. "The deadline for the offer avoids procrastination and the new conditions, force the Soviets to be realistic about terms, act in time and avoid losing an opportunity to buy abroad. Their industry is run-down and our package could be crucial. They may pressurize on price, but the firm must stand steadfast and preserve our reputation. From the magnitude of the contract, we can offer government credit—with repayment spread over 10 years."

"There can be no slippage," I intervened.

"No question!" he continued. "The firm will commit the resources, the American side will help us out. They are ready to ensure there can be no risk of delay, or over-run. The parent company has given an undertaking that the business will be followed to successful conclusion."

"Splendid! Such an undertaking from our head office must be dependable," I couldn't help interrupting, relieved to hear that our people seemed to be treating the matter seriously. He told me the technical advances available from the firm would mean more to the Russians, than the extra dollars they would have to pay for several years. He got increasingly excited, coming to my side of the desk and peering into my eyes saying: "Keep it to yourself, but I have been advised that this could be the biggest contract the group has landed—worldwide."

"It's not won!" I reminded him. "There's much to be done to satisfy demands, not to mention timetable."

"No matter!" He added. "We can do it."

"Good to have your confirmation," I said.

"I am going to remember this when I work-out your share of the bonus. My God, you deserve it! You have put the firm in a unique position to win this monster, at a critical time for development of the market," he paused a moment. "What is more, I want you to follow-up closely with the people over there and in person. You should return as soon as possible. You need to apply for a visa right away."

I submitted the application, when the embassy opened next morning. Its expected issue date allowed a margin of three weeks, within the return date promised to her. As it would be the last, before her expected move outside the Soviet Union, promptness was vital. It was a relief to know, I would be with her 'on time'.

There was a takeover. Private shareholders were selling the firm to a landmark public corporation. It wasn't just in the Soviet Union, where shuffling of leaders resulted in musical chairs and new names. Tremors would be felt throughout the organization, particularly the higher levels. Calvin worked directly for Stanford, the second man of this former private concern. An Ivy League man with a wealth of experience stretching around the globe, he had worked in ninety countries and controlled branches in ten. He was quitting and replacement from the acquisitor was master in manipulation of people, and wizard in development of forms—capitalist twin of the Soviet functionary. I realised again, it was not just politics, where boundaries became less distinct. The new man would secure results without needing to stir from his expansive desk, with its adjustable reclining chair. He was duped by Thornton's boasts from holidaying in France, to earn the reputation of seasoned traveller and Calvin would have to suffer the indignity of reporting to him. It would be a puppet show, with tiers of novices pulling the strings, dictating moves from afar. Keen to exercise newfangled authority, Thornton was issuing confidential memoranda outlining a thrifty economy plan to cut the bonuses. He resented anyone earning more than he and on latest estimates, my share from the Russian business, could put me ahead. It would have been sacred to Calvin, but now Thornton could overrule him. Moves were irreversible and Calvin was promptly instructed to assign Elliot, a young Australian, as assistant for the Russian market. Officially, it was for 'familiarization', but in practice no different from the third person at the dinner in Moscow sent to check on Ivanov and his companion. Of practical impact, the new man must accompany me on my imminent trip, for introduction of the contacts. If I were to await his visa, safety margin would be cut to two weeks. There were complications. As part of a joint visit my half processed application had to be resubmitted with Elliot's, and must start from the beginning. It was going to be tight.

At lunch, Davidson was persuasive. "It's a new arena that fills a void for the oil companies. The group has money to back this to the hilt. They look for leadership and if successful, you can win a seat on the main board—an important group, quoted on the London stock exchange. The vice chairman is convinced the acquisition is a winner." I agreed to let him set a meeting. In the unclear atmosphere with the current firm, it could provide a soft landing.

It took a week or so for Davidson to arrange, the vice chairman was a busy person. I lunched with him at his club. A middle-aged heavy man in chalk-stripe, he knew little about the firm's specialisation, but as an accountant, was adept with numbers. He expressed enthusiasm about my joining, but insisted I meet others to set the conditions, taking another week or two. Afterwards, he informed me that Davidson would be in touch. "You'll hear from him," he promised.

Unexpectedly, I ran into a friend, who knew Spencer. He said, he was surprised not to see me at the country housewarming and probably to boast his wide circle of acquaintances, mentioned he saw Anna and Spencer together at a function in London. When I showed surprise, he looked embarrassed. I was unsettled by Anna's glowing remarks about the party and the new pointer, indicated that their relationship was not as dead as she would have me believe. I realized I was hasty with my remarks on the way back to the dacha, when she asked about 'positions in the square'. When I get to Moscow, I must inform her of the probably altered scenario. Hopefully, I should hear about the new job, before my trip and will be able to tell her about both at the same time. Wherever she goes after Moscow, it should be comforting to know the possibilities for visits. I wondered whether she sent the application for the position in Athens.

Time was lost in resubmission of visas for the joint visit with Elliot. As soon as both were expected, I learned of a new delay. Elliot was unknown in the Soviet Union, and vetting would take longer. I became anxious about my promised return, and realizing I would not arrive within the seven-week deadline, called her flat. It was a Wednesday and I phoned in the evening, to be sure, she would be in. I went to the international telephone centre and after waiting more than two hours—the operator advised me there was trouble on the lines to Moscow. "Come back at the same time tomorrow, love!" she suggested. She was wrong—it was worse. I had to wait till Friday. Then, I got through in half an hour. Although the voice was faint and blocked by background noises, it was definitely her on the line. She had difficulty hearing. In spite of shouting in the mouthpiece, I couldn't be sure she understood what I said. There was no chance to give an explanation, I kept repeating: "CANNOT TRAVEL YET—VISA DELAY—COMING EARLIEST POSSIBLE," I must have reiterated the sequence six, maybe ten times. Then the line was cut. In the circumstances, mentioning 'new scenery' was out of place. It was reckless to provide ammunition to listeners-in and with the bad lines, explanation was not possible. Sensitive information had to wait till we met. I decided to call on Saturday from the office. I knew there would be no one there and told Anna, I had urgent work to complete. I went in the afternoon and ordered the call through the international operator. It took almost three and a half hours to get a line and before I could speak, it was lost. It took another hour before they reconnected me and this time, there was no reply from her number. She must have gone out. I cursed that after waiting so long I finally missed her. On Sunday, there was no connection.

I almost forgot about Davidson and the job, when he rang and spoke to Anna: "It's a shame he is not in, as I can't call again today. Are you his wife?"

"I am," she responded.

"Why don't you give him a message? Tell him the offer's firm. They accept his terms in full. All he has to do is come to my office, to sign the papers. If I am not here, my secretary will have them ready. That's what he needs to do."

"I'll pass this on."

"Something else—tell him he won't have regrets. It's a move for the better. For a start, he will have more power!"

"Right!" She added as he rang off.

Anna gave me the message later that evening. "What are you going to do?"

"Consider."

"If the position is more important, you must be paid more money. You should give his secretary a ring and fix a time to sign the papers."

"I am busy tomorrow, but I'll think about it. If he calls, please tell him I'll be in touch."

No visa was in sight and I called her home again on Tuesday, without result. In desperation, I arranged a meeting with the consular office of the embassy. I told them I was required in Moscow, for vital discussions. As I was known, I asked them to separate processing of the visas, so I could travel ahead and Elliot join me later. They agreed, but authorization must come from above, and it meant more delay.

I called her two days later on the Thursday, the operator got through late in the evening but said: "There's an unusual noise on the line, it seems out of order." Then, surprisingly, asked: "Are you sure the number is right?" It was disconcerting: Had she moved out? It was too early! The number was correct.

In Moscow, they agreed to my request and on Friday morning, I got a message to collect my visa. I booked the earliest flight on Sunday. Luckily, Thornton was absent and I could get Calvin's blessing to proceed alone. I phoned Davidson to tell him I was keen, but timing was wrong. I had to travel to deal with pressing negotiations, before I could leave the present firm. He warned the position would not be open long. "Keep in touch! If there's news, contact me at once," he added, before I rang off. Though unsure whether their offices were open, I tried two more calls to Moscow on Saturday morning. From the school, there was no reply. When I got through to the embassy, a cold but polite message informed: "We are not allowed to give information over the telephone. If you have a bona fide enquiry, please come to the embassy."

31

His arrival in Moscow was three weeks later than promised. Overcome by the communication difficulties from outside, he nonchalantly reassured himself, the problem must be a technical failure with her line, or the connection abroad, and would be resolved, when back in the city. On arrival at the hotel, he asked the operator to get her number. There was an unusually long delay and he had to call back to enquire what happened. The answer from the hotel operator was more direct than that in London: "The line could not be used, because it was cut-off and without the new number, phoning was not possible." The disconnection suggested she moved out. He had not conceived that she might have left the flat.

Had he missed the ship? Perhaps his splitting induced immunity to warnings and now he knew she was not there, the realization was brusque. Assuming the embassy suitably rewarded the social fund of the secret police, to have the case dropped and obtain the exit-visa, she must have moved home, or wherever she found a new position. He was surprised, she left so quickly—she told him there would be a 'week or so' of margin, to plan the move. He could not say why, but he had a premonition—she went to America. She belonged there and it was easier to imagine. It consoled him to think how he could arrange a business trip and visit her. He lay on the bed and thought about the repetitive encounters at the beginning, how they talked of people's lives moving in time and randomly intersecting, re-crossing the orbits of those important to them. He considered the possibilities: I might spot her ahead in a bustling crowd on the sidewalk of Madison, East of the Park, or planning to meet her at an airport, suddenly see her coming towards me along one of the wide carpeted corridors that lead down to the gates. Her face will light up, beaming, and I would hear the familiar "Hi". Thinking about meetings to come, made him more cheerful, particularly when considering that whatever country she was in, it would be easier away from Moscow's restrictions and the imposition of the party. Although sure she was in the States, it was possible that she applied and was selected for the Athens posting, then moved at once because of a time limit. It would be new and something not yet part of their life together. He would have to take time-off, to make a private visit, pretending to Anna the trip was for the firm. The place was a natural fit for her positive nature and thinking about it, made him light headed. I could go to her flat with no guards around. There will be no bugging, observation, or taking of notes. I can walk to the doorway and ring on the bell. She won't be able to show me round the mausoleum, at least not Lenin's, but in Athens, we can visit hundreds of monuments from times past.

Looking around the room, he was angry with himself at not anticipating her absence. It should have been clear that delays with the visa, might lead to his missing her, yet at no point did it seem a possibility. It made him conscious how he yearned for her. Apart from disappointment, knowledge that she was not here induced intense sadness. Without her, the city was a void again. There was no one he could call, or contact about her—not one person. He could do nothing until morning. Awareness of how long he must wait to see her dismayed him, not just the days to get through in Moscow, but now she was outside—the weeks to reach wherever she is. It was harsh retribution for delay.

It was evening and looking up at the dark sky between the open curtains, he contemplated other possibilities for what could have happened. It was unthinkable, but what if the embassy had not done as promised? Then she might be in prison. He rejected this phantasm and put it out of his mind.

On waking next morning, he was uneasy, when he thought about whom he should call at the embassy. The only person he met from the staff, was Maryellen and she had long since returned home. He decided, it would be less impersonal, to call the school. He would try to find the friendly American lady in administration, who was helpful before and he asked the operator to get the number. This time it worked. When requesting the department, they passed him directly to her and she seemed to remember him. When he told her whom he was seeking, she didn't respond directly. She did not say whether she was there, nor if she was absent and he remembered the strict secrecy conditions set by her security people. She told him he should talk with Mr. Meredith at the embassy and when enquiring which department to ask for, she gave his direct line. "I am sorry I can't be more helpful, but I'm sure Mr Meredith will give you the assistance you need. If I were you, I'd call right away. It's the best time to catch him in his office. Good luck!" She said, as she rang off.

He caught Meredith at first attempt. From his sparing manner, he could recognize him as a security man. He didn't seem surprised by the call and behaved as if he'd heard the name before. He said he would like to meet, but would be out for the rest of the day. He suggested coming to his office at 4.00 p.m. the following day. "I'll leave your name with the duty marine at the gate and he can show you right through," he added helpfully. When putting the phone down, he felt relief—almost elation. The worst part of the hunting was over. He looked forward to getting the information from Meredith. Assuming she was outside the country, which seemed the logical explanation, he was convinced he would learn where she was and the uncertainty would be over. He could phone her, as soon as he was out of the Soviet Union. Like with Monday morning calls on early visits, he had to wait, but this time, didn't have to 'stay in the room', he just needed to fill the gap and for this, there was work waiting. In his reanimated state, he set about calling the business contacts, who knew where he was and were sending a car to collect him. He could see how his luck improved and it was the same at the ministry. With satisfaction, they displayed the firm's documents, presenting him a list of comments and questions, warning he would be kept busy, over the coming days. As if the mould was reversed, they wanted to achieve as much as possible, whilst he was there, working late without breaks and none of the delays from before. It was an unfamiliar pace. When setting the programme, he told them he had to leave at 3.30 the following afternoon, to attend a pressing appointment. They agreed, providing the hours missed were compensated by an earlier start, which left less free time to worry about what concerned him most. Returning to the hotel that evening, he sorted through the papers and saw that the size of the contract had grown again. From what he gathered during the day, the business seemed certain to proceed. There will be much to tell, when he meets her. Without her insights, matters would have been different for the firm. He had landed on his feet. When seeing her, he will be able to remind her of the conversation on the way back to the dacha when he suggested—something unexpected, could alter circumstances. The news would more than mitigate upset from communication difficulties and his delay.

The schedule next day included a briefing with the vice minister, who had become affable. Most of his speech was missed, as the translator was unable to cope and eventually gave-up. In spite of the progress and cordial atmosphere, he had to depend on outward composure to conceal an inexplicable, growing unease. Impatience and anxiety over the unresolved issues, increased as the meeting approached. When he reached the hotel, he went at once to find a taxi to the embassy. Precisely as promised, a duty marine was expecting him and took care of entry formalities. As soon as he showed his passport and signed-in, he was led through a maze of corridors and doorways to a rather plain office at the rear of the building. Through an open door, he could see a balding grey haired man, formally dressed in a lightweight check suit. He was sitting behind a metal desk, shuffling through papers. He gave no hint of noticing that people waited outside and glanced-up with a look of irritation, when the marine sergeant announced his name. Then standing, the man stepped into the corridor to shake the visitor's hand. He was tall, clean-shaven and a high forehead made the narrow face appear long. He pointed at one of a group of four wooden chairs, with plastic upholstered seats and splayed arms, placed around a small circular table, set along the wall opposite the desk. "Excuse me a moment, let me get hold of a colleague," he said, disappearing out of the door. He returned with a stocky, younger man with short cut fair hair, a ruddy complexioned face and thick moustache. He had one of the metal clip ties with strings, used by people from the South. As they came into the room the second man with a thin file visible under his arm, containing loose papers, purposefully closed the door behind him and took the seat to the right. Meredith sat down in the chair facing and introduced his colleague by name, saying merely that they worked in the same department. "I am glad you were able to step-in," he started. "It's probably no surprise to you, that your name is known to us from other sources, as an associate of Miss De Sousa. Before we go further," he went on. "Do you mind telling us how long you have known her?" He told them, realizing that they must have discovered more about the relationship, than he suspected. He assumed the younger was the one she talked to, when he got in trouble at the opera. Meredith must be the more senior man, brought in after her detention, to deal with the pending charge.

From remarks between themselves, it was apparent that they met her at different times. It was a shock to learn, they appeared to know the relationship was intimate. It meant that it was not just the Russians, who were an exposure threat at home. He remembered numerous occasions when she told him, his involvement was not discussed and after their meticulous efforts to keep the affair undercover, it seemed ironic, they should find out. They must also have known that he worked for an American firm. Hopefully they would be wary to misuse such information without cause, but he must be heedful—they had power to harm.

These reflections were interrupted, when the second man coldly recited a warning about security regulations. He mentioned that the exchanges might touch on classified subjects and opening his file, laid two typewritten sheets on the table in front of him. They needed protection against disclosure to third parties for a 25-year period, he explained. Although assuring them, it was a private matter—they insisted that before proceeding, he sign the prepared secrecy agreement. After glancing superficially through the document, he signed. Asked when he last saw her, he told them it was ten weeks earlier. When probed, he admitted she talked to him about her troubles with the police. Enquiring whether he knew about the trial and the date it was to start, he conceded she informed him that the embassy were negotiating for the case to be dropped, before a trial could take place. "That's partly true," the younger man intervened. "We made it clear to her, that we would give help to arrange for the charges to be dropped, but not before the case. That step could only be taken after the case had run its course in the court." The significance of these last words was startling. Was it possible that the 'worst scenario', which she said could not happen after their pledge, had actually taken place? If so, instead of being outside, she could now be inside—locked-up, in prison. He concealed his anger, recognizing that they represented his only hope to see her in jail. However they mishandled the case, he needed their goodwill to establish contact. "You have to accept, the legal system is different here. The charge is not made at time of arrest, but fixed at the start of the trial. In Miss De Sousa's case, there were complications. For the primary charge, the sentence could not be determined in advance. It had to be decided by the judge, depending on the prosecution witnesses presented at the trial. Accordingly, negotiation of a settlement had to await the result. Our intervention could only be after and not preceding the trial." He saw them nod to one another before Meredith resumed: "As a close friend of Miss De Sousa, it's important, you appreciate the crucial difference on this point. Is it clear?"

"I recognize the difference, but must confess, I am bewildered. Miss De Sousa mentioned the problem concerning the potential sentence and the judge's dependence on the evidence presented in court, saying that this was the reason you resorted to an application under the abrogation procedure, in spite of its high cost. She pointed out that this only took effect when the penalty amount is fully paid, at least seven days before the court was due to sit. She told me it was the only course open to a 'foreigner with a pending charge', to obtain an exit visa, therefore I fail to understand, how you could get this for her, after the trial."

"You seem to know part of the story, but you have the facts confused. I can't figure where you got the information from, but in this particular case it is not correct," said the younger man guardedly.

"I got the facts from Miss De Sousa, and I am sure she will confirm to you that this was the situation the last time I saw her."

"What Miss De Sousa discussed with you, must have been based on our preamble discussions with the other side. Later, additional information became known—we found there was more behind this trial, than was expected initially. In our subsequent discussions about dropping the original charge, the Russian side mentioned, there would be an allegation of spying, supported by evidence at the trial, with documentary reports from a link." There was a pause as he thought: this conversation has assumed a Kafkian dimension—I know the allegation is fake! Meredith, looking at him intently, intervened: "I hope you realize, the gravity of this charge made it vital to check its validity, as well as the grounds to support it. In practise, our only means of investigation was to pursue the trial, as it unfolded. It was the sole source of leads, to identify the undisclosed link. We made this clear to Miss De Sousa. She knew why the procedure had to follow this sequence. She understood the trial must go ahead and run its course."

"From what you say, I assume the trial has gone ahead. What were the results? Were the charges worse than you expected?"

The second man remained impassive. Meredith however, shifted uneasily in his chair and paused momentarily. His composure altered. His face drained of colour, his cheeks sagged and the expression deepened. He seemed to be adopting an over concerned attitude, which was unnatural, like a schoolmaster talking in confidence to a senior pupil, as he said: "Before we go further, there is something else you should know,"

"Please go ahead, but I hope it's not anything unpleasant."

"I'll let you be the judge on that. It's an essential factor. You need to know about it, to get a proper awareness of the situation."

"Are you preparing me for something bad?" He asked.

"You are right, I have unpleasant news. You had better brace yourself!" Meredith added, pausing again, as if waiting for a sign of assent from his visitor, who sat motionless, frozen by the fear of what was coming.

"I have to tell you, Miss De Sousa must have been extremely agitated, about what lay ahead for her at the trial. It is probably hard for anyone not presently living here, to comprehend the full extent of the fears and stresses, induced by a trial in this autocratic State."

Impatiently, he interrupted: "For Goodness sake! What are you saying? What happened at the trial?"

"The trial did not take place. Sir, I have the unpleasant duty to inform you, Miss De Sousa took her life, before it could start."

32

I felt the sudden surge of grief—it seemed to assault the throat. I couldn't say a word. I sensed pressure from tears welling behind the eyes and an intense heat flowing through my whole body. I could feel sweat breaking out on my arms and on my back. "Are you alright? Look here! One of these might help," Meredith said, passing me an open box of little round white pills. "Go down to the men's room—on the left, at the end of the hall, there's a faucet inside. Take a few minutes to compose yourself. You'll feel better, when it starts to take effect. Take your time! There's no rush, I'll be here." In the lavatory, I hung up my coat on the back of the door, pushed the pill into my mouth and scooped water from the tap. Then I collapsed on the seat, leaning back against the cool wall, made colder by the wetness of my sweat-ridden shirt. I sat in this way for a few minutes, fighting back thought, to make my mind go blank. Then I told myself it wasn't true. That this could apply to her was inconceivable. They must be talking about somebody else. It was a fantasy! They were playing a game, trying to trick me to a disclosure. Beyond these desperate thoughts was the obstinate reason of reality—constant and undisplaceable. I made no attempt to argue with it. As the drug took its effect, I could study the reactions on my own body—a distant observer. First, I noticed a tightening of the stomach. Hidden hands were slowly clamping it in place. There was a draining of the limbs, but in an outward direction—occurring progressively away from the stomach. It was the reverse of the flood of heat from before and I could be rational. Now I was uninvolved, emotions had been systematically frozen and deadened. It wasn't I. The thoughts that now flowed in were starved of life, dreamlike, icy. Intense chill from the wall behind, prompted me to get back to what was unapproachable outside. I noticed I was shivering.

I stood to put on my coat, leaned over the small washbasin and washed my face. It was important to eradicate giveaway traces. I collected myself and returned to the room. When I got there, Meredith was at his papers again. "That's good! You look better. Those little gems make a difference, don't they? You should have another as reserve, for when the first wears off. Come to think of it, you may find it helpful to have something for sleep tonight." He took two larger elongated pills out of his drawer and when he passed them to me, I slipped them into my pocket. "Remember the bigger ones are for the night. Why don't you take a seat and I'll fetch my colleague." When the two of them came back and sat down again, it was Meredith, who addressed me: "I suppose you have some questions. You must realize they might touch sensitive areas, but I'll try to answer what I can"

"I arrived with the hope, you would let me write down her phone number, now I know I could not use it. How did it happen?"

"In her flat—with the gas from the cooker."

"When discovered, why wasn't it possible to save her? Did anyone try?"

"It took place at the weekend, some time during Saturday night, or more likely, in the early hours of Sunday morning. The occupants of adjacent flats were absent and other people in the building were out during the crucial hours. The discovery was made by one of the residents, returning on Sunday evening and detecting the smell of gas. By the time, the embassy was notified and the emergency service had opened the security lock on her door, it was already almost 9 p.m. She was immediately transferred to the nearest hospital, but it was too late. She could not be resuscitated. She was pronounced dead by more than one doctor."

"Was it the weekend immediately preceding the trial?"

"Precisely."

"It was an accident. She could not have done it deliberately."

"I have to correct you there. Unfortunately, it wasn't possible. The installation was completely safe. There was a small ventilation opening high in the external wall, and the outlet discharged directly outside. A piece of cardboard had been taped in place, to block-off the air inlet. Another had been used as a baffle, to deflect the outlet gases back into the room."

"It looks more like murder to me. It was the weekend and you said that she was not discovered earlier, because everyone was away. The locks on her building were special, but they could not have been beyond the capability of the KGB. Maybe they broke in and set it up as suicide."

"There was no evidence of such a break-in. Those who discovered her did suspect this initially, when they noticed her bookshelves emptied, but subsequent investigation revealed her books were carefully stacked elsewhere in the flat. It was concluded that this was in preparation for her return to America, or to another posting, for which she may have applied. Although the motive cannot now be established, there could be no doubt that removal of the books from the shelves could only have been done by her, or under her instructions."

"The books meant a lot to her. But maybe they were looking for microphones. Why are you so sure she made the next step herself?"

"There was other evidence, which made the verdict conclusive. She took a brown rug into the kitchen to lie on. There was no sign of a struggle. Her hair was neat and she had make-up on. She was fully dressed and wearing shoes. It was as if she had been getting ready to go out, but thought again. When discovered, she was lying in an attitude of repose."

"If she took her life, she must have left a message."

"There was none. Indisputable is the fact that she taped around the door from inside the kitchen. There was only the one door, so whoever installed the tape could not have left the room. In fact, the half empty roll was still lying on the draining board, where it had been dropped after use."

"I knew her well. She could not have done it to herself. She was a positive, out-going person."

"I share your view about that. She was a popular person among the staff she worked with. But as you may know Sir, in certain cases, this can be a facade for inner insecurities. As you may realize, members of staff here are subject to intense interviewing techniques, including psychological testing. Although Miss De Sousa displayed confidence and strong character, her background could explain subsequent traits of instability. You can say our assessment is proved by what happened."

"You promised her a deal, to win her release and the possibility of not doing this before the deadline, was unthinkable. You must have saved the bitter truth until the end—the time she expected to be free. Her action displays complete hopelessness. It was the circumstances that were abnormal, not her reaction."

"You have no right to make these assertions. You are referring to events, of which you have no knowledge."

"It was a situation to prompt despair. How could you have abandoned her in that condition?"

"Such comments are unhelpful. I will assume this is the result of the present stress you must suffer."

"Are you trying to write the evidence to suit the circumstances?"

"You have to understand, this unfortunate incident has been fully investigated, by our own staff and by the local police. There can be no question about it—we are talking of suicide. The relevant authorities are in agreement."

"Her suicide was probably as much of a surprise to you, as it is to me. She depended on your support to get through this. You have to give an explanation."

"There is no other explanation plausible. The act was self-inflicted. The incident is regrettable for everyone concerned, but the facts cannot be reversed."

"I am going to prepare a full written statement for my embassy."

"You can take whatever steps you consider correct, providing you do not infringe our confidentiality. Let me remind you of the document you signed earlier today, and the fact that the matters discussed are subject to tight security restrictions. Read the entire document carefully, before taking any step that could harm your own well-being. Staff there, may welcome information you care to disclose. Take note however—they will also be eager for information from our files, about you and your activities, including your relations with the late Miss De Sousa. I suggest you are not in a position to throw stones. If you exercise caution, you will likely conclude that any breach of our security will not be in your personal interest. Nor would such steps be helpful, to a case that is entirely outside the aegis of your country. You should acknowledge that this matter has been closed and sealed by our government and the responsible authorities here."

"I shall keep my options open and your explanation is still pending."

"We have thoroughly reviewed the whole matter. I have already mentioned the subject of character traits. On the subject of espionage, I am not in a position to discuss our findings. It is a sensitive area for us."

"I knew her. It would have been impossible for her to be involved without my notice. Had she tried to conceal it, I would have realized. It is unthinkable!"

"You are entitled to your views on this matter. Our findings are confidential and will remain so. Her file will be sealed for the statutory period. The Russian allegation will not be known outside of here—not even by Miss De Sousa's family. We cannot discuss that aspect further."

"You mentioned, there was a suspected link in this connection. I met a Mr. Curtis Weltler with her. I know he was present at the time of her arrest. Have you investigated him, as the possible link you are seeking?"

"We know Mr. Weltler and we took a statement from him, in connection with Miss De Sousa's arrest. At the time, there was criticism of the way he behaved, both in regard to the Russian police and to Miss De Sousa, but we are not prepared to discuss his affairs with you." Meredith then picked up the phone and gave some instructions. He leaned across to whisper something to his colleague, before continuing: "We have tried to be as open as possible with you, and I suggest it is now time to close this meeting."

"Just one last question. What happened to her? Where is her body?"

"Initially this was subject to the jurisdiction of the Soviet Union," the younger man responded. "The body was sent to one of the city morgues. Formalities for repatriation were arranged at the earliest moment and have been completed. The body was taken back to the United States. It is usual in such cases, for the deceased's family to take care of funeral arrangements."

While we talked, two marines entered the room and took up positions on either side of my chair. Meredith addressed them: "Here, I have signed the entry document. Please accompany my visitor back to the gate. Have him sign the book and see him securely off the premises." His final remarks to me were: "Thank you for coming in Sir. I was glad to meet you and believe me, it was an unpleasant duty to have to pass the distressing news. I am sorry I could not be more encouraging. Have a good day Sir!"

They escorted me shoulder to shoulder, back along the corridors. If it was not suicide, the Russians did not have exclusive rights. It could have been the others and they would not have needed a break-in. In renouncing her to the court and what she knew could follow, there was no need for murder, to explain her death. The prospect was enough to induce an avalanche of despair. The marines were superfluous. I wasn't planning to make trouble. What could I do? She was dead and there was not a single living person, I could contact for evidence, or rely on for support. Meredith and his colleague would say they were performing their responsibilities and could muster a range of documentary evidence. The power would be on their side and I would face the same hegemony as with the Soviets. Besides, they were not the only ones with blood on their hands. Walking slowly between my new guards, I reflected: his passivity contributed to her final action. He let the system beat him, when he should have taken control and insist to travel alone. For her, the desertion could have been as decisive, as her father's before. Despite the sadness, he denies guilt. He was unable to behave any other way. It's probably similar for them. Another time, there could have been another set of motives, another list of excuses, but denial would be the same. We are who we are! We are who we are! I repeated to myself, before signing at the appropriate point, indicated by the duty marine at reception.

My guards escorted me clear of the building, and like hers, on the day that things started to go wrong, they stood in the middle of the street, watching me, until I turned the corner and was out of sight.

33

Instead of going to the hotel, I went to the Intourist office, checking to make sure the girl with the green eyes was not on duty, the reminder of the weekend at the dacha, would not be supportable. I went in and modified my return flight to Thursday. It was the best available and it meant I only needed to get through a single day. From the hotel I sent a telex to the firm, advising that because of illness, I was coming back early. I asked them to notify Anna. Then, I went up to the room and took one of the larger pills for the night. I only had to wait for half an hour. A problem was the dreams—though many, they were of the misty kind that do not properly disentangle from each other and cannot be remembered as separate, or sequential images.

I was lying in bed, watching the shapes of light infiltrating the room, around the heavy velvet curtains at the two windows. I do not know how long I studied their shifting patterns, when I became conscious it must be time to get-up. It was then, I remembered. At first, I was not sure whether it was real or imagined, but the acknowledgement soon prevailed. They were collecting me early and I was glad to have retained the second of Meredith's small pills. When I got to the meeting, I had to break the news that it was my last day. I told them I was ill and needed to interrupt the trip to see my doctor. I promised a further meeting in a month, confirming Elliot's presence, but did not disclose that he would be alone. As the hours waned, I was not fully involved in the discussions, but somehow managed to avoid obvious irresponsibility. My slowness and absence of enthusiasm were only in part explained by my alibi. I was lucky to have a new translator that day. When they asked questions I gained time, pretending I could not understand. They did not question my symptoms and seemed to accept my situation. My report of the discussions could be minimal. The firm would be blinded by further growth of the business. They did not need more.

Late at night, I decided to take a last look at where she lived. Like the confused time when trying to spy on her, I took a taxi to the Puschkin Museum and went by foot from there. I didn't go to the back. I didn't want to see the small ventilation opening from the kitchen. I went to the front and walked on the far side of the street, to be unseen by the guard. When level with the building, I stayed where I was, looking at it from across the street, which at the time was without traffic. I stood back under one of the broad trees, taking comfort from its deep shadows and remained without moving. I could gaze directly at the gates that were decisive from the start. They would remain a symbol of our time together, their ambivalent significance stretching the whole span from lure of a refuge, to exile from a tomb. She drove me through them in both directions—going in and coming out, on every occasion. Peering across between the pillars, I could see into a part of the yard, where she parked her car. Half expecting it to be there, I looked for it, but it was already a memory. Behind the opening and above the wall with its spiked railing, hesitant against the night sky—was the house. I had not looked at it from this side of the street. In fact, I had not seen the full elevation. My view was confined to jigsaw puzzle mosaics, made-up of fragmented glances, from a multiplicity of directions through car windows. There were also close-ups, sneaked during the few paces, between vehicle and doorway, often distorted, or foreshortened with head lowered, or turned-away under the constant eye of the guard. I looked at the door that she many times opened for me, with her special security keys. It seemed more imposing than I remembered, dully lit from the overhead wall lamp mounted above. I raised my eyes higher to the windows, counting each of the rows for the five stories. It was late and only those of the landings were with light, others curtained, or in darkness. How about the back and the window of her flat, as by habit would the curtains still be hanging unclosed? They could have been taken-down. Then there would only be reflections from the glass panes, to suggest the bareness and silence of the unseen room behind. Sometime there will be light again, but not yet. As I stood alone in the dark, I could abandon myself and allow distress to surge unchecked, the anger and tears un-judged in a silent vigil—substitute for a funeral, I would not attend. How often did I sense in intimacy the closing proximity, the thinning of whatever kept us apart? We shared the feeling—but not then. When she took that last step, she was uncompromisingly alone. At whatever moment, she staged the final path of events—the barrier must have been so thick that it would seem a vault, its walls as cold and impenetrable as the granite mausoleum we visited together. No matter how many times my thoughts spun, conclusion was the same. Whatever her reason, the truth was inescapable. Had I returned as promised, the fatal step would not be taken.

Without warning, the stillness was shattered. A jeep-like vehicle drove noisily down the road and flashed its lights in my direction. I thought I heard someone shout. I must have been observed in the sudden glare. I doubled-up pretending—as a person vomiting. Alcoholics were commonplace at night. Better mistaken, a drunk lost on his way, than a person lurking. They could pick me up for that. I kept moving. They might drive around and come back to double-check. I continued in a haphazard direction, until sure they lost me. Then I looked for a taxi.

That night, my thoughts teemed with nauseating fantasies, I could not efface and from which, there was no release. At one moment, there was a stream of ordure and faeces. At another, I became a corpse, lying among a pile of decaying human remains. I tried to heave myself from disgust, through some tangible explanation. The awesome and contradictory facts persisted. When suddenly, she faced the despairing events her 'helpers' set for her—she must have felt condemned. Disillusionment from betrayal was as complete as that of Camus' 'outsider.' Hers was not: 'cowardly suicide with farewell letters and resentments.' When circumstances became defeating, she rejected the victim's role and took the lead. Following her self-professed image: 'free soul in an environment of totalitarianism,' she played both—condemned and executioner. Only that way was she sure to win. In her final drama, she 'broke-free and quit' to take control of time once, but forever. Holding to that kept me afloat.

Asphyxia, a form of suffocation, is caused by deficiency of oxygen in the inhaled atmosphere, as necessary for support of the organism. Occurrence can be through restriction of air content in confined spaces, or through contamination of the atmosphere by irrespirable gases. Domestically the latter can be from the gaseous components of town gas, natural gas, or the products of combustion of either. As the oxygen is progressively diluted, or displaced by contaminants, its resulting deprivation in the diluted atmosphere inspired through the respiratory duct, leads directly to reduction in its resultant passage from the lung alveoli, to the adjacent blood capillaries, supplied by the pulmonary and bronchial arteries. The blood pumped directly by the heart, for redistribution through the veins to the tissues, for use by the metabolic sites in the mitochondria, transports oxygen at proportionately lower levels. The starvation, or interference in its transport leads to hypoxemia, which causes progressive degeneration of the body, its tissue components and cells, as deficiency in the supply further deteriorates or as residual oxygen in the confined space, is progressively consumed. When the gas is ignited in the appliance, presence of carbon monoxide, which poisons the haemoglobin contained in the red cells of the bloodstream, is critical in the inspired gases and induces faintness and a slow loss of consciousness. Destruction of haemoglobin, as the oxygen carrying substance in the red cells of the blood, further reduces the mass transfer from the inspired air in the lungs into the blood, to accelerate promotion of hypoxemia. When carbon monoxide is not present, nerve cell degeneration begins after the initial deprivation reaches the brain, and will then spread under the conditions represented, to lead to unconsciousness and damage to the respiratory centres, which impedes, and eventually prevents, cardio-pulmonary resuscitation. In the final phase, when tissue starvation reaches its extreme form, the hypoxia leads to the condition of histiotoxic anoxia, where oxygen is entirely absent in the tissue. At that juncture, there is a complete failure of the cellular respiration in the body.

Under any circumstances, getting out of the country was intimidating and almost more complicated, than getting-in. The abundant lines of passengers hardly moved, as people stood in queues before departure desks, for declarations and countless checks of passports, visas, exit visas, permits and documents. In the cavernous baggage hall, they waited indeterminately for customs inspectors, who were elsewhere when needed. Keeping of travellers in suspense, was part of procedures applied without compromise. It went with the indignity of emptying bags, exposing intimate contents, then bundling them inside again. When finally cleared to go, it was a wonder to find that planes had not left long before. This was simply to get through the building. It did not include standing in the open-air alongside the plane, unprotected from the elements, while meticulous controls on counter-checked documents, were implemented by armed uniformed militiamen. This time—it would be the last.

34

It was illusory to think I could have carried on my life with her and Anna in parallel, as a remotely separated threesome. Although it seemed to work for Rainer and was in keeping with current trends, I should have paid more attention to what he told me about that play and the rewritten 'true-to-life' ending, added later by the author. I was halfway there.

"Whatever happened that you return early," Anna said, as she met me at the airport." They told me you were ill, but apart from looking pale, you seem OK."

"It was an official excuse. The real explanation has to do with the Russian business—an inconvenience the firm has to overcome."

"Well at least you are back for the weekend."

"It was deliberate. I want to reach Davidson tomorrow to check if the job is open."

"I thought you behaved irresponsibly, it's time for a change!"

There was no reason not to use an alibi and next morning, I stayed at home. Anna called the office, to inform them I was back, asleep and not to be disturbed. She said it was severe food poisoning. I phoned Davidson and spoke to his secretary. Like the first time, he was expected and called back promptly. He enquired, whether I had rethought. I told him the way was clear to make a decision and asked whether the offer was open. "You must be psychic!" He exclaimed. "I have a meeting set with them this afternoon, to discuss my shortlist for replacement candidates from your dropping out. If you are ready to sign on the line this time, I will call it off. You're way ahead—the vice chairman approved and it will take a few weeks to get another that far along." When I confirmed he could count on me, he suggested I call at his office around twelve.

"I'll have the papers ready for signing. When phoning them about the afternoon, I will suggest you come along. There may be questions to settle. After the set-back, they want to move fast."

I told Anna about my call. "I am going to sign and he has fixed a meeting with the group this afternoon. I should be back around six." She would be out herself, for lunch with a woman friend, she said. As there was nowhere to park at Davidson's office, I took the underground. The papers were ready and I signed them, before there could be regrets on either side. When he called the new firm to advise them all was finalised, they told him to cancel the afternoon session. There was nothing more to discuss, except my starting date. Davidson took me for a celebratory lunch at a nearby restaurant. "I'm glad you saw the light. The timing is a happy coincidence—it saves unnecessary work. I wasn't eager to begin again, in the end, the fee is the same!"

After lunch, I got a cab to take me home. As we approached the lane leading to the house, the driver pulled over to wait. A car had stopped outside one of the houses and was blocking the narrow section, about fifty yards ahead. With reflection from the windscreen, it was not possible to recognize people inside, but from the silhouettes it appeared, a couple in the front seats were embracing. As the person at the wheel didn't seem to notice us, the taxi driver hooted. A woman got out and I realized it was Anna. She went around the stationary car and up the steps, waving a kiss to the unseen driver, then disappeared behind the front door. The car started up the lane and I watched cautiously from the rear side window of the black cab, as it squeezed past. First, I saw a man driving and then recognized Spencer. Sitting well back in the seat, I could not be visible. So, that is what Anna has been doing in my absence. I asked the driver to go to the bottom of the lane, turn right along the river and then turn right again to drop me outside the church. From there, I could walk back along the main road, as if coming from the station. Anna would have no reason to associate me with the waiting taxi. I needed to arrange matters effectively and realized the benefit, from not travelling over the next months. As I went in, I said breezily: "The deal was sealed. They cancelled the meeting and I'm back early."

"It's good news!" She responded. "And I had a good lunch as well."

Davidson called me late in the afternoon, after speaking with the vice chairman. He was happy the matter was concluded, but insisted there be no more delay. "Tell the present lot, notice must be one month maximum from next Wednesday, so you can commence on the first. Good luck and give me confirmation, before the end of next week."

Whether change is real or not, I am taking the job—and not because of additional power, promised by Davidson. I am moving, because I have to. I cannot go back to that city. I must get away and this means new employment. With Calvin on vacation, I had to deal with Thornton for my resignation. He was resentful, his masterful plan for Elliot's involvement on the last trip failed. Irritated that I did not make the necessary introductions, he insisted I go to Moscow to settle the omission. It was out of the question, but I was sparring with hands bound. I could not tell him why. He had his eye on the bonus and was concerned that his would be lower, according to my grounds to claim the ample share, agreed by Calvin. This was not the diligent administrator, looking after interests of the firm. His main goal was diversion, to enrich his own account and to resolve the issue—I had to await Calvin's return from vacation. I chose another tactic and the route was quicker. I proposed to Thornton, that he unconditionally release me from further travel to Moscow and allow me to meet the one-month deadline, in return for my renouncing any claim for bonus from business in the Soviet Union. He accepted at once and the agreement was signed the same afternoon. It took two days, to reach Calvin in Vancouver and agree my date of termination, then I called Davidson to confirm the starting date. With announcement issued and debriefing set, the move was irrevocable.

Financial hardship from sacrifice of the bonus was not the only calamity to take place in previous weeks, but coming from success that would not have happened without her, it squared a debt. She did not modify my life, but the difference she made seemed the disparity between distance to the treetops or the moon. As if time in between were frozen, the 'immortalisation of her memory' preserved her unaltered. Just as familiarity with her bookcase made it possible to use glints from shiny book jackets to make out its shape in the darkness, so glints from patterns in my mind, allow me to trace the contours of her body, or the inimitable image of her face. I did not say goodbye, but I thought of Max with happiness and pride . . . also with a bitter touch of shame.

35

'Change is a mirage'. My position is the same as the 'true-to-life' ending of that theatre piece Rainer talked about—rewritten by Goethe more than two hundred years ago. She ('Mistress' in play) has poisoned herself with gas. By quitting the firm and giving up the bonus, he or I ('Hero' in play) has ruined himself financially. My life with Anna ('Wife' in play) is falling apart and she will enjoy the spoils. I have not shot myself, but after this, who knows? 'Time' is a match frame, centuries, or not. Nor will the job make a difference. Advancements are photocopies in files and print fades. It will not bring fulfilment. As on early visits to Moscow, circumstances set the rules. Nor will it offer gratification. Like the vodka, it can create a thirst for more. Offices may seem larger, furnishings grander and lists of phone numbers longer, but the work involves talking, arguing and defending interests with people—and they do not change. Terms might look better, but new disappointments will likely out-match the dissatisfactions of before. As in nature, differences mutate to similarities and in time, become indistinguishable.

I stopped in Athens and went to the American embassy. A secretary let me talk to the head of the school. There were several applicants and at first he did not recall the name. When I described her, he confirmed she was on the list. She was unmatched and the withdrawal upset them. Cordially, he suggested I call the Moscow embassy to find her. I thanked him and instead, called Elektra.

36

A year later, I visited a restaurant in South America not far from the sea, picked by colleagues with whom I spent the evening. It had a transitory air, perhaps from arcaded mirrors, lining the walls and was almost full. Unexpectedly, everyone turned their heads as a boisterous troop of foreigners—a film crew, stormed in. I had seen them before, shooting a street scene in the centre. Standing on the kerb among spectators, a local next to me held not a briefcase but a chain with a cheetah, its head inches from my right hand. I didn't spot the danger, as someone in the crew took my attention, a woman clutching a sheaf of papers, at the director's side. She was sun bronzed and her straight auburn hair hung down loosely around an unusually interesting face. There were fifteen or more in the group that burst through the revolving door. The owner must have expected the late arrival and held back a large table along the wall, to the right of where we sat. I could not resist glancing at them from time to time. It was not their antics, but the woman in the crew—the one, who caught my attention earlier. Now dressed in black, she sat the other side, facing our direction. The principal actor with his recognizable face enjoyed himself, repeatedly acknowledging his sallow image, in the cascading reflections behind. He almost took over from a waiter, helping to serve his lively companions amidst shrieks and howls of laughter.

Experience taught me that in a congested room, it is possible to distinguish words spoken by a person quite far away, when studying the face and mouth intently. That is how I realised the woman I was watching spoke English, with a slight American accent. The words contained an expression, heard from Max. As well as watching her face, I could turn my head to catch its profile in the mirror and follow the way she played with her hair, while talking with others in the group. Later, she saw me looking. As our eyes met, she smiled.

Walking back from the restaurant, he came upon a setting that seemed timeless. A square led into an *avenida,* running between old but unremarkable buildings, several stories high. It was in a poorer sector of the city and the surroundings had an air of neglect. For a political event, the street was decorated with strings of flags, stretched from side to side at first floor level and repeated at regular intervals. The small pieces of red cloth with white lettering, hung down above his head, fluttering. From where he stood, he could not decipher them, nor read what was written on manifestos pasted high on the walls. Traffic was barred and stalls, or vehicles that might normally clutter the area, were out of view. A crowd had collected, sauntering around, waiting for something to happen. They looked alike, men and women indistinguishable in their drab workaday clothes. Numbers increased and before long, the space was filled. Someone was speaking and he could hear the voice, persistently droning from loudspeakers, perched on windowsills above. Unacquainted with the city, he knew he could not navigate the maze of alleyways that meandered behind the facades. He decided to remain where he was until the speeches were over. He looked for somewhere to sit, but with nowhere free on nearby benches, stood propped against a lamp post. After a while, he became impatient, anxious to return to where he stayed. Wary of straying from the thoroughfare and losing his way in the backstreets, he went forward through the crowd. People stood in groups, conversing in an unfamiliar dialect, but he kept silent, realizing they would not understand if he spoke. Moving between them, he looked at the faces hoping to see someone he recognized, but not having been there before, knew it was unlikely. As he continued, no one turned their head, or nodded. Not one among them gave a sign of acknowledgement. Even when he had to push, there was no response. Nobody in the crowd seemed to notice. They appeared not to see him. It was as if he did not exist.

When he reached about halfway, he altered direction and veered to the side. He needed to lean against a wall, pause and rest a moment. As he stood completely still, looking around him, he felt unsettled. He knew where he was, but it might have been somewhere else. He knew when it was, yet it could have been another period. Though manner of dress hinted at date or place, expressions on the faces were changeless and would be the same anywhere, anytime. Glancing across the congested space, to the rear and in front, he was disconcerted by a sense of alienation, from what he passed through and what lay ahead. He was not sure where he must go to reach persons he knew, nor how long it might take to get among objects that were familiar.

END